Rival Seduction

Alexandrea Weis

This is a work of fiction. Names, characters, places, and incidents are products of the author's imagination cr are used fictitiously and are not to be construed as real. Any resemblance to actual events, locations, organizations, or person, living or dead, is entirely coincidental.

Copyright © Alexandrea Weis 2015
Weba Publishing

Licensing Notes

All rights reserved. No part of this book may be used or reproduced in any manner whatsoever without written permission, except in the case of brief quotations embodied in articles and reviews.

Cover: BookFabulous Designs
Editor: Maxine Bringenberg

Alexandrea Weis

Chapter 1

The air was heavy with the promise of rain as thunder rumbled in the black skies above Kenilworth Farms. Cool October breezes swirled the dirt around the well-trod entrance to the show ring as a sleek, dark bay thoroughbred approached. Atop the horse, dressed in the customary black jacket, black riding pants, black-velvet helmet, and shiny black boots, a woman gazed out over the jumping course before her. In the distance, the ever-present whinnying of excited horses rose, while the thud of the mighty hooves of the horse in the ring pounded the ground.

The woman's powerful horse gave an excited snort and pivoted his back end around, anxious to head into the ring. The thick, carved muscles in the animal's rump had been bred for speed, but like so many unfortunate throwaways of the racing world, show jumping had become his salvation.

"Easy, Murphy," the woman cooed as she patted the horse's bulging neck. Her eyes traveled to the elegant black gelding currently taking a turn at the fences on the course. "The asshole's almost done."

Scanning the faces gathered around the ring, she marveled at how everyone's eyes were glued to her competition. Glimpsing the horse working the course of high jumps, she could understand the crowd's fascination. The massive animal lifted his thick body over the fences with such grace that he looked as if he had sprouted wings and could take flight at any moment. However, it was the rider on the back of the black beast that captivated the woman's attention. The man commanded just as much envy as his fine mount. Athletic, assured, and with a perfectly carved profile that caught every woman's eye, he was a dangerous competitor both inside and outside of the show ring.

Closing her bright blue eyes, the rider waiting at the gate tried to calm the swarm of butterflies rising from the pit of her stomach. Pushing back a stray ringlet of brown hair that had fallen from beneath her helmet, she then rubbed her hand along the curve of her wide chin and pressed her thick red lips together. She hated this part; that moment before you entered the show ring, when all you could concentrate on was the mistakes you prayed you didn't make.

"You need to make sure you push Murphy through that last touch and go, Heather," a man's smoky voice said beside the horse. "He gets lazy through the second half of the course. You need to cut your time in this jump off."

Heather opened her eyes and beheld the square jaw, slightly bent nose, and thick, wavy, almost black hair of the man next to her horse. His sunken cheekbones accentuated the tan on his face, while his brow was etched with a few worry lines that seemed to deepen as he frowned up at her. When he set his riveting gray eyes on her, Heather wanted to shrink down in her saddle.

"I know, Trent. I can't let the bastard beat me again."

Dressed in form-fitting brown jodhpur pants and a white T-shirt, Trent Newbury kicked up the dust around his short brown boots. Shifting his eyes to the show ring, he waited as the black brute hurtled over a wide triple combination of fences on the course. "How many times have you and Grant Crowley ended up in a jump off?"

Heather tightened her grip on her reins. "Five times in the last five shows. Son of a bitch beats me every time, too. I really hate that guy. I'm gonna make him eat that cocky smile of his."

Trent slapped her black boot, drawing her attention. "You're fixating on the rider in the ring and not on what I'm telling you."

She peered down at him. "What's up your ass? I'm not one of your students, Trent. I'm one of your top riders. I know what I need to do."

"Then do it! My job as riding master of Southland Stables is to make sure you and Murphy win this damn class. You need to cut your turns this time, and not take the long approach to the fences."

"Murphy needs to see what he's jumping," she argued.

"Murphy only needs to see the fence, not paint a picture of it. Shorten your approaches." Trent glowered up at her. "I hired you to ride for Southland, remember, and I can fire you just as easily."

"You won't fire me, Trent. You need me to pick up Rayne's riding classes at Southland. You're short good instructors, admit it."

Chuckling, Trent's eyes followed the outline of her black jacket over her curvy figure. "I fear for those kids. You always were an intimidating bitch, Heather."

"That's rich coming from your arrogant ass. I seem to remember you made it a point to sleep with damn near every woman at Wescott Stables."

"It wasn't every woman. I didn't sleep with you."

Her eyebrows went up. "And you wonder why I turned you down?"

"Repeatedly turned me down, as I recall." He brought his dark brows together. "Why did you keep turning down my dinner invitations?"

"Because I didn't date assholes back then," she quipped with a tepid sneer.

"What about now?"

Heather looked up just as the black gelding in the ring cleared an impressive blue and white oxer fence. "At my age, there is nothing left to date."

"Your age? Christ, you're the same age as my wife. It can't be all bad out there."

She didn't feel like explaining why she had given up on the opposite sex. The happily married could never understand the disappointments endured by the lonely hearted.

Out of the corner of her eye, Heather spotted a pretty woman with unruly honey-blonde hair waddling toward them. Wearing blue overalls that did little to hide her protruding belly, she looked as if she was about to go into labor at any moment. For an instant, Heather envied the woman. She had the birth of her child and a life with someone to fill her heart.

"Rayne, what in the hell are you doing out here?" Trent scolded.

"Trent, please stop being such an overprotective ass," Rayne grumbled.

Trent went around to her side and held her arm. "You know the doctors said no horses. That means even being around them, in case you get kicked or hurt. I can't afford for anything to happen—"

"Trent," Heather cut in. "As a nurse, I can tell you that the doctors meant no horses in terms of riding. Rayne is fine to walk around the show area."

Trent shot Heather a dirty look. "Is she your wife?"

"No, but she is her own woman."

"Thank you," Rayne replied, waving up at Heather. "See?" She smirked at her husband. "She even thinks you're nuts."

"You've got my vote on that one," Heather edged in.

"It's bad enough I can't ride Bob, but don't ask me to stay away from the stables, Trent," Rayne implored. "I'll go crazy if I can't be around the horses. Besides," she playfully elbowed her husband, "I came to support Heather, not talk to you."

Trent shook his head, appearing fed up. "Fine, I can't fight both of you."

"You're lucky." Rayne smiled up at Heather. "I usually can't get him to cave so easily at home."

Trent frowned as his gray eyes returned to the ring. "I'm not caving, baby. I'm merely being tolerant because you're very pregnant with my son and I don't want to upset you."

Heather chuckled at the pair. "You're better at training men than I thought, Rayne. When we taught together at Wescott Stables, he would never cave to anyone's demands. Most stubborn instructor I ever met."

"That was several years ago, Heather, when I was used to getting my own way," Trent admitted. "Marriage has changed me."

"Really?" Rayne raised her eyebrows. "If you ask me, you're still trying to get your own way … especially when I am the one having the baby."

"Let's not start that again, Rayne." Trent gave his wife an indulgent smile. "I told you before, I think natural childbirth is healthier than using all of those drugs."

Rayne glanced up at Heather. "You're a nurse. If you were having a baby, would you go natural or use all the drugs you can get?"

Thunderous applause broke out as the black gelding cleared the last fence, sparing Heather from having to answer Rayne's question. Spying the eager faces in the crowd, Heather was mystified at how the imposing man on the prancing black gelding always remained the crowd's favorite.

If they only knew what he was really like, then they would despise him.

"Get your mind back on the course." Trent pointed to the jumps in the show ring. "Crowley jumped clean."

Heather glimpsed the time clock set next to the white judge's stand at the side of the ring. The digital clock flashed its orange numbers back at her, making the butterflies in her stomach quiver.

"You've got to beat two minutes and eighteen seconds," Trent broke in, reading her thoughts.

"Damn," Rayne mouthed. "Crowley is good. Glad he's not jumping in my division."

"Rayne, you're not helping," Trent chided. "Just because he owns Crowley Stables doesn't make him better than either one of you."

Sighing, Rayne rested her arms on her large belly. "Yeah, but being part of the wealthy family that owns Crowley Ranch sure affords him the luxury of hiring the best trainers, purchasing state of the art equipment, and buying the most gifted horses."

"Well, he doesn't have me," Trent insisted with a smirk.

"He doesn't have you yet," Rayne added.

"You know why I keep turning him down, Rayne, so let's not rehash…." Trent grew quiet as the black gelding that had just been in the ring came alongside of Murphy.

At over eighteen hands the animal was intimidating as hell, dwarfing every horse on the show grounds. What Heather found even more disturbing was the man who sat atop the behemoth creature. As she lifted her eyes past the horse's thick neck to his rider, a clap of thunder shot through the air, making both horses take a nervous sidestep.

Toned and teeming with self-confidence, Grant Crowley cut an imposing figure on the back of the horse. With the slightest hint of his exquisitely carved cheekbones that peeked through his smooth-shaven cheeks, a pointy chin, wide mouth, perfectly straight nose, and a long, pensive face, he seemed better suited for a print advertisement for some wildly sexy cologne instead of riding an ill-tempered mount. But his eyes were the one thing that always bothered Heather. Amber in color with an iridescent yellow hue, they reminded her of some reptilian creature rising from the depths of a black swamp. They were cold, calculating, and appeared to see into the very depths of her soul.

"At it again, I see, Ms. Phillips." Grant Crowley's deep voice sounded as boastful as the man who possessed it.

"You know I'll never quit," Heather asserted through gritted teeth.

His hypnotic smile was unwavering. "I like your persistence. It's a very admirable quality."

"Pit bulls are persistent, Crowley; people are determined." Heather noted the way the black gelding's nostrils were flaring as he stood alongside Murphy. "Maximillian seems awfully tired this afternoon. Sure you haven't put on a few pounds?"

"Heather, none of that." Trent directed his gaze to Grant. "Crowley, you looked good out there."

Grant tilted forward in his saddle, letting his reins drop from his hands. "When are you going to leave Southland and come and work for me, Trent? I could use a riding master like you in my ranks."

Trent gave a throaty chuckle. "Yeah, like Gigi would allow that. Your sister hates men, Crowley. We could never work together."

Grant Crowley dismounted and came around the front of his horse. "Well, Gigi doesn't own the stables, I do. And I can hire whomever I choose to run it." He nodded to Rayne, standing next to her husband. "How much longer do you have, Rayne?"

Rayne smiled for him, patting her round belly. "Two weeks, if I make it that long."

Grant gathered up his reins. "Tell your husband to come and see me after the baby is born. I can make him a handsome offer." His uncanny eyes found Heather. "Ms. Phillips, good luck in there." He motioned to the show ring. "Watch out for that touch and go. It's tricky."

He strode away, leading his horse from the gate and back toward the red stables of Kenilworth Farms.

Heather seethed as she tried to think of something witty to call over her shoulder, but words failed her. They always failed her around the exasperating Grant Crowley.

She had closely observed him at the different horse shows since she had started riding for Southland Stables a few months back. Heather had always been intrigued by the subtle swing of his hips, the kick of his long stride, and the way he constantly hooked his finger through the belt loop of his pants as he listened to others speaking. Whenever they ran into each other outside of the show ring, he had been cordial—called her Ms. Phillips—but had never offered one glimmer of warmth in his daunting eyes. In the beginning, she had found it an aggravating characteristic. Now, his distinctive eyes were awakening a whole host of awkward feelings. For Heather, such feelings were best suited for someone who wasn't a bitter rival.

"Good-looking man," Rayne mused. Her eyes followed Grant and his horse.

"I'm standing right here, Rayne," Trent admonished.

"Just an observation, darling. I can look, can't I?"

Trent frowned at her, drawing his gray eyes together. "No, you can't look." He focused on Heather. "Get your ass in that ring and show that son of a bitch who is the better rider."

Rayne hid her slight grin as Trent walked beside Murphy while Heather guided the horse to the gate. A loud rumble of thunder rolled across the darkening sky, making Murphy take a leery sidestep.

"Remember what I said about cutting those turns, and push him through the second half of the course," Trent instructed as they stood before the gate, waiting for the judge's cue to enter the ring.

When the demure woman judging the event waved Heather into the show ring, Trent slapped her right boot.

"Push him, hard," he ordered. "You need to beat this guy."

Trent's words haunted her as she rode Murphy in the ring. The dark bay pranced as he viewed the fences. His neck arched a little deeper and his muscles tensed with excitement. Gathering up her reins, Heather straightened her back and took in a deep breath. Reviewing the course in her head, she eyed the fences, mapping out her strategy. Again, thunder boomed across the sky, and a whip of wind pushed her to hurry before the heavens opened up.

"All right, Murph. Let's do this," she whispered to the horse, watching as his black-tipped ears swung back and forth, listening intently to her every word.

Circling Murphy in the front portion of the ring—making the customary courtesy circle before starting the course—Heather forced her mind to concentrate on the fences. However, as the first black and white triple oxer loomed before her, all Heather could think of was Grant Crowley. His words infuriated her, while the look in his eyes still enthralled her. Everything Trent had advised completely dashed from her mind. Disgusted, she tapped Murphy's flanks, urging him to pick up his speed as they came to the time marker right before the first fence.

They cleared the first hurdle, and then cantered on to the big blue oxer. After taking three more fences, she looked to the clock on the side of the ring. She needed to pick up the pace if she was going to challenge Grant Crowley's time. Images of Grant once again plagued her; his walk, the curve of his riding pants over his tight ass, even his disturbing eyes. Her interest in the man had started out innocently enough; he was attractive and always turned heads, so Heather had thought sneaking glances at him was normal. Yet, as time had gone on and their interactions had become more strained, Heather sensed the change in her stomach whenever he was around. Instead of churning with the embers of hatred, a more pleasant tingling sensation had started to take over.

Murphy's back hoof grazed the last pole on a fence, bringing Heather back from her contemplation. Tightening her legs around the saddle, she berated her lack of concentration and spurred Murphy on. How could the man invade her thoughts in the middle of the show ring?

After clearing two more jumps, she spied the last touch and go Trent had warned her of. The two closely compact fences were meant to challenge the horse, only allowing them to touch their hooves to the ground before forcing them back into flight to clear the second hurdle. Many show jumpers dreaded such combinations, because it was the ultimate test of fluidity between horse and rider. If the rider or horse were off, even to the slightest degree, they would never clear the second fence.

Urging Murphy on, the horse responded by digging his hooves into the soft earth. On the last two strides before the fence a loud strike of lightning hit very close to the show ring, startling Heather and her horse. The effect was enough to put them out of position for a solid approach to the touch and go. Murphy strained to clear the first part of the combination, touching his hooves to the ground for only a second, but all Heather could do was try and help the horse over the second jump and pray he cleared it.

Unfortunately, when Murphy touched the ground on the other side of the fence, that dreaded thud sounded. The collective gasp from the audience told her what she already knew. They had knocked down a pole on the last fence in the jump off. She had not ridden a clean round, and Grant Crowley was once again going to best her in the show ring.

After racing Murphy through the time markers at the end of the course, Heather glanced back at the last jump and spied the bright red and white pole taunting her from the ground. Turning to the gate, she saw Trent waiting for her. The dark scowl on his face said it all.

"What in the hell is wrong with you?" he began as soon as she was through the gate. "You were all over the place in there. Where was your head, because it sure wasn't on the fences, Heather?" The anger in his voice added to Heather's humiliation.

She pulled up the horse just beyond the gate and dismounted. "He got spooked by the lightning before the touch and go."

"Bullshit," Trent barked. "You should have had him lined up better in the approach. What happened to cutting your corners? Jesus, Heather, you were still three seconds off Crowley's time. Even without the four faults for knocking down that pole you would have come in second place."

She ran up her stirrups, avoiding Trent's intense eyes. "I tried, but obviously it was too much. He needed a wider approach to the touch and go."

Trent came up and slapped his hand over the pummel of her riding saddle. "No, you weren't paying attention. I watched you. I know you well enough after all these years to see when you're distracted, Heather, and you were as distracted as shit in that ring. What's going on with you?"

"Trent," Rayne spoke out. "Let it go." She came up to her husband's side and pulled on his arm. "Heather feels bad enough without you yelling at her."

Trent was about to turn to his wife and say something when another loud snap of lightning tore through the sky.

"I guess the gods of winning were against you again today, Ms. Phillips," Grant Crowley's voice said from the other side of Murphy.

Heather careened her head over her horse's withers to see the confounding man staring back at her.

He had removed his riding helmet and his blond curly hair was matted and a touch sweaty. His chiseled cheeks were pink, and a stain of dirt ran along his sharp chin. When his liquid gold eyes bore into Heather, she clenched her jaw.

"I saw your misstep at the touch and go. So sorry about that. I was rooting for you."

Heather swallowed hard, fighting back the explosion of expletives she wanted to wield, and then an unwelcome tingle erupted in her gut. Quickly dropping her eyes to her saddle, she searched for something ... some cutting remark to give the man.

"One day she'll beat you, Crowley," Trent warned as he stood next to Murphy's shoulder. "You know Heather is just as good a rider as you."

Grant came under the horse's thick neck, grinning. "Would you like to put a little money on that, Newbury? How about at the Riverdale Farms Show in two weeks?"

"She'll beat you. I'm willing to bet on it," Trent shot back.

"All right, enough, both of you." Rayne put her round belly in between the two men. "Nobody is going to bet anything on the Riverdale Farms Show. Heather just had a bit of bad luck with the weather, that's all. Stop acting like this is some kind of brawl."

Grant Crowley raised his head as he took in the crowd around the ring. "Of course you're right, Rayne. Any horse would have shied like Murphy did in this weather." He eyed the black clouds above. "Wouldn't surprise me if the rest of the classes today get postponed." When he returned his gaze to Heather, she bit down on her tongue. "Tough break, but you did ride well."

"Not well enough to beat your cocky ass," she mumbled.

"Grant, yoo-hoo, darlin'," a woman's voice called from the warm-up area just beyond the show ring.

All heads turned to see a leggy blonde looking completely out of place next to an array of swishing horse's tails and dirt-caked riders. In a pair of designer, form-fitting blue jeans, a white silk top, and high black stilettos, she appeared to be heading for an afternoon of intense shopping. Her long hair was swept strategically to the side of her lovely face while her hands sparkled with an array of rings and her wrists jingled with gold bracelets. Her face was powdered and penciled to perfection, highlighting her collagen-enhanced lips, sculptured nose, carved cheekbones, and wrinkle-free skin. To Heather, she seemed to be everything that a man could want; blonde, big-boobed, beautiful, and bereft of the slightest hint of intelligence.

"Honey," the woman fussed as she came up to Grant. "I told you I can't walk that fast in these heels. Why didn't you wait for me at the stables?"

Grant shot her a menacing scowl. "I told you before not to wear heels to a horse show, Vanessa."

"Nonsense, these feet can't be caught dead in anything under two inches." Vanessa giggled, attempting to appear cute and coquettish, but the effect made Heather yearn for the days when public executions were considered a form of entertainment.

"Vanessa, didn't think we'd see you here," Rayne commented. "I thought you preferred to stay away when Grant showed. Last time you said his jumping made you nervous."

Vanessa placed a manicured hand over her ample bosom. "Oh, it still does, Rayne. But I feel guilty if I don't come out and support my man here." She nestled a twig-like arm about his waist. Her beady brown eyes dug into Heather. "So, another red ribbon for you, Heather? How many is that this season?"

"Vanessa, perhaps you should head back to your car." Grant motioned to the dark skies. "I don't think it's wise for you to get caught out in the rain. You might … catch cold."

Vanessa squealed, sounding more porcine than human. "Aren't I just the luckiest girl to be dating such a caring man? He's always looking out for me."

Rayne snickered. "Yes, you two have been going out for quite a while now. How many months is it?"

Vanessa put on her best beauty queen smile. "Five months."

Trent grinned. "That's got to be some kind of record for you, Crowley. It must be true love."

Vanessa frowned, bringing her bulbous red lips together. "Of course we're in love. How could we—?"

"Vanessa," Grant cut in. "I think you should head home now."

Vanessa wiped away a bit of dust from the lapel of Grant's black riding jacket. "Of course, sweetie. But I have to find Gigi first."

Grant nodded toward the red-painted stables of Kenilworth Farms behind the show ring. "She's back at the barn, seeing to Maximillian."

"Let me just speak to her, and then I'll meet you back at the ranch later tonight, all right?"

He gave her a tolerant nod. "Fine."

Leaving a red lipstick stain on Grant's cheek, Vanessa gave a halfhearted wave to Trent, Rayne, and Heather and then carefully began to make her way back to the stables, balancing precariously on her black stilettos.

"You two should be getting ready." Trent motioned to Grant and Heather. "They'll be calling for the winners to enter the ring in a few minutes."

Heather reached for Murphy's reins as Grant stepped over to Trent's side. "I'll look for you inside the ring, Ms. Phillips."

Heather watched as the man strutted toward the gate entrance. The cut of his black riding pants hugged the tight round curve of his butt, momentarily mesmerizing Heather.

"I'll take Murphy back to the stables while you collect your ribbon," Trent informed her.

Heather damn near jumped out of her skin when Trent touched her to take Murphy's reins from her hands. Hoping to cover up her reaction, she rubbed her hands together.

"You all right?" Rayne whispered beside her.

Heather spun around to her. "I'm just worn out."

Rayne patted her belly. "I know what you mean."

"Rayne, are you coming back to the stables with me?" Trent inquired. "I need to get Murphy cooled down before this storm hits."

Rayne's curious hazel eyes studied Heather. "In a second."

Trent clucked to Murphy. "Better hurry before it starts raining, baby. I know you like to think you're tough, but all the orange juice in the world isn't going to help if you're sick and pregnant." He winked and then walked away.

Heather gestured to Trent. "Is he still on you about natural childbirth?"

"All the time." Rayne gave a perturbed snort. "I've been trying to talk him out of it. Natural childbirth scares the crap out of me."

"Then use the drugs. Tell your husband to launch a watermelon out of his ass and see how it feels." Rayne's little-girl giggle made Heather smile. "Go back to the stables, Rayne. I don't need you to watch me get my second-place ribbon."

Rayne spied Grant, who was waiting by the gate to the ring. The handsome man cordially dipped his head to her.

"Somehow, I get the impression you're not coming in second place anymore," Rayne muttered under her breath.

Heather shot her a curious side-glance. "What are you talking about?"

"Nothing." She waved Heather to the gate. "Better get up there." With one last knowing grin, Rayne turned around and waddled toward the bright red stables.

Furrowing her brow at the woman, Heather headed for the ring entrance. When she spotted Grant Crowley watching her, that nagging sense of nervous excitement rippled through her bones. Why did he always make her feel that way? Maybe it was his sinister eyes or the way he studied her as she moved. One thing was for certain, Heather was becoming more unhinged by the disarming man with every passing day. If she didn't get a handle on these feelings soon, she was going to end up with a really big problem, both inside and outside of the show ring.

Chapter 2

The winners for the Junior Division class were announced over the loudspeaker just as the heavens burst. Rain pummeled the show ring and stables, sending the crowds scurrying for cover. The formal ceremony where the winners were marched into the ring one by one to receive their ribbons from the judge was replaced by a hasty handing out of ribbons at the gate by the show steward.

As the rain left dark droplets on the sleeve of her black jacket, Heather gripped the long red ribbon in her hand. The color red was becoming a familiar sight for her, and she wondered how much longer she would have to wait before finally getting ahold of that coveted blue ribbon.

"You're getting wet," Grant said, grabbing her arm as the rain began to come down really hard. "Come on. We can't stay out here." He pulled her to the right of the gate and toward a shed several feet away. Used by the timekeeper to reset the clock, the wooden structure was painted white, raised a few feet off the ground to offer an unencumbered view of the show ring, and enclosed on three sides.

As they climbed the steps, a gust of wind sent rain droplets pelting against Heather's face. She could hardly see where she was going, and then once she stepped inside everything went uncomfortably still.

"We'll be fine in here until it passes." Grant flicked the rain from his black jacket.

Heather kept her eyes on the wet ribbon in her hand, suddenly uneasy about looking up at the man.

He tucked his blue ribbon inside his jacket. "Second place is admirable, Ms. Phillips. You jumped a great round, but the show ring is my world, and you will never be able to beat me in it."

Heather's eyes flew to his. "Your world? Why are you such an asshole, Crowley? You parade around the show grounds like you own them, and treat your competitors like dirt. Do you enjoy being such a … dick?" She clapped her mouth shut.

A leering smile spread across Grant's wide mouth, causing Heather's stomach to shrink.

"I had heard you were bold and blunt. I'm glad the rumors about you are true."

She stepped to the opening in the front of the shack that gazed out over the jumping ring. Her heart was slamming against her chest like a terrified deer caught in the cross hairs of a hunter's scope. She wanted to flee the confining space, but the rain drumming on the tin roof reminded her that she was trapped along with her rival.

She squared her shoulders, anxious to appear strong. "People talk a lot of bullshit around stables. You should know better than to believe what you hear." She unclasped the chinstrap of her helmet.

"Yes, I know. Nevertheless, there are quite a few juicy rumors making the rounds about you."

"Don't believe any of it," she growled.

"I wholeheartedly agree. However, there are the innuendos about your sex life that I find hard to ignore."

"My sex life?" She spun around to face him. "You're joking?"

"Afraid not. Many believe you're a lesbian because you avoid relationships with men." He came alongside her, his eyes drinking in her figure. "I have to say I find that particular rumor difficult to swallow."

"Why is it when a woman is assertive and prefers her own company to men, she's a lesbian?" After removing her black-velvet helmet, a few wisps of her long brown hair fell from beneath her hairnet. "Do you believe I'm a lesbian? Is that what you are trying to find out?"

"No, I don't believe it. Personally, I seek out the facts on an individual before I draw conclusions, Ms. Phillips."

"Why do you do that?"

He turned to her, crinkling his wide brow. "Do what?"

"Call me Ms. Phillips. My name is Heather." She dropped the red ribbon inside her helmet.

He slowly nodded his head. "Yes, I know it's Heather, but I was raised never to call a lady by her first name until invited to do so."

The response took Heather off guard. Was he trying to play the gentleman card with her; the man who had taunted her and beaten down her self-esteem in the show ring?

"What is it with you?" She took a wary step away from him. "First you condescend to me, then attack me in the show ring, and now you—"

"When did I ever condescend to you or attack you?" he questioned with a raised voice.

"Are you kidding me? You're always calling me Ms. Phillips and making little snide comments to me. Then you try to pass yourself off as some kind of gentleman. What kind of hypocrite are you?"

The comment gave Grant pause. As he studied her, Heather felt her insides heating up.

What in the hell is wrong with me? This is the enemy.

"I've never meant to be rude or condescending, and if I have, I apologize," he cut into her thoughts. "That was never my intention. You've always been a bit of a mystery to me, and if my teasing was taken the wrong way, again, I apologize. I was merely trying to … figure you out."

"'Figure me out'?" The words rolled around in her head as she tried to decipher their true meaning. "Why?"

"Don't you try and get inside of the head of the competition, learn their weaknesses and strengths, so you know how to fight them in the ring?"

"Jesus, it's a horse show, not a military operation." She shook her head, suddenly feeling out of her league. "Do you always take everything so seriously, Crowley?"

"Grant, please. Trent Newbury may call me Crowley, but I would prefer for you to call me Grant."

"What difference does it make what the competition calls you?"

He hesitated, taking in her face with his disconcerting amber eyes. "You are much more than the competition, Ms. Phillips."

"Heather. No more Ms. Phillips, please. It's so … maddening."

The hearty laugh that came from him sent Heather reeling. His warm chuckle was nothing like his long, somber face. It was musical, instilled with a childlike exuberance she would not have expected from such a serious man.

"I have to admit you've been something of a thorn in my side for quite a while, Heather."

"Me?" The surprise in her voice reverberated about the small structure. "How have I been a bother to you? Nothing seems to bother you."

The grin that careened across his lips stopped Heather's heart. It was a knowing kind of smile that imparted more of a lustful intent, rather than a playful one.

"Let's just say I have had my eye on you. You're a gifted rider, but you just need a bit more polish to start winning those blue ribbons."

"I disagree." Heather faced the ring beyond as she watched the rain begin to pool in large mud puddles around the jumps. "All I need is you out of the show ring and I could take home the blue ribbon every time."

"What accomplishment would there be for you in that? I would think beating me would give you a hell of a lot more satisfaction than seeing me … put out to pasture."

When she veered her eyes back to him, the lurid smile on his lips was still there. *Damn the man. If he was going to use logic….*

"You're right. What would be the fun in winning if I couldn't beat you? I'd love to kick your ass in the ring, Grant."

His eyes lingered over the curves of her black jacket while his finger hooked the belt loop of his pants. "Now that is something a champion would say. Never take a hollow victory, Heather. To truly know you're the best, you must best those who challenge you."

Holding the helmet against her chest, she leaned back against the unfinished wall. "Did you read that off one of the numerous trophies you have decorating your mantle?"

He viewed the rain clouds above. "No, it was something my father always told me. He never wanted me to settle for second, but to push until I had everything I wanted. It's a philosophy I live by to this day."

Heather drank in the sharp angles of his profile. She found it funny how his almost cruel countenance had mirrored her initial impression of him. While she looked on, the standoffish coldness she had first seen in his face warmed into an attractive kindness. In the space of a few minutes, her opinion of the man was being upended, and that was not a good thing.

"I've never seen your father at any horse shows," she said, thinking out loud.

His amber eyes returned to her and he raised his hand to his curly blond hair, patting down the wet locks. "My father gave up going to my shows once I passed the age of eighteen. That was many years ago. Show jumping has always bored him."

"What about your mother?"

He rubbed his hand across his chin. "She left when I was eleven. Let's just say we were never close."

A knot formed in the center of Heather's chest. "I'm sorry. I know how hard it is to lose your mother at such a young age."

He took a step closer to her. "Yes, but my mother simply left, she did not die. There's a different kind of pain in knowing someone you cared for volunteered to leave you behind." His eyes wandered over her figure. "I must admit I've heard numerous stories about the unhappy events in your life. First your father and his ... tribulations, followed by the death of your mother. It must have been hard for you and your brother."

She let go a short snort. "Nothing is hard for Stewart. He has his work to keep him going."

"Yes, he's carrying on your father's legacy. Heading up the cardiology department at Baylor and forging new ground in cardiac research has made him quite the celebrity in Dallas."

"My brother is far from a celebrity. He's just a doctor trying to do good."

"And you're a nurse trying to do the same. I'm told you do a very good job in the ER at the Medical Center of Lewisville."

Heather's apprehension bristled. "How do you know where I work?"

He pressed his back against the frame of the wide window that overlooked the show ring. "My family contributes a lot of money every year to that hospital. Dr. Ben Eisenberg and I have become friends."

"My boss is your friend?" She rested her shoulder against the opposite side of the window.

"He's the one who told me about you. Ben admires you a great deal."

Another loud crack of thunder shook the little stand, making Heather flinch. She contemplated the now muddy show ring and noticed that the rain was beginning to let up.

"I need to get back to Murphy."

"He's a fine horse." Grant angled out the large window. "How did you come by him?"

"A rescue organization contacted me. He was marked for termination because he had lost one too many races."

Grant turned back to her, his lips drawn together. "I can abide many things, but the inhumane treatment of horses is one of my big pet peeves."

"That's rich, coming from a cattle rancher."

His brows drew together. "It's simply a family business, Heather, not a choice. We treat our cattle very well. I'm sure you, like many other people, don't want to know the cow you're about to eat."

"I'm a vegetarian."

He appeared surprised. "In Texas? I thought they ran all of your kind out after the Alamo." He chuckled as he eyed the rain. "Should we attempt to make a run for the stables?"

"I think we'd better." Heather was itching to put a little distance between her and her nemesis.

"I'm glad we had a chance to talk outside of the ring, Heather."

She went to the door. "Why is that? So you could learn more about my weaknesses?"

He opened the door for her. "No, so I could learn you don't have any weaknesses."

She thought she should give him some snooty reply, but then reconsidered. Taunting her competition didn't hold the same appeal as it had before the thunderstorm. She was seeing Grant Crowley in a whole new light ... and Heather definitely didn't like how it made her feel.

* * *

By the time she and Grant had crossed the threshold of wide doors at the entrance of Kenilworth Stables, Rayne was waiting. When Heather ran through the doors with Grant at her side, she could not help but notice the smug smile on Rayne's pink lips.

"I'd better see to my horse," Grant said as he shook the rain from his black jacket. "Heather, I enjoyed our chat. I hope we get to do it again."

He strode down the wide shed row, his boots kicking up the dust from the thin layer of shavings covering the ground. Heather found it even harder to turn away as she watched his tight round ass walk away.

"So...." Rayne began next to her. "What's going on with you and Grant Crowley?"

Heather faced her, determined not to give in to the curiosity dancing in Rayne's gold-flecked eyes. "We were in the timekeeper's shack. We ducked in there when the storm hit."

Rayne took the helmet containing the wet red ribbon from Heather's hands. "What did you two do for twenty minutes? I mean, he's obviously still alive, so that rules out all of the usual modes of homicide."

"We talked," Heather told her.

"Talked?" Rayne's smile widened. "About what?"

Heather let her eyes wander over the shed row. "Nothing in particular. Just small talk."

Rayne pulled the red ribbon from the helmet and held it up, inspecting it. "You can't fool me, Heather Phillips. I saw the way you were watching his ass. Butt watching is a sure sign of interest on a woman's part."

Snatching back her black-velvet helmet, Heather smirked. "Nice try, Rayne, but I'm not interested in Grant. I've got enough trouble keeping one temperamental twelve hundred pound man between my legs … I don't have room for another."

"You always did have a way with words, Heather." Rayne chuckled, rubbing her hand over her swollen belly. "No one would blame you if you were interested in Grant Crowley."

Heather felt a rush of warmth rise up her body and settle right below the high collar on her white dress shirt. "Crowley is an arrogant piece of shit who needs to be put in his place. I could never … he's in a relationship."

"I'd hardly call that a relationship. He can barely stand to look at the woman. You saw them together. She's a bimbo."

"Men like bimbos," Heather argued. "Former Ms. Dallas beauty queens who know how to smile the right way, laugh at their jokes, and please them between the sheets."

"What makes you think she pleases Crowley between the sheets?" Rayne's hazel eyes narrowed on Heather. "Did you see the way he looked at her? I sure did, and it wasn't lust I saw in his face; it was contempt. The man can't wait to get rid of her."

"Men don't get rid of that kind of woman. Vanessa Luke knows how to keep a man coming back for more."

"What if Grant Crowley wanted you instead of Vanessa?" Rayne curiously raised her eyebrows. "Would you go for it?"

She considered the question, and then shut down the X-rated visions clouding her judgement. Heather had learned long ago that where men were concerned it was best not to daydream. Daydreaming only led to disappointment and eventually heartache.

She had suffered through enough doomed relationships to know that the good ones only existed in fairy tales.

"No. I wouldn't get involved with him," Heather finally affirmed. "A man like that only uses a woman for what he can get from her and then tosses her aside."

"Wouldn't you want to be used by the likes of Crowley, at least for one night?"

Heather hooked her finger inside her tight collar, desperate to get a little air beneath her sweltering black jacket. "I'm not what he wants."

"You're wrong. You may think he's into those beauty queen smiles and vacuous personalities like every other man in Texas, but he wants more from a woman. He looks at you the way Trent looked at me when we were first together."

"And how is that? Like I'm the competition?"

Rayne's lips twisted into a devilish grin. "No, like you're the prize."

Alexandrea Weis

Chapter 3

Monday morning Heather arrived at the glass entrance to the Medical Center of Lewisville. Wearing her usual blue scrubs and with her long brown hair pulled back in a ponytail, she meandered down the stark white halls, following the signs to the emergency room. As her tennis shoes squeaked on the polished white-tiled floors, she thought back to her encounter with Grant. Heather had spent the entire weekend analyzing his every word, trying to find some hidden meaning, but once she had climbed out of her bed that morning, she found herself more perplexed than ever by the man.

"Hey, Heather," a voice called from behind the curved oak sign-in desk for the ER.

"Hi there, Cali. Are we busy yet?"

The coffee-skinned receptionist with the bright brown eyes laughed. "Hell yeah. Got several admits still being worked up. And you know who is on, and he's in a major tizzy this morning, so watch out, girl."

Heather went to the wide double doors to the side of the desk and hit the round metal button on the side of the wall. The doors slowly opened, offering a glimpse into the ER.

"I appreciate the heads up, Cali."

Making her way down the corridor, Heather snuck peeks into the exam rooms on either side. Tugging at the leather backpack over her shoulder, she noted that several of the rooms were occupied, but the hallway seemed pretty quiet.

"That's a good sign."

She approached the nurses' station set at the end of the hallway and saw two heads bowed low behind the high counter. Easing around the counter, Heather spied two women making last minute notations on charts.

"Busy night?"

A blue-eyed blonde looked up. "Hey, Heather. No, just the usual."

The dark-eyed beauty sitting next to her reached for a white paper coffee cup. "Three asthma attacks, a broken wrist, two with chest pain, assorted stitches needed for various stupid accidents, and one drunk driver who hit a tree and is sleeping it off in twelve."

Heather dumped her backpack on the counter. "Cali told me you know who is on."

Both women rolled their eyes in unison.

"Oh my God," the dark-eyed woman uttered. "He's in a foul mood this morning, so steer clear of him."

Heather shifted her hip on the counter. "What's so special about this morning?"

Both women looked at each other, flashing mischievous grins.

"Aw, come on," the blonde offered. "You know why. The only time the man gets out of whack is when you're on the schedule." She stood from her chair, holding a red binder in her hand. "You really should do all of us a favor and sleep with him, Heather."

"Jesus, Babs." Heather waved her hand down the ER hallway. "Want to say that a little louder so the patients can hear?"

The dark-eyed nurse wearing blue scrubs sat back in her chair while inspecting Heather over the rim of her coffee cup. "So when are you going to make poor Ben Eisenberg's dreams come true? The man only has eyes for you, Heather."

Heather folded her arms over her chest, pouting. "Really, Cassandra, we're just friends. Why do you guys insist that there is anything more?"

"Girl," Cassandra clucked. "You're about the worst liar there is. Everyone, from maintenance all the way up to administration, knows poor old Ben is in love with you. Hell, I heard the guys in security have a pool going on when you two are going to sleep together."

Heather bolted up from the counter, grabbing for her backpack. "Very funny."

Babs slid the red binder in her hand into a circular rack above the desk. "You can't blame everyone in the hospital for talking about it, Heather. You've led that poor guy on for years."

Heather's mouth fell open. "I have not led him on. If anything, I keep—"

"Babs, I need the labs on eight," a man's high-pitched voice called from down the hall.

All three women turned to see a lanky man, dressed in green scrubs and a white coat, making his way toward the nurses' station. With a lumbering stride and jovial round face, the physician had thin black hair that fell over his eyes like a comma. His cheeks appeared a little too large for his face, reminding Heather at times of a chipmunk stuffed with nuts for the winter. He wore a red T-shirt under his scrubs, allowing just a smidge of his dark chest hairs to poke out over the collar. His eyes were a deep shade of blue and surrounded by thick black lashes, and his forehead was short and came to an abrupt stop at his brow, causing a slight ridge. His lips were thin, his mouth small, and his chin was round and dimpled.

"I'm on it, Dr. Ben," Babs said, reaching for a chart in the rack.

When Ben Eisenberg raised his eyes from the binder in his hands, he spotted Heather behind the desk. The momentary hush across the ER was unnerving, especially for Heather.

"Heard we were on together for today," he said, coming up to the desk.

Heather slung her leather backpack over her shoulder. "Sure looks that way."

"Good." He turned his attention to Cassandra. "Ten needs their IV disconnected, and twelve needs their discharge instructions signed."

Cassandra stood from her chair and put her coffee cup down. "Sure thing."

Ben Eisenberg lifted his penetrating blue eyes to Babs. "I need you to push five of Lasix in fifteen. Let's see if we can get some more fluid off her before we send her home."

Babs diverted her eyes to Heather and slowly smiled. "I'll do that first, and then get your labs, Dr. Ben."

Heather's stomach flipped as the women quickly vacated the nurses' station. After Babs and Cassandra had disappeared down the hall, Ben Eisenberg came around the high desk to Heather's side. After tossing the red binder in his hands to the countertop, he softly uttered, "You've been avoiding me."

She nervously tucked a stray tendril of brown hair behind her ear. "I haven't been avoiding you; I've been taking some time off to work with Murphy. I've got a lot of big shows coming up."

He hiked his hip up on the corner of the desk, never taking his eyes off her. "How is Murphy?"

She held her head up. "We had a show over the weekend."

He tucked his pen in the top pocket of his white coat. "Really? How did you do?"

"Came in second … again, to my rival, Grant Crowley." She peered into Ben's blue eyes. "He said you two know each other."

"His father is a big contributor and general pain in the ass to the hospital board."

She hesitated, her curiosity eating away at her. "Grant said that he asked you about me," she finally divulged, attempting to sound casual.

He paused, taking in the curve of her jaw. "He mentioned you rode together when I ran into him at a benefit two weeks back. He asked me some questions about you."

"Oh." She made a move to turn toward the nurse's lounge to the rear of the station, but he held her arm.

"We need to talk, Heather."

The sigh that left her lips sounded as frustrated as she felt. "There's nothing to discuss, Ben."

He stood up. "Ever since you ran out on me a month ago, you've been juggling your shifts around so we don't work together and ignoring all of my phone calls." He tilted closer to her. "What is it? What did I do wrong? Was it because I brought up living together? I thought you wanted that."

She anxiously scanned the nurses' station, hoping no one overheard them. "Jesus, Ben. We had a few nights together, and then you start making this a relationship. It was just sex."

He let go of her arm, his eyes growing round with anger. "It was more than that. I want more than just sex with you. How long are you going to keep running away from relationships, Heather?"

She took a step away from him. "I don't run away from relationships."

"Bullshit. You're what, thirty-three? How much longer do you think you can keep pushing men away before they stay away for good? I know you liked being with me just as much as I liked being with you. We have something. Let's not ruin it because of your—"

"Dr. Ben," Babs shouted from one of the exam rooms. "I need you."

"I'm on my way." His eyes veered to Heather. "This conversation isn't over."

Heather's body sagged at the thought of the confrontation to come. Shaking her head and debating the possibility of finding a job at another facility, Heather went to the door that led to the nurses' lounge.

Placing her hand on the silver doorknob, she muttered, "This day is going to suck."

* * *

A little after ten that morning, Heather was walking out of a room after helping a patient with congestive heart failure. She was removing her rubber gloves when Emily, the unit secretary, came up to her. The heavyset mother of five put on a strained smile.

"We've got a VIP coming. Administration just phoned Dr. Ben."

Heather dropped her gloves in a wastebasket in the hallway. "Any idea who?"

Emily shrugged. "Someone big. I suspect … money big. You know how much this hospital kisses ass to donors. They just told him it was some kind of farming accident."

"I'll get six set up." Heather glimpsed the door to the larger of the ER rooms close to the nurses' station. "Better have radiology, respiratory, and CT standing by."

"Already done," Emily admitted. "Your boyfriend even called the head of orthopedics and cardiology himself to tell them to get ready."

"He's not my boyfriend, Emily."

Emily snorted with amusement. "Not yet, but he will be."

"You're not buying into the gossip, are you?"

Emily tittered, a light tinkling laugh that matched her demure appearance. "All bullshit is based in fact, Heather."

Watching Emily waddle back down the hall to the nurses' station only added to Heather's resolve. "I've got to get out of here."

She was heading to the entrance of exam room six when Ben came alongside her. "We've got a VIP coming."

"I heard." She grabbed some supplies from a cart by the nurses' station. "I'm on it."

"ETA five minutes," he told her, and rushed to the ER entrance.

As he strutted away, Heather became distracted by the sway of his white coat as it whipped around his long legs. Flashbacks of their time together floated through her head.

Their affair had started out innocently enough. After months of hinting at a date, Ben had finally asked her to dinner at one of her favorite restaurants. Deciding to tempt fate, she took a chance on the man. He had been courteous and sweet, even avoiding kissing her until the end of their date. Standing before the door of her simple ranch home, his good-night kiss had been warm, soft, and utterly boring. That was what she remembered most about their time together in bed; he had been enthusiastic, catered to her wants, but it had all felt … dull. Like a meticulously rehearsed ballet, sex with Ben had lacked that spark of spontaneity she had hoped for. It hadn't been bad; it just hadn't been enough to leave her wanting more.

Turning away, she entered the exam room, forcing her mind to prepare for the coming trauma. As she flushed IV lines and set up a code cart in the room, she began to wonder what was wrong with her. Grant Crowley's words from the previous Saturday at the horse show were still fresh in her mind.

"Just because I don't like to date idiots doesn't make me a lesbian," she mumbled. "Do people honestly think that I would want—?"

"Thirty-seven-year-old male found down on the scene," a man shouted as a gurney barged through the exam room door. "He was helping to move cattle out of a pen when he got pinned."

The two emergency medics dressed in dark blue jumpers were on either side of the gurney, with Ben coming in the door behind them.

"No obvious broken bones," an older medic with silver hair went on. "His airway is intact, and there is an eight-inch laceration on the left chest. Vitals are stable, he responds to all commands but is groggy. A loss of consciousness was reported at the scene."

Heather went into full trauma mode, rushing to the head of the gurney and helping to transfer IV bags to the hospital bed. She was busy checking the lines in her patient's arms when she spotted the blood along the right side of the man's torn and muddy white dress shirt. Taken aback, she inspected his mud-covered businesslike attire and pondered why someone would be wearing such a shirt and black suit pants around cattle. Without hesitation, her eyes traveled to the face of the man lying on the gurney.

"Oh shit."

The two medics and Ben went silent.

"What is it?" Ben posed, sounding more concerned about her reaction than his patient.

Heather pointed at the unconscious man on the gurney. "That's Grant Crowley."

"We know that, Heather." Ben went around her to the head of the hospital bed. "I told you a VIP."

He grabbed the edge of the red back board under Grant's head as Heather reached for the side of the board beneath his legs. The two technicians stood on the other side of the gurney, waiting to transfer him to the bed.

"On three, nice and easy," Ben instructed, gripping the red board.

After Grant had been safely transferred to the hospital bed, the emergency technicians began moving the gurney out of the room.

"Thanks, guys," Ben called to the men.

"His father followed the ambulance in," the older of the two medics said as he pushed the gurney to the door. His blue eyes twinkled as he gave a gap-toothed smile. "Get ready. He's a real piece of work."

As the exam room door closed, Heather began cutting open Grant's shirt and placing the white leads on his chest to monitor his heartbeat and respirations. She eyed the large bruise forming on his right cheek and temple.

"You should have told me," she softly said to Ben.

While pulling his black stethoscope out of his jacket pocket, Ben went around to the other side of the bed. "And ruin the surprise?"

Heather wrapped the automatic blood pressure cuff around Grant's left arm. "What in the hell does that mean?"

Ben inspected the discoloration down the right side of Grant's temple. "He asked me a lot of questions about you, but I didn't know why at the time. By the look on your face after they wheeled him in, I'd have to guess there is more to the two of you than just a friendly rivalry."

"Christ, Ben. This isn't the time to—"

Grant began to stir. His eyes opened and he blinked several times, as if trying to focus on his surroundings.

"Grant?" Heather angled over him. "Do you know where you are?"

When his amber eyes settled on Heather, the change in them was instantaneous. The confusion was gone, and he examined every curve of her face.

"Ms. Phillips?" His voice was raspy, but still strong and deep. "We meet again." He searched the room. "What happened?" He struggled to sit up.

"No, Grant, don't move," Ben advised, grabbing his other arm. "You've had a bad accident and have been knocked unconscious. We need to see what else is going on with you."

Grant settled down and Ben released his arm. "Jesus, you got a hell of a bedside manner there, Ben."

Heather hid her grin. Ben had always been abrupt with patients. The staff had given him the nickname Dr. Frost, but no one had ever shared that little tidbit with Ben. Next to his curt tone and lack of empathy, his snapping turtle temper was well-known about the halls of Lewisville Medical Center.

"What the hell am I lying on?" Grant complained.

"It's a backboard," Heather told him. "We'll take it away in a minute after Dr. Ben examines you. Can you tell us what happened?"

"I was on my way to a business meeting when I got called to the back pens to look over some of the new calves born this season." He raised his hand to the cervical collar around his neck. "One of the men got caught in the pens by a pissed off heifer. I went to help him and she cornered me." He tugged at the foam collar. "That's the last thing I remember."

"Looks like this wound is going to need some stitches," Ben declared, inspecting the laceration down Grant's muscular chest.

Heather diverted her eyes from his face to his trim body, eyeing the thick, ropelike muscles in his arms and washboard abs. The mysterious tingle she felt in her belly whenever he was around surged to life.

"Why is it so bright in here?" Grant croaked, placing his hand over his eyes.

"Follow my finger," Ben directed as he passed his right index finger back and forth in front of Grant's face. "How many do you see?" Ben held up two fingers in front of Grant.

"Two, I think," Grant replied. "They're awfully fuzzy."

"Call CT." Ben looked up at Heather. "Let's get him in there first thing." Ben gazed down the rest of Grant's body. "Are you hurting anywhere else? How about your neck? Any numbness or tingling in your hands or feet?"

Grant shook his head. "Just sore all over, and I've got a bad headache."

Ben removed the cervical collar from about Grant's neck. "Get x-rays of his neck and spine just to make sure." Placing the collar to the side, Ben motioned to Grant's legs. "Wiggle your toes."

Grant did as requested. "I had shoes on before I was hit."

Heather smiled for him. "EMS probably took them off at the site as part of their evaluation."

"Heather, why don't you make those calls to X-ray and CT while I finish my assessment?" Ben coolly suggested.

She was about to leave the room when shouting erupted from the hallway outside the exam room door.

Ben's shoulders seemed to sag. "I can guess who that is."

Heather furrowed her brow. "Who?"

"My father," Grant grumbled from the bed. "Christ, this is all I need."

The exam room door flew open and a tall, robust man with sparse silver curly hair and deep amber eyes stared into the room. Wearing pleated blue jeans, a pressed white dress shirt, black cowboy boots, a shiny gold Rolex, and carrying a black cowboy hat in his hands, Tad Crowley was the epitome of a Texas ranch owner. His angular features, tanned skin, and sharp eyes matched his son's, and the added wrinkles on his face and soft skin around his neck were the only hints to his true age. When he spied his muddy and half-naked son on the bed, Heather could almost see the man's blood pressure rise, adding to the redness in his cheeks.

"Son of a bitch!" The older man slapped his hat against his jeans. "Who is the stupid asshole who let you in those pens, Grant?"

"Mr. Crowley, you need to wait outside," Ben asserted, trying to sound authoritative, but Heather swore his voice trembled as he spoke.

"Which one of the little ass-kissers on staff here are you?" Tad Crowley roared.

"I, um…." Ben's brow beaded with sweat. "I'm Dr. Eisenberg, Mr. Crowley. I'm administrator of this ER at Lewisville—"

"Do I look like I give a shit? What are you doing to help my son?" Tad Crowley stepped into the room, walking with a slight limp, but when his eyes fell on Heather he stopped in his tracks. "You wanna tell me what's wrong with him?"

Ben went around the bed to take up position right in front of the worried father. Squaring his shoulders, he raised his head to meet the beady eyes of Tad Crowley. "You need to wait outside while I finish my assessment. As you can see, he is awake and talking."

"Are you talking, Grant?" the older man yelled into the small exam room.

"Jesus, Dad," Grant groaned from the bed. "Give it a rest."

Tad Crowley nodded his head. "He sounds fine to me."

"I have yet to make that determination, Mr. Crowley," Ben argued.

Tad Crowley peered around Ben's shoulder and his eyes connected with Heather. "You take care of him, ya hear me?"

Heather nodded and then felt Grant's hand wrap around hers. The simple gesture had an unsettling effect; her stomach fluttered with excitement and her heart quickened. She didn't understand what was happening. No one had ever elicited such a response from her. But Grant's touch had definitely awakened something. In that instant, everything changed between them. She couldn't put her finger on how, but she knew their relationship would never be the same again.

Tad Crowley gave a contemptuous humph and exited the exam room. After he was out in the hall, Ben shut the door and returned to Grant's bedside.

"Let's draw a full chem profile, CBC, UA, then get X-ray in here." He lowered his eyes to Grant. "Once I've got the films to confirm there are no broken bones, I will remove that board from underneath you."

Grant sighed and nodded his head. "Fine. Just hurry up and get me out of here."

Ben placed his hands on Grant's chest and began palpating along the long gash on his left side. "Pretty safe to say you will be staying the night, Grant. We need to observe you for a while."

"No way. I've got to get back to the stables tonight."

When Ben's eyes connected with Heather's hand wrapped in Grant's, he scowled at her. "Go to the desk and call radiology, CT, and the lab. Then let admitting know we'll need a VIP room. I'll finish my assessment."

Slowly, Heather pulled her hand away from Grant's grasp. She could see the apprehension in his eyes, and she yearned to give him some encouragement, but Ben was watching. Placing Grant's hand at his side, she went to the exam room door.

"Send Babs in here while you make those phone calls," Ben ordered when she reached for the handle. "She can assist me with this patient."

Outside in the hallway, she quietly shut the door. For a brief second, she could still feel Grant's hand in hers and pictured his anxious eyes looking up at her from the bed. A spark shot down from her belly to her groin. Resting a shaking hand over her stomach, Heather tried to cool the fire building inside of her.

"Shit. What just happened?"

Chapter 4

Grant was being prepared to be moved to a private room on the fifth floor. His father had been pacing like a mad tiger in front of his exam room door, yelling into his cell phone and chomping on an unlit cigar. Many of the staff had avoided making eye contact with the ornery older man, but when Heather approached the room to check on her patient, Tad Crowley caught her arm.

"You know my son, don't you?"

She put on an engaging smile, but could not help but cringe as she saw the man's amber eyes sweeping up and down her figure. "Yes, we ride together ... well, not ride, but we have competed against each other in several horse shows."

A flicker of interest lit up his craggy face and he lowered his gaze to her ID badge hanging from her tunic pocket. "Heather Phillips. You're the woman who always comes in second behind him at those horse shows of his."

Heather was amazed that a busy man like Tad Crowley would be aware of such a detail. "How did you know about that?"

He let go of her arm. "Gigi, my daughter, spoke about you. She always likes to tell me how Grant does at the shows. She's mentioned you on several occasions. She calls you 'the brainy brunette with boobs who can ride.'"

Heather chuckled. "Not sure if I should feel flattered or insulted, Mr. Crowley."

"Coming from Gigi, I would suspect you were meant to feel a little bit of both. She's tends to push people the wrong way." He removed the foul-looking cigar from the corner of his mouth. "I'm glad you're watching out for my son, Ms. Phillips."

"The entire ER staff is watching out for your son, Mr. Crowley."

"I knew your old man, Dr. Carl Phillips. He and I met several times at a few benefits for Baylor Hospital. If you're anything like him, then you're good people."

Heather's heart rose in her throat at the mention of her father. "I'm surprised to hear you say that after everything that happened."

"I never liked what they did to Carl. He didn't mean to harm anybody. I was sorry to hear about his arrest … and about your mother. Jessie Phillips was a good woman."

"I appreciate that," she softly said, and made a move toward the door.

"I don't want my boy left alone in some hospital room all night. I want someone with him the entire time." Heather turned and faced him. "I've had enough experiences with these places to know people don't always come when you need them."

"I can assure you, Mr. Crowley, that your son—"

"I want you to stay with him," Tad Crowley cut her off. "Stay in his room and make sure he gets everything he needs."

Heather took a step back, searching for the words to handle the situation. "Ah, Mr. Crowley, the hospital has sitter services if you feel your son needs—"

"I want you." He pointed the cell phone in his hand at her. "Already discussed it with your hospital administrator, Tim Wellborn. He said that would be fine with him."

Heather didn't know what to say. She had already put in a full eight hours in the ER, and she had a show to prepare for and needed to get to the stables to practice with Murphy.

"I'm sorry, Mr. Crowley, I've already had a long day here and I need to get home and see to my horse."

"That wasn't a request, missy." Tad Crowley chuckled, sounding like a malevolent wizard in a children's fairy tale. "Your administrator guaranteed me that you would stay with my son."

Heather balled her hands into fists. Having a riding master tell her what to do was one thing, but she was damned if she was going to take it from anyone else. "Mr. Crowley, I'm not one of your ranch hands. You cannot boss me around."

"Yes, I can," he edged in with a smug grin. "As far as I'm concerned, one nurse is as good as another, but I saw my son holding your hand in there earlier. That means he trusts you." He tossed his cigar on a cart by the door. "Now, I'm not one to hand out praise, Ms. Phillips, but if I were you, I'd take that as a compliment. My son trusts no one. Coldest son of a bitch I ever met, even if he is mine." He paused, and then added, "I'll pay you triple what you make in one night here."

Heather was floored by the proposal. The prospect of additional money was very alluring. She had bills to pay, and keeping Murphy in the show ring had stretched her budget to the breaking point. She considered spending the evening with Grant, and the tingle in her gut began to spread throughout her body.

"I will do it for your son, Mr. Crowley. We may be competitors in the show ring, but he is a fellow rider, and therefore a friend."

"Friends are just people who haven't fucked you over yet, Ms. Phillips. Excuse my French, but I'm an old cattle rancher who has seen my fair share of lies and trickery." He dipped his head to her. "Grant will be discharged in the morning, and after that he will be transferred to my house on Crowley Ranch. Doc Ben said you only need to stay a few days at the house to make sure he is back on his feet. I 'spect there won't be much for you to do, but—"

"What are you talking about?" Heather interrupted. "I agreed to stay the night with him, not babysit him at your home."

"Three days to babysit him, make sure he is back on his feet and doesn't overexert himself, and I will pay you a month's salary." His gray eyebrows went up. "Is that agreeable?"

"No, it is not agreeable. I have a job here. I'm on the schedule for the next three days and I cannot—"

"Already taken care of, Ms. Phillips. Tim Wellborn has handled everything so you will have the next week off to take care of my son."

"But I have responsibilities," she maintained.

"What responsibilities? You have no husband, no children. The only thing you take care of is your horse. My daughter tells me you're known for not giving a damn about people, which I personally think is an admirable quality. If it makes you feel any better, Gigi has already contacted Rebecca Harmon at Southland

Stables. She's agreed to see to your horse, Murphy, for a few days. Not to worry, Ms. Phillips, I've taken care of everything."

She shook her head, feeling any further protests were pointless. "What did Grant say about all of this?"

He wiped his hand over his mouth, his intense eyes glowing with irritation. "He doesn't know. He would only refuse any offer of help. Just tell him you're doing this for me. I hired you, Ms. Phillips, not my son. I'll be expecting you in the morning at my home." He turned away and was heading into the hall when she stopped him.

"What if I had said no, Mr. Crowley?"

He halted and showed her his profile. "No is something I just don't like hearing, Ms. Phillips. So I do everything in my power to make sure the answer will be yes."

As he strode down the hallway, Heather reached for the door handle. She hated being manipulated by people, but reasoned that Tad Crowley would have gotten what he wanted from her, no matter how hard she fought back. Experience had taught her that money always spoke louder than dignity. She needed to swallow hers in order to keep her job and continue paying for Murphy's upkeep.

Stepping inside Grant's room, she saw him resting on the bed, a cooling pack wrapped over his eyes. When he heard the door to the exam room close, he raised his head.

"Am I going to my room?" He put the cooling pack on the side of the bed.

Noting the pale color in his cheeks and how the blue in the hospital gown draped around his shoulders offered a clear view of the white bandage on the left side of his muscular chest, she approached the bed. Heather forced herself to think of him as a patient and not a good-looking man ... but it wasn't working.

"Yes, patient transport is coming to take you to a suite on the fifth floor."

He tugged at his hospital gown. "Are you sure this is necessary? I'd prefer to sleep in my own bed."

"This is safer. Just in case you have any problems during the night, there will be help close by."

He sat up in the bed, ignoring the gown as it slipped from his shoulders, offering a better glimpse of his muscular chest. "I want to thank you for all of your help today. I appreciate your … kindness."

"I was doing my job, Grant, and it seems I will continue taking care of you for a few more days."

His lips turned sharply downward. "What are you talking about?"

"Your father hired me to be your nurse for tonight and after you go home. It seems I will be returning to Crowley Ranch with you."

His eyes melted into hers. "How much is he paying you?"

"Enough, but that's not why I'm doing it."

He closed his eyes and rubbed his fingers over his temples. "Why are you doing it? To torture me?"

She stood next to his bed, acutely aware of his semi-naked body. "I think maybe I'm the one being tortured here." She cleared her throat. "Your father went to the hospital administrator and demanded I stay with you. It seems my job is on the line."

"Why didn't you to tell him to go to hell?" he asserted in a milder voice.

"I can't afford to do that. I'm not independently wealthy."

"This is all I need." Grant got comfortable in his bed. "I don't want a nurse."

"Let's just pretend for a few days that you do. It will make your father happy, keep me gainfully employed, and you can learn more things about me so you can continue beating me in the ring. I'm sure that will make you happy." Heather went to the IV pole next to his bed and rolled the stopcock down, halting the drip.

"I'm not the twisted bastard you think I am, Heather."

She turned to him and was jolted by the glint of fire in his eyes. "What I think doesn't matter."

His eyes wandered over her round face, full lips, wide jaw, and olive-toned skin. When he came to her bright blue orbs, he smiled.

"Maybe we should start over. I think I would very much like the chance to be friends, and not rivals."

"Nice try, Grant." She directed her attention to the IV tubing taped to his right arm. "You made the ground rules the day you set out to destroy me in the ring."

He folded his hands over his lap. "I never set out to destroy you, merely dent your ego a little."

Pulling at the tape that secured the IV in place, Heather tried not to grin as he flinched when the tape pulled at the hair on his arm.

"I think you're enjoying this," he murmured.

A satisfied smile curled her lips. "Maybe I am. We're not in the show ring anymore. You're in my world now, and there is a whole different set of rules here."

He shifted his head closer to her. "I don't like following the rules, Heather. I'm better at breaking them."

She peeled the last of the tape away and removed the IV line from the catheter. Stringing the tubing up on the IV pole, Heather avoided his eyes. "I'm just here to make sure you don't die, Grant. As long as you don't break that one rule, we'll get along just fine."

After making a hasty retreat for the exam room door, she slipped into the hall. Once safely outside, she fell back against the door and closed her eyes, fighting to steady her galloping heartbeat.

"You okay?" Ben questioned.

Heather opened her eyes and nodded. "Fine, just a little tired."

Ben's blue eyes inspected her features. "Tim Wellborn just called me and told me about Crowley's demand you sit with his son for a few days. Are you sure that's wise?"

Heather pushed off from the door. "Wise, no; profitable, yes."

"I wish you wouldn't. You don't know what kind of man Grant Crowley is."

"He's a man, Ben. Aren't you bastards all the same?"

Heather was about to step away when he stood in front of her. "Grant is well-known for setting his sights on a woman and hunting her down until he gets what he wants."

She sighed, knowing where this was going. "That won't happen with me. Grant has nothing but contempt for me."

"That's not what I witnessed before when you were holding his hand. You two seemed pretty cozy."

"I was being a good nurse."

Ben arched closer, dropping his voice. "He may look appealing, Heather, and his name and money may seem awfully tempting, but I'm telling you the guy is no good. I've heard stories about what he does with women. He's got a reputation for liking it real rough. I don't want you alone with him."

She stepped away, her mouth ajar. "Jesus, Ben. You're acting like we are married or something. As far as what Grant Crowley does or doesn't do with women, it's none of my business. I'm not going to sleep with the guy. He's involved with someone and I don't—"

"That beauty queen isn't going to last. Everyone knows he has grown bored with her. You're not safe around him."

Heather held up her hand. "This has gone far enough. What I do, who I do it with, where I go, are none of your concern, Ben." She glanced around the ER, hoping no one was taking in their little tete-a-tete. "This is exactly the reason I left that night. You started talking about the future in terms of we, and it scared the shit out of me."

"I asked you to move in with me and you took off running for the door," he argued, raising his voice.

Concerned about who could hear them, Heather took the elbow of his white coat and pulled him along the corridor toward the supply closet. Once in front of the closet door, she turned to him. "You asked me to move in with you after three weeks together. What the hell was I supposed to think? I told you I didn't want to get serious, and then you go and ask me something like that. What did you expect me to do?"

"I expected you to consider it. Not run out my front door half-dressed. We could have talked about it. Who cares how long we've been dating? We've known each other for over two years."

"This is exactly what I'm talking about, Ben. You can't just jump into living with someone. I need to work up to something like that."

He tossed up his hands. "Fine, we'll work up to it. You can start by turning down Crowley's offer and going out with me tonight. We'll talk, we'll set ground rules, we'll figure out how to split the bills … whatever you want. Just don't go with Crowley."

Heather gauged the look of desperation in his eyes and it disturbed her. She had seen him handle numerous life and death situations, but in all their time in the ER together she had never seen him appear so terrified.

"I've already agreed to take care of him, Ben. I can't go back on my word."

"Old man Crowley won't care if you change your mind."

"I'll care, Ben." She stifled her growing aggravation and put on a warm smile. "I appreciate the concern, but I will be fine."

"Will you at least think about my offer?" He took a strand of her hair in his fingers. "Please?"

Heather knew she should shut him down, but the hint of hope in his eyes was too much to ignore. She wasn't the kind of woman who could leave a man in the dust and then walk over him with her pointy high heels. She could never be that cruel.

"Sure, Ben, I'll think about it," she heard herself saying before she hurriedly walked away.

Chapter 5

It took another hour before Grant was finally situated in his hospital suite. The room had an adjoining sitting area set against windows that looked out over a man-made lake. Painted in muted earthy tones of brown, it reminded Heather more of a hotel than a place for the sick. The sofa and recliner were done in brown leather with velvet throw pillows. Hanging on the walls were prints of green mountaintops and wooded forests.

"Never been in this room before," Heather professed as she set a green blanket at the foot of Grant's bed.

"It's for VIP's," Tad Crowley explained, hovering close to his son's bed. "Your administrator said they always have it on stand-by."

Heather refrained from telling him that she thought all patients should be treated as VIP's. Tad Crowley didn't seem like the kind of man who gave a damn about anyone other than himself.

"I have an ambulance set up to transport you to the house tomorrow morning," Tad Crowley informed his son.

"An ambulance?" Grant griped. "I don't need a goddamned—"

A flash of red flew in the door, cutting him off. When the blur stopped next to Grant's bed, Heather almost laughed out loud. Donning a red tennis outfit with a pleated skirt and brilliant white tennis shoes, Vanessa Luke was a caricature of the wealthy Dallas housewife. Her hands were covered with an assortment of shiny rings, and her long blonde hair had been teased to perfection and pulled back in a fashionable ponytail with a red bow.

"Honey," she cooed with all the sugary sweetness of a scorpion. "I was at the club when Gigi called me." She stood by the bed, gazing down in horror at his body. "Are you in pain? What can I do? You had me worried sick. Do you want me to stay the night with you?" She took a breath. "Gigi said you got attacked by some mad cow. Did they shoot the stupid animal that did this to you?"

"Vanessa, why are you here?" Grant questioned without a trace of emotion in his voice.

Heather eagerly watched the interaction between the couple as Rayne's words came back to her. Grant's features were flat; his attitude toward the woman appeared distrustful at best. She had never noticed it before, but their interaction was strained and almost uncomfortable to watch.

"Baby, I had to come. As soon as I found out, I bolted out of that club like a pig from a slaughter house. The idea of you being in the hospital, all alone—"

"He's not alone," Tad Crowley intruded. "He's got Heather to watch over him."

The mention of Heather's name made Vanessa spin around from the bed. When she faced Heather, Vanessa looked as if she were about to spit nails.

"What in the devil is she doing here?"

Tad Crowley closed the open room door. "I hired her to care for my son."

"What about me?" Vanessa challenged. "I can take care of him. He doesn't need her. She despises him. She might try to hurt him to keep him from riding." Vanessa waved to Heather. "You can't be serious, Mr. Tad. I can take better care of my—"

"Vanessa, you couldn't care for a pet rock." Tad Crowley moved toward the bed. "Heather is a professional and better equipped at handling blood than you. Last time you came down to the pens and saw a calf being born, Grant had to carry you all the way back to the house."

"But, Mr. Tad," Vanessa whined, sounding like a two-year-old having a tantrum.

"You're his girlfriend, Vanessa, not his nursemaid." Tad Crowley took her elbow. "I think we should go and let Grant rest." He urged her toward the door.

Vanessa scurried away from Tad Crowley's side. After planting a kiss on Grant's cheek, she declared, "I'll call you later, baby."

"Don't," Grant begged as he reclined on the bed. "I'll probably be asleep."

After his father and Vanessa had left, Grant sank into the bed, looking as if a great burden had been lifted from his shoulders.

"That woman drives me nuts," he muttered under his breath.

Heather contained her desire to giggle. "That doesn't sound good."

He leveled his eyes on her. "She's an even bigger thorn in my side than you."

"If she bugs you so much, then why continue seeing her?"

He lowered his eyes to the IV in his arm. "She has certain charms."

"Charms?" Heather snorted. "I'll bet."

Grant played with the tape securing his IV. "Do I detect a hint of jealousy in your voice?"

This time Heather did not hold back her sarcastic chortle. "Jealousy? Why on earth would I be jealous of her?"

He lifted his eyes. "Maybe because she's so successful with men."

Heather folded her arms over her chest, tempering the anger welling up in her gut. "I don't need to be ogled over and spoiled by a bunch of men who are more intrigued by my bra size than my brain. I only need one good man to make me happy."

"So where is he? Where is this good man of yours?" He waved his left hand over her figure. "Why aren't you married with a house in the suburbs and a kid or two on your knee?"

"Why aren't you married?" she returned, not wanting to answer his question.

He folded his hands on his lap, grinning. "I asked first."

"Jesus," she almost shouted. "Are you always this obnoxious?"

"I'm not being obnoxious." He rested his head on his pillow. "I'm getting to know you."

She tossed up her hand. "What's the point of that? So you can lull me into a false sense of security, get me to open up, and then use everything you learn against me later? Isn't that how your kind operates?"

"My kind?" He closed his eyes. "I know you think me a heartless bastard, Heather, but for the sake of argument, can we try to have a conversation that doesn't descend into name calling?"

"I make no promises."

"I guess that will have to do." He chuckled, sounding just like his father. "All right … to answer your question, I've never married because I never found a woman I wanted to marry." He sighed, sounding frustrated. "Most women bore me after a time."

Heather moved over to the leather sofa. "What about Vanessa? You obviously haven't grown bored with her yet."

He opened his eyes and peered over at her. "Vanessa is different, but not in the way you're thinking. She is more of a … profitable venture."

Heather had a seat on the sofa. "Profitable venture? I don't understand."

"Vanessa's family owns a large cattle ranch. Her father and my father have entertained the idea of merging the two properties, but I've yet to warm up to the idea of marrying Vanessa to seal the deal."

Heather's jaw fell. "Your father asked you to marry her for the business?"

"Now you can understand why she has become a thorn in my side. Lately, she and my father have been putting a lot of pressure on me to announce our engagement."

Heather nervously fidgeted and then stood from the sofa. "So you're thinking about marrying her."

"It's not something I want to do, but I may have to, yes."

Heather went to the bed and grasped the side rail. "That is the stupidest thing I've ever heard. You have a choice, Grant."

Sitting up a little, he grinned, amused by her reaction. "You really are naive, aren't you? Do you think everyone in the world marries for love?"

She let go of the side rail and stood back. "No, of course not, but marrying a woman you don't love out of some sense of family duty is idiotic. You're going to spend the rest of your life being miserable with a person you can't stand for what … your cattle farm?"

"I won't be miserable all of my life … just until a suitable amount of time has passed. Then we can resume our separate lives."

"You're kidding? What are you going to do ... keep mistresses, have affairs?"

"It's simply business." He repositioned himself in the bed. "What difference should the happiness of an obnoxious asshole like me make to you?"

Heather had to stop and think for a moment. He was right; why was she getting upset about his possible marriage? It wasn't like she was really attracted to the man ... or was she? "Well, what about your children?" she interrogated, ignoring the nagging questions whirling around in her head. "What will they think of your loveless marriage?" she added.

"Vanessa and I will never have children." He waved his hand in the air, disregarding her question. "Children are not a priority for me."

"What about down the road? When you're older? You may change your mind."

His eyes were on her again, sizing her up like a Hollywood director checking out a fresh young starlet. "I might. If that time comes, I'm sure Vanessa and I could come to some kind of arrangement."

"Arrangement?" She glared at him. "Children should be planned, wanted, not considered as an afterthought. After all, your children will be the ones paying for your mistakes. It may be nothing more than a business contract to you, but for them it will be a lifetime of living with the question of whether or not they were...." Her voice died away.

A heavy silence filled the air. Heather chastised her inability to keep her mouth shut. Her anger always got the better of her.

"Is that why you are the way you are?" he inquired, breaking the tension between them. "Because of what happened to your father and mother?"

She raised her chin, appearing defiant. "The way I am has nothing to do with them."

"Yes, it does. You're always so angry with everyone. It's as if you blame yourself for what happened to them." He adjusted his pillow and sat back in his bed. "Why don't you tell me about your father? I read about the trial in the newspaper, but that left more questions than answers for most people."

"Is learning the truth about my father going to help you rip me apart in the show ring?"

His amber eyes shot to hers. "I'm not the enemy, Heather. I'm trying to be your friend."

"My friend? You must be joking."

"Why not? I think you need a good friend." He smirked up at her. "Do you even have any friends?"

"I have friends. And I don't need—"

"I'm talking about friends you confide in, friends you can talk to about whatever is bothering you. I know you don't have relationships with men, but then who do you share your hopes and dreams with?"

A sickening wave rolled through Heather's stomach. How could she tell the man she had given up on those kinds of friends? Confiding anything to anyone was just giving them ammunition to use against her later. "I don't need to confide in anyone. I'm better off without friends like that."

"Are you?" His eyes turned to the windows. "I think you've been carrying so much around inside of you for so long that if you don't talk to someone soon, you'll lose touch with your heart."

"What would you care about my heart?"

"Your heart is what makes you a winner, Heather. It's the difference between blue ribbons and red ones."

She chuckled, letting off a little pent-up steam. "Now I know that bump on the head has affected you. That doesn't sound like something Grant Crowley would say to me. I'm your competition."

"Not after today." He shook his head. "When you held my hand in the exam room, I felt … I hoped something had changed between us. Was I wrong to think that?"

Heather couldn't come up with an answer. She had felt the change between them, but her suspicious nature doubted the validity of it.

"I was doing my job," she finally blurted out.

"Your job?" He raised his eyebrows. "I don't buy it."

"Think what you like, Grant." Heather backed away from the bed. "You need to stop talking and get some rest."

"You don't have to stay if you don't want to, Heather. I'm fine."

She went to the sofa and had a seat. "I told your father I would stay, and I'm staying."

"My old man could care less if you stay. All he wants is to make sure his interests are protected." He closed his eyes and tilted his head back on his pillow. "Bastard has never cared about anyone. He's one cold son of a bitch."

"Funny, he said the same thing about you."

His body relaxed in the bed. "He's right. But everything I am, he taught me to be."

After a few minutes, she noted the steady rise and fall of his chest beneath his hospital gown. Letting her eyes travel over his strong profile, she mulled over their conversation, making her wonder how much of what the man told her was genuine. She knew of his reputation, but somehow when she was with him, away from the show ring, she just couldn't see the ruthless competitor anymore. It was as if she were being offered glimpses of the man underneath all the bravado. As warnings from Ben, and words from Tad Crowley, flooded her mind, something Rayne had said came back to her. Could he be interested in her as more than just the competition? Heather hated to entertain such hope, but that was the problem with hope, once you allowed it into your heart, it had a pesky habit of never letting go.

Alexandrea Weis

Chapter 6

Heather had tried to keep her mind occupied while Grant dozed on and off throughout that evening. She had checked his vital signs and done routine neurological assessments to make sure he was still stable, but short of sitting by his bed and watching him sleep, there wasn't much for her to do. Finally, about eleven that evening, when Grant was soundly asleep, she decided to sneak out of his room to find some reading material to keep her awake during the long night ahead. She had successfully slipped outside his door when she was startled by a deep voice from behind.

"You wanna grab some coffee?"

Spinning around, she saw Ben outfitted in his street clothes of baggy blue jeans and a white button-down shirt. His hair was still wet and he smelled of his usual strong, musky cologne.

"What are you doing here?" she whispered, edging the door closed. "Your shift ended at seven."

"I know." He shrugged his hands into the front pockets of his jeans. "I went home and changed and decided to come back and check on you. I know we can't go out, but maybe we could grab some coffee and talk."

"I don't know, Ben. I shouldn't leave him alone for too long."

"I wish you would leave him alone. I don't trust him. Has he tried to put any moves on you?"

Heather fought to suppress her laughter. "Moves? What are we, in high school?"

"Men are men whether in high school or nursing homes, and all men have a set pattern of moves they use on women to lure them into bed."

She gawked at him. "Is this in a rule book or something?"

"No, all guys know this stuff." He pushed the comma of black hair from his eyes. "Every guy has a tried and true go to plan when it comes to women."

"What is your move? Did you try it on me?"

He shook his head. "I honestly tried all my best lines on you, and you shot me down every time. When I was finally honest with you, about just being friends, that's when you agreed to have dinner with me."

Friends. She thought of what Grant had told her.

"Do you think I confided in you when we were together … as a friend, I mean?"

Ben smiled, his blue eyes filled with mirth. "You confiding anything to anyone is a real stretch. You aren't the kind of woman to share your feelings, Heather. That's what I like about you. You're strong and capable."

Heather scrutinized his blue eyes. "What if I did want to confide in you? How would you feel about that, Ben?"

He suddenly appeared nervous. "Is this some kind of test? It's just not you, Heather." He took her elbow. "What about that coffee? We have some things to talk about, plans to make."

"Plans?" She was jarred by the word. "What plans?"

"Your place or mine for starters," Ben suggested with a beaming smile.

Heather dropped her head, hiding her frustration. "Ben, I said talk about getting back together, not moving in together. I agreed to consider it."

Setting his hand beneath her chin, he lifted her head. "I think we should just go ahead and do this. Jump in with both feet and see how it goes. What do you say?"

As she took in the hope gleaming in his eyes, Heather felt lower than dirt. She didn't have the strength to refuse him. She wanted to … wanted to push him away and shout out that she didn't need anybody, but she didn't believe that with the certainty that she had once possessed. Time was taking a toll on her resistance to Ben. One day she would need someone. No one could make it in this world without someone there to hold their hand, and maybe Ben was who she needed.

"You're not jumping all over me, so that must mean I have a chance here, right?" he probed, watching for her reaction.

Heather slowly nodded. "We can discuss all the details later. Right now, I need to see to my patient."

"When?" Ben persisted.

"After I get back from Crowley Ranch. We can talk then."

Ben's blue eyes lit up. "You're serious?"

"Yes," she reluctantly agreed. "Maybe you're right. I've spent enough time running from relationships. I need to grow up and embrace one."

His arms flew around her. "We're going be good together, you'll see." His lips came down on hers.

Heather gave in to his kiss, willing for her insides to tingle as they had done with Grant. But nothing happened. His lips were cool, soft, but did nothing for her.

Ben urged her lips to part. She went along, thinking maybe a more ardent kiss would stir her insides, but there wasn't even a hint of interest coming from her body.

What was wrong with her? Here was a successful, single man with a great career, but she didn't want him. She considered the possibility that relationships shouldn't be based on emotions. Maybe the time had come for her to be practical about life and about her circumstances. Ben was right, she couldn't go on forever being alone, and she was getting tired of trying.

Pulling away, she lowered her eyes. "We shouldn't do that here."

He caressed her cheek. "I don't care who sees us."

Stepping out of his embrace, she mustered a warm smile. "I'll call you when I'm back from Crowley Ranch."

Ben nodded and lowered his arms. "You do that. Call me when you're there, anytime. I want to know you're safe."

Before Heather would have chided him for being overprotective, but something inside of her snapped. It was time to change her ways.

"Sure. I'll call you after I get settled." She motioned to Grant's hospital room door. "I should get back."

"You've made me very happy, Heather." Ben added as she turned for the door. "I'm going to make you happy, too."

Heather had her doubts, but didn't voice them. She had never met a man who could make her happy, and didn't know if she would ever find one. Perhaps it was time to choose a man who could keep her comfortable. Happiness was a dream meant for the young; security was a necessity for the old.

After hastily sneaking back inside Grant's door, she was surprised to see the television on and Grant sitting up in bed, wide awake.

"You're up," she voiced, approaching his bed. "Do you need anything?"

He hit the remote connected to his hospital bed as he stared at the television. "I could use a whiskey and soda."

"Sorry, all out." She noted the ugly bruise forming on the side of his right cheek. "How's the head?"

"Pounding," he curtly replied.

"I could get you some Tylenol."

His eyes never left the television. "I'd prefer the whiskey."

"How about something to eat?"

"Forget it." He dropped the remote on the bed. "Let's talk."

Heather shrugged her shoulders and moved away from the bed. "All right. What do you want to talk about?"

He folded his arms over his chest as she took a seat on the sofa. "How about telling me what's going on with you and Dr. Ben Eisenberg for starters?"

"Were you eavesdropping?"

He sat up in the bed. "No, I was asleep and your voices outside my door woke me. So how long has it been going on?"

Heather's stomach dipped. "Me and Ben? We're friends."

"Friends?" He snickered. "You told me you didn't have any friends. From the conversation I heard, I would say there was more to the two of you than friendship." He threw off his green blanket. "You're actually going to consider living with him." He pushed back the side rail on his bed. "Really, Heather, I thought you had better taste than that."

She rushed toward the bed. "What are you doing?"

"Getting up," he flatly told her. "I'm sick of being in this bed."

"Grant, you need to take it easy. Your body has had a shock and you—"

"Stop worrying about me." He waved his hand in the air, dismissing her concern. Scooting to the edge of the bed, he stood up.

Heather placed her hand on his shoulder just as he wobbled slightly to the left. "You're not fine. Sit down on the bed."

He turned his eyes to her. "I have to go to the bathroom."

Heather grabbed for the plastic urinal hanging from the opposite side rail. "Use this."

He frowned at her. "I'd rather not."

She glimpsed the bathroom door on the opposite end of the room. "I'm not sure you should be getting up and walking—"

"I'm walking to the bathroom, Heather. I'm not an invalid; I just got kicked in the head."

She eased her arm around his waist. "Then I'm going with you."

"Fine." He wavered for a second or two. "You can take me to the bathroom door."

She started walking him slowly across the room, making sure to keep her arm securely about his waist.

"Glad you're starting to be reasonable," she commented.

"What are you being with Ben Eisenberg? Complacent?"

She stopped and abruptly turned to him. "What in the hell is that supposed to mean?"

He kept on moving toward the bathroom and Heather had to take a step or two to catch up. "It means that you have nothing in common with a man like that. He probably bores you to death."

"You've got a lot of—" Heather gritted her teeth. "I have a lot in common with Ben. We're both practical medical professionals and he ... I shouldn't be discussing this with you."

"And in bed? What do you have in common there?"

When they reached the bathroom door, Heather pushed it open for him. "That is none of your business."

He held on to the doorframe while taking in her blue eyes. "Admit it; he's too soft and polite. You're a woman who needs a man to be powerful and forceful with you." He dipped his head closer to her. "You like to be taken, not escorted to bed. There's a difference."

She gulped back a rush of nerves. "How would you know what I like in bed?"

His face lifted in a half-smile. "It's a gift I have. I can usually read what a woman likes in bed … and I always give it to them."

Heather was overcome by a sudden pang of longing. She scrambled to gather her thoughts. "Ah … I should go in the bathroom with you. To make sure you don't fall down."

"Stay out here," he ordered. "I'll call if I need you."

Deciding it was better not to argue, she waited by the door as he shuffled inside. Standing outside of the bathroom, she listened for sounds of crashing.

"Everything okay?"

"So tell me about you and Ben," he shouted through the closed door.

Rolling her eyes at his persistence, Heather had a feeling he would bug her until he got what he wanted. "There's nothing to tell. We dated for a while, things got serious—well, Ben got serious—and then … that was it. What you overheard was him wanting to start over again."

"What I heard was him begging you to live with him. You, on the other hand, didn't sound very enthusiastic."

Heather leaned against the doorframe, shrugging with acquiescence. "I'm warming up to the idea."

She could hear the sound of rushing water, and then the door opened. "No you're not; you're giving in to the idea. You don't want to live with that man any more than you would want to give up riding."

He stepped out from the bathroom, and she hooked her arm about his waist. "I don't know why you keep insisting that I don't want him. We're good together."

Grant slowly started toward his bed. "What if I could convince you otherwise?"

"What are you talking about?"

He halted and turned to her. "What if over the course of the next few days I convinced you to give up on Ben? Would you do it?"

"This isn't some kind of competition, Grant. It's my life."

When they reached the bed, he wobbled slightly and Heather put her other arm around his waist, holding him tight. When he lowered his head to her, letting his lips hover in front of hers, Heather's stomach twisted into a thousand knots.

"There's no one better than me to show what a mistake you would be making with Ben." His hot breath brushed against her cheek.

Looking away, she tried not to think about how his lips would taste. "I don't want you to show me anything, Grant."

His arms went around her. "Yes, you do. I think you will like what I will show you. You'll like it a lot."

The feel of his arms, the heat from his skin, and the lull of his achingly close lips were getting the better of her. Shaking off her momentary lapse in judgement, she pushed him onto the bed.

"This is strictly professional, Grant."

Reclining back on the bed, he grinned up at her. "I'm going to change that."

Without commenting, Heather turned from the bed just as the knot in her stomach melted into that bothersome tingle. When she reached the sofa, the tingle began to spread, awakening an unexpected heat in her belly. This time she did not analyze the sensation ... she feared it.

Chapter 7

After rushing back to her home in Copper Canyon to pack a bag and grab a quick shower, Heather made the long drive heading north toward Denton, home of the Crowley Ranch. Behind the wheel of her black Pathfinder, she let her thoughts drift over the night she had spent on the sofa next to Grant's hospital bed. Not being a night nurse, she had found herself on several occasions dozing off, only to startle awake and fear she had been caught sleeping on the job. Grant, on the other hand, had spent a peaceful night in his room, and in the morning had been a lot better rested than Heather. Despite the cramp in her back from staying on the lumpy sofa, and her lack of sleep, she was still anxious about spending the next few days at the Crowley Ranch.

As she drove along—yawning incessantly—Heather remembered frequently looking over at his bed to check on him during the night. She had made a detailed examination of his countenance, debating on whether she would call him good-looking or handsome. He didn't have those beefy, playboy features that young girls swooned over. He wasn't overtly muscular, but more sinewy in appearance. His face wasn't round and boyish, but carved with a hint of cruelty to it. The angular line of his jaw and pointy chin gave him an air of authority, as if he was a man who would take charge in all things.

During the wee hours of the morning her contemplation had taken a more lurid turn, and images of her and Grant lying naked together had crept into her foggy mind. With two cups of strong coffee coursing through her veins, she chalked up her late night fantasies to fatigue and nothing more. But as the tall black iron gates to the Crowley Ranch appeared before her, she felt that insidious tingle return to her belly.

"You just need a good night's sleep, Heather," she reasoned. "You always get jittery without enough sleep."

The main winding gravel road that meandered through the ranch was surrounded by rolling grassy fields. Various herds of brown, blue, and blonde Beefmaster cattle that had been developed and bred in Texas since the early 1930's were scattered about the pastures. Intermixed with the cattle were the long white cattle egrets that frequented this part of the state and feasted on the bugs that often pestered the herd.

It took several minutes of slow maneuvering along the gravel road until she viewed the shiny tin roof of the famed Crowley Stables. Situated to the left of the road, the stable was built to house over a hundred horses and boasted heated and air-conditioned stalls to maximize owner and horse comfort. The blue and white stables were rectangular with stalls facing outward, and had shutters attached to the perimeter to enclose the barn during extremes in temperature. Today, the white shutters had been pushed open to let in the cool October breezes. A white-railed ring was in front of the stables with a complex array of fancy colored fences set up in a practice jumping course. On either side of the main ring were paddocks with shady oaks set in the middle. Horses were out in the paddocks and could be seen in another open field behind the stables that sloped down to a shimmering lake.

"Damn. This makes Southland Stables look like a ghetto."

In the distance, she saw the red rooftop of the main house rising from a high hill. As she drove closer, the majesty of the old home came into view.

Built to resemble the great plantations in Louisiana and Mississippi, the neoclassical structure was coated in stucco and painted a pale shade of yellow. Three stories high, with the first two floors completely encased in long white Doric pillars, two red bricked chimneys rose on either side of the three dormer windows that topped the red-tiled roof. Along the grand galleries on the first and second stories of the home, wide french doors were decorated with unfinished wood shutters. Great potted ferns hung from the rafters on the first and second floor, while gardens of crape myrtle and gardenia bushes were set on either side of the curved red-bricked steps. Beyond the steps was a wide arched doorway surrounded by leaded glass windows and topped with a fanned transom.

After parking her car on a small shelled lot to the side of the house, Heather skeptically inspected the mansion. She knew the Crowley's had great wealth, but considered such an ostentatious display a bit tacky.

"The house is just as arrogant as the rest of them," she sighed, climbing from her car.

Lugging her overnight bag and purse over her right shoulder, she made her way to the front porch. Just as Heather was placing her foot on the first bricked step, the wide front doors flew open.

"There you are," Tad Crowley proclaimed. "I was beginning to wonder if you had forgotten about us."

Heather approached the door, staring at the man's pressed blue jeans, sharply creased button-down shirt, and shiny black cowboy boots. "Sorry," she mumbled, tugging at her bags. "I had a quick shower and some coffee before I left my house."

He waved her in the door, eyeing the fit of her snug blue jeans. "No need to apologize, Ms. Phillips. Grant tells me he had a quiet night."

"Yes, he did." She stepped into a white marble foyer with an eighteen foot ceiling and a large brass chandelier. "He slept most of it."

"Good." Tad Crowley slammed the front door closed and eased the overnight bag from her shoulder. "Let me take this." He set it on an antique walnut table to the right of the door. "I'll have Elise, the housekeeper, bring that up to your room." His hand went around to the small of her back. "Come, let me show you my home."

They headed across the foyer and Heather marveled at the breathtaking paintings of western landscapes covering the gold-painted walls. Just ahead a wide spiral staircase done in oak, with a bannister carved to resemble the long neck of a horse, rose to the second story of the home. Standing at the base of the steps, Heather admired the detailed carving of the horse's head at the start of the bannister. The flaring nostrils and wide eyes resembled an animal in the throes of a wild gallop.

"Beautiful," she whispered while her fingers lovingly traced the carved head.

"The house was built by my grandfather. Through the years it has been renovated several times. The last renovation was done when my wife and I first took over the ranch."

Heather took in the paintings of horses covering the walls along the stairway. "Yes, Grant mentioned her."

"I'm surprised he spoke of her to you," Tad Crowley reflected. "Considering he hasn't seen the woman since she left over twenty-five years ago."

"I got the impression their relationship was strained."

He motioned to a tall door to the left. "It's not strained, my dear girl, it's dead. Gigi is the one who has kept in touch with Maureen through the years, but still they're not very close. I never restricted either of my children from seeing their mother. Grant is the one who cut all ties with her the day she left."

His heavy footfalls reverberated in the wide foyer as he went to an ash-colored oak door. "This is the best room in the house," he declared, placing his long hand on the brass doorknob.

After he pushed the door open, Heather froze. The room beyond was covered from floor to ceiling with bookcases stuffed with books. Heather's mouth remained open with amazement as she hurried into the room. Done in dark wood with a rich rippled inlay of light-colored rings, the bookcases were embedded in all four walls and connected by a brass railing that allowed a rolling ladder to circumvent the room. In the center of the main wall was an arched hearth. The mantle above the hearth was covered with the same drizzled wood, and above the mantle was a life-sized portrait of a stunning black-eyed brunette wearing a white ball gown and holding a radiant pearl fan.

Heather's eyes were glued to the beautiful woman. Her slender figure and small cinched waist made her look delicate and graceful … the exact attributes Heather felt she lacked. She had porcelain skin, and sharp pointy features that added a sinister quality to her looks. As Heather gazed up at the portrait, she recognized those same features in Grant.

"That's Maureen, Maureen Delessops Crowley," Tad Crowley announced. "But now she is Stevens. Not such a grand last name after the first two." He inched closer to the mantle. "She's from New Orleans. Born into an old, well-established family there, she was even queen of some Mardi Gras crew. This was the portrait her father had commissioned to celebrate her crowning." He nonchalantly waved his hand across the air. "She told me the name of the crew several times, but I've forgotten. We met one summer when I was down there on business with her father. I fell in love right away." He smiled up at the painting. "Took Maureen a while to warm up to the idea of marrying a Texas cattleman, but she eventually did."

Heather came alongside him, nervously clutching her brown leather purse. "You make it sound like she didn't want to marry you."

"She didn't." He chuckled under his breath. "Her father was the one who pushed for it. He wanted to set up a beef export business with me, and hoped that marrying his daughter would sweeten the deal, which it did."

Heather warily eyed him. "Your marriage was arranged?"

"It was love on my part. I was mad about Maureen, but after a time—once we got to know each other—she finally agreed to the match." He gazed lovingly up at the portrait. "She hated living out here. Always did. She missed the excitement of the city. I guess coming from New Orleans, this place would seem pretty dull."

Heather browsed the older man's angular profile. "How long were you married?"

"Seventeen years." He shrugged. "Then one day she turned to me and said she was done." He shook his head and placed his hands in his back pockets. "I don't force people to stay in my life, Ms. Phillips. I may be many things, but I'm not cruel. I gave Maureen a divorce and whatever she needed financially to be independent. She met Howard Stevens after our divorce. My children are the ones who never forgave her for leaving." He turned to her. "Grant refuses to set foot in this room, so I would steer clear of mentioning Maureen to him too much."

Heather snuck one more glimpse at the portrait. "I'll keep that in mind."

Tad Crowley strolled toward the library entrance. "The house has six bedrooms, each with its own bath. There is a game room with a billiard table, if you like that sort of thing. We have a gym and movie theatre on the second floor. Grant usually lives in the apartment above the four-car garage, but I had him moved into a bedroom upstairs next to yours until he is well enough to be on his own again." Heather scurried to keep up with his long stride. "Elise, the housekeeper, comes in five days a week, and the cook, Lola, prepares lunches and dinners five nights a week for the family. Breakfast is up to you."

He waited at the library door as Heather stepped into the grand foyer. "I'll show you the kitchen. This way." He ambled along the foyer's white marble floors, heading toward the wide oak staircase. Walking beneath the grand winding staircase, Heather gazed upward at the logarithmic spiral design that reminded her of a nautilus hemi-shell.

Emerging from beneath the shadows of the intricate staircase, Heather found herself in an airy room decorated with white plush leather sofas and chairs set against windows that opened on to a sunroom. The ceilings were beamed with dark, roughly hewed wood, and the floor was done in a matching dark hardwood with a shiny finish. Along the far wall, surrounding a white mantle, were family photographs of what looked like Grant and his sister sitting atop various horses and holding on to brightly colored ribbons.

"The family wall," Tad Crowley explained when he caught her getting a closer look at the photographs. "Every horse show they attended when they were kids, we framed the pictures. Maureen started the wall. All of the pictures date back to when Gigi and Grant were younger."

"Grant told me you don't attend his horse shows anymore," she said, eyeing one photograph of a very young Grant astride a black pony.

"No need to. Grant is his own man."

Heather gazed back at him. "If my father was still around, I know he would come to all of my horse shows."

"Excuse my candor, Ms. Phillips, but you know nothing about my relationship with my son."

"I know he respects your opinion," she countered, coming toward him.

"Grant is my heir and will inherit Crowley Ranch. He respects my opinion because he wishes to hang on to that inheritance." Tad Crowley veered toward a short hallway to the left. "If it were any different, my son and I would have parted company years ago," he insisted over his wide shoulder.

Heather scrambled to keep up with him, but stopped short when she passed beneath a stone archway and entered a massive family room combined with a kitchen and breakfast area. Done in alternating shades of yellow and white, the warm room had a stone fireplace that climbed all the way up the high wall, and a luxury kitchen done in light oak with cabinets covering the walls, shiny stainless appliances, a double Viking oven, and an oval island covered with deep blue granite countertops. The floors were done in smooth stone and matched the ones in the wide hearth.

Tad Crowley went to the built-in refrigerator and opened the oak-inlaid door. "The fridge is always fully stocked, so help yourself to anything. If you have any special needs, leave a note for Lola. She does all the shopping." He shut the door. "I always insist my children dine with me in the formal dining room through there." He pointed to the double doors at the side of the kitchen. "I will expect you to join us. It's nothing fancy, mind you, just an opportunity to discuss the business of the day. The only time I see Gigi and Grant is during dinner. Vanessa usually joins us, as well. It allows her and Grant more time together, since he is always so busy handling the ranch."

"Was that your idea or Grant's?"

Tad Crowley zeroed his deep amber eyes on her. "Keeping my son happy is a priority of mine, and keeping the woman that he intends to marry close by seemed like the logical thing to do."

"So is Grant going to marry Vanessa Luke?" Heather probed, knowing she was treading into dangerous water.

"Eventually," Tad Crowley answered with an edge of aggravation in his voice.

"Does Grant know that?"

He took in a deep breath, sounding frustrated. "Your job here is to attend to my son's physical needs, Ms. Phillips. His head is my domain."

"And his heart?" Heather pressed. "Who watches out for that?"

Tad Crowley clasped his hands behind his back as he came up to her. "He doesn't have a heart, Ms. Phillips. Never did."

"I would disagree, Mr. Crowley. Everyone has a heart. Sometimes it's just buried beneath a whole lot of pain."

"His heart is none of my concern." With a dismissive side-glance, he raised his hand, showing her out of the kitchen. "I'll take you to your room now."

Climbing the spiral staircase, Heather looked up and spotted an intricate stained glass dome in the roof on the third floor. Gazing up at the bright morning sky, she admired the unique architectural feature.

After stepping onto the second-floor landing, she was escorted down a short hallway with deep brown carpet and red oak wainscoting running along the lower third of the walls. Tad Crowley stopped before a white cypress door and turned the shiny brass doorknob.

"This is one of the guest rooms I had it made up for you." He pushed the door open.

Inside, the bedroom was done in alternating panels of forest green and gray. Thick mahogany furniture hugged the walls, while a mahogany four-poster king-sized bed was nestled between two french windows. A forest green fuzzy throw rug was on the floor and matched the comforter on the bed. Portraits of green forests and mountain landscapes adorned the walls, and a two-tiered brass chandelier hung from a plaster medallion in the pale gray ceiling.

"The bathroom is through there," Tad Crowley said, coming up behind her and gesturing to a darkly stained door. "There is a closet in the corner." He motioned to two shutter doors on the far side of the room.

Heather went to the bed and put down her purse. She then went to the long french window next to the bed and moved the deep green curtain aside. "Can I go out on the balcony?"

"Of course. The bedrooms on this side of the house open on to the second-floor balcony. It makes for a beautiful way to take in the sunsets."

Her eyes did one last tour of the room and then she faced her host. "Where is my patient?"

He dipped his head to the right. "Next door." Tad Crowley turned for the bedroom door.

Out in the hall, Heather only had to take a few short steps before she stood in front of an open bedroom door. Peeking inside, she immediately spotted Grant sitting up in a walnut four-poster bed and typing away on a laptop. The pink color had returned to his cheeks, and his curly blond hair was tossed about his head. Heather could not help but notice the long strip of gauze on the left side of his naked chest.

"Someone is feeling better," she announced, entering the room.

Grant raised his eyes to her and for a moment her belly burned.

"Your nurse finally arrived," his father declared, following Heather in the bedroom.

Grant lowered his eyes to his laptop. "Did you give her the grand tour and tell her about your rules?"

Tad Crowley eased closer to the bed. "I gave her a tour, but as far as—"

"My father," Grant interrupted. "Always insists on family dinners, and that no one wander the grounds after dark."

Tad Crowley glanced over to Heather. "We have packs of livestock guardian dogs that roam the ranch to protect the cattle from predators. They have been known to attack a few of the workers who walk around late at night."

"No one has been attacked in years, Dad."

"Despite that," Tad Crowley went on, "I always insist that guests stick to the main house after dark."

"But Heather isn't a guest, Dad. She's an employee, right?"

The older man's face turned downward in a sour scowl. "Just get him back on his feet, Ms. Phillips. I need him running the ranch."

"I'm already back to work," Grant professed, flourishing his hand over his laptop. "So you can just send Heather home. I don't need a nurse."

"Let's not rehash this, Grant." Tad Crowley waved abruptly at his son. "She stays. You might not think you need someone to take care of your sorry ass, but you do." He marched to the door. "Anything you need, Ms. Phillips, we can discuss it at dinner. Good luck."

After his father shut the bedroom door, Heather waited for Grant to look up from his laptop, but he never did.

"He's worried about you, Grant. You took a nasty hit to the head."

When Grant raised his eyes, Heather couldn't tell if he was angry or amused. He held her in his gaze for several seconds before he finally spoke.

"I never figured you to be on his side."

Heather inched closer to the bed, noting the ugly bruise on his right cheek and temple. "I'm not on his side … I'm the employee, remember? It's my job to make sure you get back on your feet. Snapping at me and your father isn't going to help your recovery."

A grin snuck across his thin lips. "Now there is my determined little pit bull."

She came up to the side of the bed and snatched up his laptop. "Pit bull or not, you're not fully recovered and this can wait." She carried the laptop to a walnut dresser decorated with silver handles.

"Hey, I was using that," Grant complained behind her.

When she turned around, he was tossing the beige covers aside. Catching a glimpse of his blue pajama bottoms and naked, muscular chest, Heather hesitated, searching for the strength to order him back in bed. But when Grant stood too quickly from the bed, she became alarmed when she saw the blood drain from his face. He was wobbling on his feet as she hurried up to him.

"See, you're not better yet." She eased him back into the bed. "This isn't something that is going to go away overnight like a virus, Grant." She lifted his feet and then settled the covers around him.

He placed his hand over his eyes. "Christ, I got dizzy all of a sudden."

"You have a concussion." She inspected the white strip of taped gauze over his left chest. "We need to change your bandage, too."

When her fingers touched the bandage, he reached for her hand. "Why are you doing this?"

She pushed his hand away. "Doing what? Caring for you?"

"No, giving a damn about me."

She eased the edge of the white bandage down, peeking beneath. "I'm not a heartless bitch, Grant."

"I never thought you were anything but forthright and determined, Heather."

"There's that word again," she joked.

"Well, it suits you. I see so many riders who give up when they continue to lose. They blame the sport, their horse, other riders, but then never vow to change their fortunes. They never work hard to achieve their dreams. You do."

As she peeled the bandage away, studying the long row of stitches, a wisp of brown hair fell from her ponytail. "I haven't beaten you yet, Grant, so I haven't achieved my dream."

"But you will," he sighed, tucking the tendril behind her ear. "You'll defeat me one day."

The touch of his hand sent a firestorm of desire tearing through her body. The sensation was unexpected and almost sent her crashing to her knees. Heather desperately tried not to show how much the gesture had affected her. "Ah...." She raced to collect her thoughts. "We need to clean this wound and get you a fresh bandage." She searched the room. "Where are the medical supplies I sent home with you?"

He pointed to his bathroom door. "Elise put them in there."

Wanting to put some distance between them, Heather darted for the bathroom. Once out of his line of sight, she placed her hands on her knees and gulped in several deep breaths. Straightening up, she went to a cardboard box on the white-granite countertop with veins of gold imbedded in it. Standing next to the double vanity, she caught her reflection in the mirror. The terrified woman in the mirror shocked her.

"Keep it together, Heather," she softly pleaded. "Just do the job and then you have to forget about him."

Heather prayed that she would be able to heed her own advice, but with every passing minute she spent at Grant's side, it was getting harder to cast off those stirrings of desire squeezing her insides. Never before had she experienced such a sensation with a man, and she hoped never to suffer through such torment again. If this was lust, she could see why so many became swept away by it. Like quicksand ensnaring an unwilling victim, such passion terrified Heather. A long time ago she had convinced herself that letting her carnality have free rein over her emotions would eventually lead to the destruction of her well-ordered life. Heather had worked too hard to throw away everything she had for a man like Grant Crowley.

Chapter 8

That evening Heather arrived at the door to the formal dining room with Grant beside her. Wearing jeans and a loose fitting shirt, he had insisted on dressing for dinner.

"You don't understand, I can't appear weak around my father," he had argued, while climbing from his bed and stumbling to his closet.

"Christ, what is it with the two of you? Why do you hate each other so?"

"That would take a very long evening filled with a lot of whiskey to explain."

"I'm not going anywhere, Grant," she had asserted.

"I know, but tonight I have other demons to conquer."

Standing in the entrance to the red oak-paneled room with its long mahogany dining table, Heather felt as if she were about to head into the lair of a great dragon.

"Why does your father insist on these dinners?" she asked, gazing about the eerie portraits of men in period clothing on the dining room walls.

"Tradition," he explained. "Dad believes we have to keep up certain traditions on the ranch. Family dinners were something he was raised on and insists we continue, along with a whole host of other stupid ideals."

"What other traditions does he adhere to?"

Grant slowly ambled to a chair at the end of the table set with blue and white china. "Arranged marriages," he disclosed.

Heather pulled out the chair next to his. "He told me about your mother."

Grant settled into his chair. "I guess he showed you that damned portrait in the library. He incessantly moons over that thing. Every stick of furniture, every picture on the walls, he keeps just as it was on the day she left. He's adamant nothing changes around here."

She sat down on the mahogany chair with a thud. "So is that why he is insisting on your marrying Vanessa? Because of some family tradition?"

Grant removed a white-linen napkin from his place setting. "That and the prestige of owning one of the biggest cattle ranches in the country. Nevertheless, I have no intention of going through with it."

"You don't ... but before you said—"

"Lying around has afforded me time to think," he inserted as his eyes traveled over her face. "I've decided there are other things I want."

"Damn, not dead yet, little brother."

The acerbic voice came from the entrance to the room. When Heather turned in her chair, she was hit head on by a pair of black eyes. With long legs, short black hair, and a stellar smile, Gigi Crowley was the spitting image of the woman in the portrait she had seen earlier that day. Wearing a pair of dirty brown riding pants, short brown boots, and a black AC/DC T-shirt, Gigi sauntered into the room, swinging her slim hips from side to side.

"I heard the old man corralled you into taking care of the prodigal son," Gigi said while coming up to Heather. "Never thought you would end up on Crowley Ranch, though."

"Gigi." Heather nodded. "Good to see you again."

"How's that lovely horse of yours, Heather?" Gigi went across to the opposite side of the table and pulled out a mahogany chair. "I love watching you compete against my brother in the ring. You always make it such a suspenseful drama." She plopped down in her chair. "You two really should work out some kind of act ... you know, to take on the road and sell tickets."

"Jesus, will you shut up, Gig?" Grant berated. "Can't you just walk into a room and say hello like a normal person?"

Gigi slapped her napkin across her lap. "When has anyone in this godforsaken family been normal?"

Heather smiled at the attractive woman with the mischievous eyes. "How have you been, Gigi?"

"Good, Heather. I've been getting my riders ready for the Riverdale Farms Horse Show coming up. Big event. Last show before the state finals in November."

Heather fingered her silver fork next to her plate. "Yes, I know."

"Where's Vanessa?" a deep voice questioned from the entrance.

"Migraine," Gigi declared. "She called earlier and said she would stop by in the morning."

"Typical," Tad Crowley huffed as he hurried into the room. "How are you fitting in, Ms. Phillips?" He took his chair at the head of the table.

"Fine, Mr. Crowley."

"You're looking better, Grant," his father admitted with a slight smile. "Glad to see you out of those pajamas."

Grant gave Heather an "I told you so" side-glance. "I knew you wouldn't want me wearing a robe and pajamas to the dinner table, Dad."

Tad Crowley motioned to a mahogany sideboard with detailed carvings of farmers harvesting their crops. "Where's the salad? Lola always has the salad out when I come down."

"Maybe she's running behind, Daddy," Gigi suggested. "Not everyone is on your strict timetable around here."

He eased into his high backed chair. "Couldn't you have at least changed for dinner, Gig? You reek of horse."

Gigi stretched across the table for a decanter of red wine. "I like the smell of horse. Reminds me of my place in this family. I'm nothing more than a glorified stable hand."

"Jesus, don't start that again," Tad Crowley snapped. "We have a guest."

"I thought she was an employee," Grant proposed with a smug grin.

Heather's insides were winding up tighter than a spring at that point. She yearned to snatch the decanter of wine from Gigi's hand and pour herself a glass; however, she knew she would need to keep her wits about her at this table.

Tad Crowley grabbed his napkin from atop his plate. "I see the bang on the head has done nothing to improve your demeanor." His small eyes turned to Heather. "Forgive my ill-mannered children, Ms. Phillips. I'm afraid I neglected in educating them in the finer points of polite society."

Gigi poured a Baccarat crystal goblet to the top with the deep burgundy wine. "Yes, my brother and I are mere heathens next to the pious propriety of our father. Tell me, Daddy, how many people did our illustrious forefathers screw over?" She nodded to the portraits on the walls. "Which one was the train robber again?"

"Enough, Gig," Tad Crowley barked. "I wish you wouldn't drink. You get nastier than usual when you drink."

Gigi lifted her wineglass to her lips. "What in the hell else is there to do around here?"

Heather took in the varied portraits of men around the room. "Are these the former owners of the ranch?"

"Yes, they are." Tad Crowley puffed out his chest. "Every male heir to the ranch is on these walls. I plan on adding my portrait and Grant's to the collection very soon."

"It's an all-boys club in here, don't you know, Heather," Gigi cracked. "The women's portraits are relegated to the attic."

"Sorry for the delay, Mr. Crowley," a round woman with thick gray hair piled high on her head called from the door to the kitchen. In her arms was a white porcelain soup tureen. "I have your favorite beef stew tonight, along with a green salad, fresh home baked potato bread, and apple pie for dessert."

"Sounds wonderful, Lola." Tad Crowley rose from his chair and went to the sideboard.

"Is there anything else besides stew?" Grant asked. "Heather is a vegetarian."

Heather felt that spring inside of her snap as Tad Crowley, Gigi, and Lola turned her way with looks of absolute disbelief carved into their faces.

"It's all right," Heather spoke up. "I can eat salad and pie."

"Nonsense." Tad Crowley motioned to his cook. "Lola can throw something else together for you. Can't you, my dear?"

Lola smiled, appearing sincerely concerned about Heather's dining pleasure. "What would you like, miss?"

"I'm fine, really."

"It's no trouble, miss." Lola flashed a cherubic smile. "I'll make sure I cook more vegetable dishes for tomorrow night."

Heather felt a twinge of panic bolt through her. "No, really, salad is plenty for me. Please don't go to any more trouble on my account."

"At least someone around here knows how to eat like a lady." Tad Crowley glared at his daughter. "Wouldn't hurt you to take some cues from Ms. Phillips."

Gigi gulped back a portion of wine and then directed her gaze at Heather. "My father has always been extremely disappointed that I wasn't born a man. You know, the backup heir to his kingdom. Since I'm a girl, he has given me more womanly duties, like running the stables."

Tad Crowley returned to the table. "You must ignore my daughter's taunting, Ms. Phillips. She has always liked to put on a show for guests."

"Really, Daddy, her name is Heather, not Ms. Phillips." Gigi nursed her wine glass while reclining in her chair.

Grant wrapped his hand around the neck of the red wine decanter. "Gig, give it a rest."

He was about to fill his wine glass when Heather placed her hand over the top of his goblet. His angry eyes burned into hers, but she pried the decanter from his hand and put it out of reach. Picking up his water goblet, she set it down in front of him.

A burst of applause broke out from across the table. "Well done, Heather," Gigi exclaimed. "I like a woman who can put a man in his place." She ran her fingers over the rim of her wine glass. "Tell me, do you like to do the same with women?"

"Gig, enough!" Tad Crowley shouted. "None of your ... antics tonight."

"My antics?" Gigi thumped her wine glass down on the smooth surface of the oval table. "But Ms. Phillips likes my antics." Gigi's taunting smile made Heather's flesh crawl. "She's just like me. You know, Daddy, one of those lesbians you hate talking about."

"Oh God," Grant groaned beside her as he sank in his chair.

"Damn it, Gigi Lauren Crowley, I will not have you use that word in this house!" Tad Crowley roared.

"I'll just get the salad," Lola muttered, and then made a hasty exit through the double doors to the kitchen.

"Heather is not a lesbian," Grant calmly announced.

Gigi smirked at him, her dark eyes shining. "How would you know?"

Tad Crowley's eyes swerved to his son.

Grant shook his head, snickering. "Because I happen to know the man she is seeing."

"Really?" Gigi's black eyes swept over Heather with a renewed interest. "Anybody I know?"

At that point, Heather didn't know if she should walk from the house or run. She wasn't sure if she should speak up or continue to let Grant deal with his sister.

Heather shifted nervously in her seat. "No one you know, and it isn't serious."

Grant leaned over to her, edging his thin lips into a teasing grin. "Really? I heard you were moving in with him."

"Oh, now I have to know who he is," Gigi said with a malicious intonation in her voice.

"Enough, all of you!" Tad Crowley banged his fist on the table, sending a loud bang echoing throughout the dining room. "I will not allow this conversation to continue." He gestured to the white soup tureen. "Let's eat and find something more palatable to discuss."

Gigi winked at her brother, and Heather heard Grant let loose a long defeated sigh.

"Still want to stay?" he whispered to her.

Heather grasped her salad bowl from the left side of her blue and white plate. "I don't scare easily, Grant."

She was about to stand from her chair when she felt his hand rest on her thigh. "Just steer clear of Gigi," he softly advised. "She's the biggest gossip in Denton, Texas."

But Heather was hardly registering his words; she was more astonished by the feel of his hand on her thigh. The heat his touch elicited made her grip tighten on her salad bowl. Instead of rising from her chair, she remained seated.

How many more days of this can I take? Instead of an answer, her mind only raced with images of her and Grant, naked and holding each other in her four-poster bed.

"You all right?" Grant queried beside her.

When she confronted his deep amber eyes, her stomach clenched. This wasn't good. In fact, this was about the worst thing that had ever happened to her. Heather wasn't prone to infatuations with men; if anything, she had always prided herself on her ability to push men away. However, this man was different. Instead of asking why this was happening to her, Heather began to consider another possibility; when would she finally act on the desire that was beginning to consume her?

* * *

"I'm sorry about dinner," Grant apologized as they climbed the winding spiral staircase to the second floor. "But you know Gigi."

"Yes, I know how she is, but I didn't know she was a lesbian."

"I'm surprised you didn't hear about it from Trent. It's one of the main reasons he continues to refuse my offer to take over Crowley Stables."

Heather stopped on the light oak steps. "Trent may be many things, but he is not a bigot, Grant."

"I never said he was. He and Gigi never got along, not because of her sexual orientation, but because of her profound hatred of men. She has driven away several male riding masters I've hired for the stables. Her temper tantrums and screaming rants at men are legendary. Trent is smart to avoid such a problem."

"Then why keep asking him to take over the stables?"

Grant started back up the steps. "Because I'm hoping that if he accepts, Gigi will quit the barn and help me run the ranch."

Heather jogged up a few steps to keep pace with him. "Doesn't she help you already?"

He shook his head. "No. My father has always insisted that women stay out of ranch business. As long as he has maintained control over the ranch, he has kept Gigi's activities curtailed to stable duties only. All that animosity at dinner was because of my father's rather antiquated views. She hates that he doesn't trust her because she's a woman."

Heather followed him up the last step to the second-floor landing. "Why don't you talk to him?"

Grant's husky chuckle filled the air. "Because he doesn't listen to me; he doesn't listen to anyone. If you haven't noticed, I try to avoid my old man as much as possible."

His long legs strode along the landing, and Heather struggled to keep up. When he stopped at her room door, a tic of concern arose in her belly. As he waited for her, his eyes swept over her tight blue jeans and soft yellow top.

"In the morning I will take you to the stables and let you ride Maximillian."

Her eyes connected with the ugly black bruise on his cheek. "Perhaps you should rest tomorrow."

"I'm better, and tomorrow I will be fine. I need to get back to work. I can't have you hovering over me all the time. It's distracting."

"You're not a hundred percent, Grant."

He raised his hand to her cheek. "I'm ninety percent, which is good enough." His fingertips stirred her desire. "Get some sleep. I know you must be exhausted after tending to me last night. I don't need a nurse tonight, Heather."

Unexpectedly, Grant kissed her cheek. The touch of his lips sent a current of electricity shooting to her toes. Heather was riveted to her spot on the brown carpet. Caught up in the frenzy zooming around her insides, she gulped back her yearning to press her lips to his.

"Why did you do that?"

He arched back from her. "Because I desperately wanted to."

Her eyes searched his. "Sometimes I feel like you're toying with me."

"I don't play games, Heather."

"Then what are you doing with me?"

The sinful gleam in his eyes made Heather's heart skip a beat. "Tempting you."

"Tempting me? For what possible purpose?"

"There is only one purpose I can think of. Can you think of another?" Opening her door, he ushered her inside. "Good night, Heather." With one last wicked smile, he shut the door.

Devastated, Heather fell back against the door, bumping her head on the hard wood.

"Shit," she uttered, while rubbing her head.

Glancing about the room, she felt edgy. How in the hell was she supposed to sleep now? Her eyes fell on a speck of silver moonlight sneaking in through the dark green curtains. Darting across her room, she shoved the curtains aside and debated on whether or not to take a late night stroll on the balcony.

"To hell with it." She turned the handle on the door and stepped into the chilly night air. Outside, she took in several deep breaths, hoping the night air would settle her nerves. Regrettably, the nip of the October breezes did little to allay her edginess. Further down the balcony, where Grant's room was located, she saw a flash of light shine through the french doors.

Closing her eyes, she pictured him undressing and preparing for bed. As her imaginings turned to sexual fantasy, a dog howling in the distance made her eyes fly open.

Rubbing her hands up and down her arms, she mumbled, "That's creepy."

Turning back for her bedroom door, she peeked once more at Grant's room. Thinking about the touch of his lips on her cheek only seemed to fuel her yearning for him.

"Damn! I'd better get out of here before I do something really stupid."

Chapter 9

The following morning Heather was up early, anxious to check on Grant. After quickly changing into her jeans and a T-shirt, she was surprised when there was no answer at his bedroom door. Heading down the spiral staircase, she stepped on the white marble floor and was instantly hit with the aroma of brewing coffee.

Following her nose, she eventually came to the large family room. At the breakfast table, she found Vanessa and Gigi huddled together and giggling like schoolgirls. Gigi was still wearing her blue robe and fuzzy white slippers, while Vanessa was sporting another one of her colorful tennis outfits, complete with unblemished white tennis shoes.

"What did I miss?" Heather questioned, coming up to the round pine table.

The two women immediately stopped giggling and looked over at Heather as if she had interrupted an important discussion. Vanessa flopped back in her chair and ran her fingers through her blonde ponytail.

"You're up early," Gigi remarked, lifting her white coffee mug.

"Where's Grant? I tried his bedroom door, but got no answer." Heather went to the kitchen and began opening cabinets in search of a mug.

"Try the one above the coffeemaker." Vanessa pointed to another cabinet. "You just missed him. Grant was heading to the stables to check on Maximillian."

Heather found the cabinet with the array of coffee mugs and retrieved a bright blue one with a bolt of lightning across it. "I hope he isn't planning on riding. He hasn't been cleared by the neurologist to ride yet."

"Really, Heather. Do you think my brother would listen to some silly doctor?" Gigi stood from her chair and strutted to the kitchen. "If it makes you feel any better, no, he wasn't going to ride. Maximillian has been fighting some kind of bug for the past few days. I have had the vet out twice to examine him."

Heather frowned while filling her mug with coffee. "Anything I can do?"

"Are you a vet?" Gigi smartly replied.

"You just worry about my future husband," Vanessa chimed in as she carried her coffee mug to the deep stainless sink next to Heather. "Mr. Tad hired you to watch out for him, not his horse."

Heather replaced the coffeepot on the warmer. "How can you be so sure Grant is going to be your future husband, Vanessa?" Heather sipped some of her hot coffee. "I know you two are dating, but the man does have a hell of a reputation where women are concerned."

Gigi curled her red lips into a smile and lifted her mug to Heather. "Bravo."

"Shut up, Gig." Vanessa dropped her mug in the sink. "Don't forget your place, Heather. You're nothing more than a hired servant. When Grant is well, your job will be finished." Vanessa stormed out of the kitchen and through the stone archway at the family room entrance.

After she had disappeared into the house, Gigi let loose an overly dramatic sigh. "She really needs to invest in Midol."

The rib broke the tension in the air, making Heather smile. She took in Gigi's dark brown eyes, exquisite cheekbones, pouty red mouth, and short, almost black hair. For a moment, she felt sorry for the beautiful woman next to her. Heather couldn't imagine how hard it must have been over the years to live in her brother's shadow.

"You're right about my brother." Gigi put her mug down on the counter. "He has no interest in marrying Vanessa, even though my father and Vanessa feel differently."

Heather thumbed the arched doorway Vanessa had just barreled through. "Why don't you tell her that?"

Gigi tossed her head to the side. "Already have, but she won't have any part of it. She has her sights set on Grant, and being married to a wealthy cattle rancher appeals to her. Vanessa is one of those vindictive women who wants to flaunt her husband's success in the face of everyone who snubbed her in the past. Particularly those who denied her the Miss Dallas crown."

Heather thought of how Vanessa's beauty queen looks had ensnared Grant, and for a moment she envied her. "I doubt a woman like Vanessa will ever make Grant happy."

"Funny, I was thinking the same thing." Gigi pointed a delicate finger at Heather. "I bet you're the kind of woman who could make Grant happy. Don't you think?"

Brimming with suspicion, Heather cocked an eyebrow at her. "I'm his rival, remember?"

"You were never a rival, Heather. Even I could see that." Gigi pulled at the belt on her robe. "You'd better get to the stables and check up on him."

"I'll do that." Heather took another needed sip of her coffee.

"And don't worry about Vanessa." Gigi sauntered into the family room. "She comes across as a real bitch, but she isn't like you and I at all. She's not a fighter. She'll never fight for Grant, but she can make life interesting."

* * *

Twenty minutes later, Heather was strolling along the shaded shed row of Crowley Stables. As she moved along, heads would emerge from each of the stalls and nose her, looking for a treat or a bit of attention. Always a pushover, Heather stopped as she went and petted each and every one of the horses that came out to greet her.

Taking a few moments to interact with the horses reminded her of how much she had always adored the graceful creatures. It wasn't just their majesty and power that had fascinated her since childhood; it was their innate gentleness. They never used their strength to maliciously harm or injure, unlike many humans. Growing up, horses had been a welcomed escape from Heather's unhappy home life. On the back of a horse, she had found a respite from her father's tirades.

"You look like you belong here," a smooth voice said behind her.

She was playing with the soft muzzle of a shy palomino mare when Grant came alongside her.

"I grew up in a stable very much like this one outside of Dallas. I guess being around horses has always felt like home to me."

He nodded in agreement. "Same for me. My earliest memories are of sitting with the horses and feeding them carrots while my mother rode around in the ring."

"I didn't know your mother rode." Heather gave one last pat to the sweet mare's head and then faced Grant.

The corners of his mouth dipped downward. "She was the show jumper in the family. Gigi always preferred barrel racing, and my father only rides Western. He hated show jumping, which is probably the reason I took it up in the first place." His face changed and he nodded to her. "How did you start riding?"

"My father. He wanted me and my brother to pursue sports. Stewart he pushed into tennis, me into horses. He put me on the back of my first horse when I was four. Scared the shit out of me, but he made me get over it."

"Made you? How?"

"My father always pushed us, hard. I didn't understand why at the time, but now I do. He was making us tough." Heather inspected the black bruise on the right side of his face. "How are you feeling?"

"I'm good."

"Still, you should take it easy for another day or two."

"Too much to do around here for that." He motioned down the shed row. "Was Vanessa still at the house?"

Heather fell in step as he walked along the aisle. "Yes, and when I asked where you were she made it quite clear that I was nothing more than the hired help. Once you are well, she will happily kick me out of here."

"She's jealous of you," he disclosed. "She sees you as a threat."

"Me? I'm hardly a threat."

He placed his hand on the small of her back, making her insides jump. "You have no idea what a danger you are to her … and to me."

Just when Heather was about to ask why he felt that way, a boisterous whinny erupted from the end of the row of stalls. Pawing at the ground outside of his stall with his long black leg, Maximillian was clamoring for attention.

"I know you're there, old man," Grant called to the horse.

When they came up to the wide stall, Maximillian strained to reach out his head to be petted. Laughing at the horse's blatant appeal for affection, Grant rubbed his hand up and down the white blaze that ran from the animal's black forelock to his black muzzle.

"How long have you two been an item?" Heather joked.

"Six years. I found him on a track in Louisiana about to be killed for the insurance money. A groom I know there gave me a call to see if I wanted him. The groom loved him and hated to see him put down. So I loaded up a trailer and drove ten hours to the New Orleans Fairgrounds." Maximillian instantly calmed as Grant stroked his head, and the horse closed his eyes, appearing content. "When I got him here, took a few months before I could ride him. He was weak, woefully thin, and had a constant hacking cough that it took months to get rid of."

"Gigi said he hasn't been feeling well."

Grant's eyes swept over the animal's shiny black coat. "He may seem big and strong, but years of neglect and abuse on the track have made him vulnerable to sickness. He's been off his feed, and we've had to up his vitamins and change his diet a bit lately."

Heather stroked the horse's sleek neck. "You two always seem so in sync in the ring. It's as if you are the same being."

"You have the same captivating way with Murphy. When you two are in the ring, it's hard to look at anyone else." He dropped his hand from Maximillian's shoulder. "However, there are a few things you could do to improve your performance."

She tipped her head to the side, letting a tendril of hair fall from her ponytail. "Such as?"

Grant brushed the stray strand behind her ear. "Why don't we tack up one of the show horses and I'll give you a few pointers? Call it blue ribbon 101."

Heather liked the glimmer of happiness she saw in his eyes. He wasn't the harsh man she had seen as her rival anymore. This was a kinder, more easygoing Grant Crowley. She wondered why she had never seen this side of him before.

"All right, Mr. Crowley, I'm in."

* * *

The Grant Crowley that came to the jumping ring with her twenty minutes later was hardly the affable man she had glimpsed before. After helping her saddle a dark bay gelding with a tendency to toss his head, Grant ordered Heather to the rail and began barking instructions at her.

"I want to see how you manage some flatwork with Tyke."

Gathering up the reins, Heather applied some pressure with her legs to urge the horse onward. Tyke proved to be not only stubborn, but hard to handle. She was used to Murphy's laid-back manner, and to be mounted on a horse who tested her at every turn was proving exhausting.

"You're letting him take the reins, Heather," Grant shouted from the center of the ring. "Tighten your legs and get control of him. You're all over the place."

"I'm trying," she growled back, "but he's fighting me."

Grant jogged across the ring toward her, making her bring Tyke to a grinding halt. When he was at the horse's side, he grabbed the reins and tugged on the bit.

"Hold them here," Grant snapped, positioning the reins over the horse's withers. "Make him bring his head in and he will stop fighting you."

Heather wiped the sweat from her brow. "Are you sure you want me to school on this guy?"

He let go of the reins. "Yes. He's the toughest horse to ride in the stables. If you can master him, then you can master anything."

"Jesus, Grant. Why are you being such a dick all of a sudden?"

He eyes turned frigid. "You want to win blue ribbons, Heather, then act like a winner." He waved to a combination of fences set up in the center of the ring. "Let's work him over the touch and go, since that combination always seems to be your downfall."

"You're not my goddamned trainer," she grumbled under her breath as she steered the horse toward the first fence.

"No, I'm not ... not yet, anyway."

Heather ignored his remark and guided her ornery beast toward two fences made up of two-tiered red and white poles that were set closely together. Digging her legs into the horse, she could feel her arms straining to hold his head. She hated to admit it, but Grant had been right ... keeping Tyke's head tucked allowed her a lot more control.

Breaking into a canter, the first jump came rushing toward them. Heather felt the horse fighting harder for speed, but she strained to hold him back. When she finally gave him his head, he leapt over the first fence. Rolling forward to keep her weight off his back, she waited until his front feet touched down on the other side, and then immediately urged him to the next jump without allowing him to take a stride. Pushing the horse over the second fence took everything she had, and by the time they cleared the red and white poles, her arm muscles were screaming.

"Now you're getting somewhere," Grant called to her. "Take him through it again. This time wait a little longer before pushing to the second jump. You were a little early."

Instead of telling him her arms were burning and she was fed up with his bossy temperament, Heather took the horse around the ring again. This time when she went through the combination, she followed his advice and waited a few seconds before pushing Tyke to the second fence.

"Better, much better." Grant's voice echoed across the ring. "Now I want you to cut your approach. You always lose in the jump offs because you take too long in your approaches."

"But Tyke isn't Murphy. I always have to give Murphy a good approach ... otherwise he—"

"The approach is for you, Heather, not the horse." Grant came strutting up to her. "You hesitate coming to the fences in every jump off. Murphy doesn't need to see the fence. He takes his cues from you." He waved to the touch and go. "Now cut your approach."

"But he—"

"Do it!"

Heather flinched when he raised his voice. Trent had his days when he could be a real curmudgeon in the ring, but he had never shouted at her like that. Deciding it was best to do as Grant asked—so she could hurry up and get the hell out of there—she turned back to the rail and asked Tyke to canter. Keeping her eye on the approach, she found her spot to cut her turn, allowing less than fifteen feet to the touch and go. Feeling the anxious butterflies in her stomach, she gripped the reins tighter and pressed her legs into the saddle.

The sharp turn forced her to use every ounce of effort to guide Tyke to the fence. After taking the first jump at a slight angle, she realized they were in a bad position to clear the second hurdle. When Tyke was about to take off over the second fence, he abruptly halted, refusing to go on. The sudden stop took Heather by surprise, and she toppled over the horse's head.

After she hit the ground, Heather did not know what hurt worse: her butt that had broken her fall, or her ego for being thrown in front of Grant.

Instantly, Grant was kneeling beside her, his hands going over her sides and back. "Are you all right?"

The sudden warmth of his touch sent a trickle of electricity down her body, curling her toes. When his arms went around her, pulling her to him, she sucked in a gasp. Heather took a few seconds before she responded, wanting to relish the feel of his arms for just a few moments longer.

"I'm fine," she assured him, eventually pulling away. "Just a dented ego."

He let her go and took her hand, helping her to her feet. "You know what you did wrong."

"Yeah, I know."

She was brushing a bit of dirt from her blue jeans when Grant grabbed Tyke's reins next to her. At least Tyke had not added further insult to injury by taking advantage of the situation and making a beeline for the stables.

"Here." Grant handed her the reins. "Get back on and do it again."

Heather didn't know if she wanted to punch him in the nose or kick him in the balls. Sure, she knew she needed to get back on the horse that threw her—it was the first rule of riding—but Heather thought she would at least get a minute to catch her breath.

"Can I take a break to—?"

"No," he cut in. "The longer you take the more your fear will grow. Get back on now and take the combination again. No discussion."

Heather bit her tongue, stifling the flurry of expletives about to explode from her mouth. Pulling Tyke to her, she mounted the horse and gathered up the reins. Without looking back at Grant, she clucked to the animal and proceeded to the rail.

Now she was pissed. She had to show the smug son of a bitch that she could handle what he dished out. Fed up with Tyke's antics, she tugged hard on the reins, forcing the horse to do her bidding. Digging her heels into the dark bay's sides, she asked him to canter and then turned him to the combination. She cut the angle even tighter this time, determined to clear the touch and go no matter what.

As she sighted the first jump ahead, a funny thing happened; she realized she wasn't afraid any more, she was furious. Her anger was taking away all of her doubt about whether or not she would clear the jump and fueling her resolve. Right before the fence, she lifted Tyke's head with every ounce of strength she had, making the horse tuck into the needed position. Having cleared the first hurdle, she was relieved to see that her position for the second fence was damn near perfect, making Tyke's take off much easier.

When they easily sailed over the second jump, Heather felt a rush of pride. Grant had been right. She had always been afraid to cut her corners, because deep down inside she feared the jumps. Or more to the point, she feared knocking them down. Heather had always believed that a good approach mattered in order to clear a fence. She had just learned a valuable lesson; it wasn't the approach that helped master a fence, it was the rider's ability.

Murphy had sensed her apprehension and it had rattled his confidence and hers.

"That was perfect." Grant came across the ring. "Did you feel the difference?"

Heather was catching her breath as he came up to Tyke. "Sure did." She nodded her head and let the reins slip from her hands. "You were right, Grant. I had been hesitating at cutting my corners. I guess I was just ... scared."

He eased the reins from around Tyke's neck. "Now you understand why I had to push you. You needed to get over your fear."

"Why didn't you just tell me that instead of screaming at me the entire time?"

"Because you wouldn't have listened to me. I could see your fear whenever I competed against you in a jump off, but if I had said anything you would have chalked it up to our rivalry. I had to let you figure it out for yourself." He clucked to Tyke and began leading him to the gate.

Heather took a moment to appreciate his round butt beneath his blue jeans as he walked ahead of her. "What if I hadn't figured it out today, what would you have done?"

"I would have kept yelling at you until you did."

"Interesting tactic you have for schooling students, Mr. Crowley."

He glanced back at her, sitting atop Tyke. "You can see why I'm not an instructor, Ms. Phillips, just a rider."

There was no grating on her nerves when he called her Ms. Phillips as there had always been in the past. Now she simply smiled, amused at the reference. As he led her horse back to the stables, Heather realized that a lot of things about Grant no longer tried her patience. The distrust she had felt for him was gone. It had been replaced by a much more daunting emotion. For the first time, what was on the inside of Grant Crowley was becoming just as appealing as his good looks and tight body.

Back at the stables, Grant unsaddled a sweaty Tyke outside of his stall door and took him to the walker behind the barn to cool down. Watching him lead the horse away, Heather briefly considered what life would be like with a man like Grant. Unlike other men she had known, he seemed to have some special insight into her psyche and could break through all of her defenses. Others had tried to figure her out, but none had succeeded quite like Grant.

And Ben? The unwelcome voice circled in her head like a hungry vulture.

She had forgotten about the persistent ER physician since coming to Crowley Ranch. Not sure if that was good sign, Heather quickly put the doctor's demand to live together out of her thoughts. She wasn't ready to consider his offer just yet.

Taking the English saddle and bridle from a post in front of Tyke's stall, Heather trudged down the shed row listening to her stomach rumble, making her regret skipping breakfast.

At the end of the aisle, she came to a red door where all the tack for the school horses had been kept. In the simple eight-by-eight room she found an empty post on the wall and slid the saddle onto it. Then she placed the bridle onto a row of hooks, and as she was shaking out the sweaty saddle pad a shadow blocked the light coming in the open door.

When she looked up, Grant was standing in the tack room doorway.

"Are you sure you're all right?" he inquired, his voice sounded softer and strangely seductive.

"I'm fine, Grant." Her hands shaking, Heather tossed the blanket on the post behind her.

He stayed in the doorway, folding his arms over his chest. "When I saw you hit the ground, it scared the shit out of me."

Heather chuckled, trying to hide her embarrassment. "I bet you were hoping your rival was out of the way for good."

He stepped into the room. "Is that what you really think?" Grant kicked the door closed, instantly bathing them in darkness. "Perhaps it's time to change your perception of me."

"What are you doing?" Heather demanded.

"Starting over ... with you," he whispered, his breath against her cheek.

Before she knew what was happening, his arms were around her, pressing her to him. His lips came down hard on hers and the heat from his kiss was overpowering.

Is this real? Can this be happening?

Heather eagerly held him close as her lips parted, begging him to taste more. His tongue flicked in and out, arousing her, and when his hands kneaded her round butt, she moaned. The sensation of being in his arms was way better than any fantasy she had entertained. He felt strong and certain against her, and as his lips moved along her cheek and down her neck, she fought against her impulse to start ripping his shirt off his back.

Unexpectedly, the tack room door flew open and they were immersed in the revealing light of day.

"Makin' out in the tack room, Grant?" Gigi's sarcastic voice flooded the small room.

Heather jumped out of Grant's arms, surprised to see that he was not at all alarmed by his sister's unexpected appearance.

"Do you ever knock, Gig?" Grant sighed.

"On a tack room door?" Gigi laughed. "Grant, I haven't caught you doing this since high school."

He ignored his sister and grasped Heather's hand. "Come on. Let's get out of here."

"Dad's looking for you," Gigi related, while he escorted Heather out of the tack room.

"Let him wait," Grant snapped. With his arm about her waist, Grant guided Heather down the shed row.

"Where are we going?" she questioned, glancing back at Gigi, who was still standing outside the tack room door, smirking.

"Are you hungry?"

Heather gazed up at him. "I'm starved."

"Good." His arm tightened around her. "I'm taking you someplace where we can have some breakfast and get to know each other."

* * *

The place Grant took her to was his apartment above the four-car garage in the rear of the mansion. The simple two-story structure was built out of red brick and surrounded by a garden of purple pansies and evergreen bushes.

"There's an entrance around back to my apartment," Grant told her, walking past the two wide garage doors at the end of the building.

Tugging on his hand, she stopped him. "You want to tell me what happened between us back there?"

"I thought that was obvious. I kissed you."

Heather let go of his hand. "I know what you did, Grant. The question is why? First you're yelling at me in the ring, and then kissing me in the tack room. To say that I'm a bit confused by your attentions would be putting it mildly."

"I yelled at you to make you better. I kissed you because I've wanted to for quite a while now."

"You expect me to believe that?"

Grant took her hand. "Let's have something to eat first, and then we'll talk more."

Heather silently agreed, figuring she could deal with him better on a full stomach. Still gripping her hand, Grant led her up a straight wooden staircase to a plain oak door. There was a window box filled with blue and white pansies to the side, and a decorative brass knocker in the center of the door. Engraved on the knocker were the words Grant's Place.

She eyed the knocker and then arched a brow at him.

Working the lock, he shook his head. "Gigi's idea of a welcoming present when I moved in here from the main house a few years back."

"Why did you want to leave the main house?"

"Do you really have to ask?" Once he had opened the front door, he faced her. "During college, I moved to a house I had purchased in Highland Park in Dallas. Unfortunately, after grad school I had to come back to help run the ranch. I've kept the house in Dallas and stay there when I have to work in town. When I'm on the ranch, I prefer this apartment to the main house."

Stepping inside the entrance, she was surprised to find a spacious living room with a wood beamed ceiling inlaid with copper panels. There was a red-bricked hearth and a wall of windows that overlooked the manicured gardens in the rear of the main house. An open, modern kitchen connected to the living room. Glistening stainless appliances stood out against dark wood cabinets with shiny silver handles on them. A Viking oven with four burners on top and a griddle in the middle was set next to a matching stainless Viking refrigerator. Recessed lighting shone down on the polished bamboo floors while behind the kitchen a recessed alcove contained an unfinished pine table and chairs.

He waved to a hallway to the left. "The bedroom is through there."

She was surprised he made no move to take her there. "You're not going to show me your bedroom."

Grant's eyes swept down her figure. "Eventually, we'll get there."

"Eventually?" Heather snickered. "You're optimistic."

He came right up to her. "I told you before … I can read what a woman likes in bed … but you I'm having a hard time figuring out." Grant wrapped a tendril of hair that had fallen from her ponytail around his finger. "You intrigue me, Ms. Phillips."

The admission shook Heather. "Maybe with a man like you that is a good thing."

His roguish grin seemed to add an enchanting glimmer to his eyes. "It just might be." He turned away and headed to the kitchen.

Heather placed her hand over her jumpy stomach. She needed to find something less distressing to talk about. "So, how often do you travel to Dallas?"

He went to the refrigerator. "Usually once a week. I try to arrange my meetings on Fridays, that way I can spend the weekends in the city."

"What exactly do you do in the city? For business, I mean." She walked up to the pearl countertop next to the refrigerator and rested her hip against it.

"I manage the family investments." He retrieved a carton of eggs and some cheese from the refrigerator. "I started diversifying our assets out of cattle several years ago. Crowley Investments owns stock in a lot of major companies, as well as a few startup companies in the Dallas area."

"Crowley Investments? When did you get into this?"

"After I finished my MBA. My undergraduate degree was in finance, so after I was done with graduate school I told my father we needed to spread our assets into other business ventures. He gave me control over the ranch finances, and I have been steadily building our portfolio for the past decade." He placed the eggs and cheese on the countertop and reached inside again for a green bell pepper and a carton of mushrooms. "I hope you like omelets."

Heather gaped at him as he moved over to the stove. "You studied finance?"

He shrugged and grabbed a pan hanging from a rack above the stove. "What did you think I studied in college ... agriculture?"

"I never thought you went to college. I thought there was no point for someone like you. You would inherit the ranch and run it just like your father."

A flame on the stove sparked to life. "I'm nothing like my father. One of the reasons I started Crowley Investments. The company is worth ten times what the ranch and all the cattle combined could fetch."

She stared at him in amazement. "How come nobody knows about this? Everyone I talk to thinks you're a cattle rancher."

"You talk to people about me?" He smiled at her.

"You know what I meant, Grant."

He drizzled olive oil into the pan and placed the bottle back on the shelf above the stove. "Some in our riding circles know of my finance background; Trent Newbury for one. We have mutual friends in Dallas, and often run into each other at various meetings."

"Trent?" Heather couldn't believe Trent never mentioned anything about Grant. "But he's an engineer."

"Who works for several oil companies that I have holdings in, as well as financing a few of their speculative ventures."

"If your other business is so successful, why do you come back to the ranch?"

"It's the family business, and still provides a great deal of income to maintain the house and stables. My father can't run it alone. Despite how we feel about each other, I won't abandon him or the ranch." He nodded to a coffeemaker on the countertop by the sink. "Can you make the coffee? Filters and coffee are in the cabinet above the sink."

Heather went to the cabinet and started rummaging around for the coffee. "All this time I thought you were stuck under your father's thumb."

"It only appears that way. He knows the investments have become much more lucrative than the ranch, but he still tries to maintain control over me. You have to understand one thing about my father; he likes to always believe he is in control. I discovered years ago it's best to allow him that little fantasy instead of confronting him with the truth."

She put the coffee bag down on the countertop with a thud. "What about Vanessa? He wants you to marry her."

He turned to a cutting board to the left of the stove and pulled a knife from a block next to him. "Marrying Vanessa would be a boon for the ranch and double our land holdings, but I won't be forced into a relationship I don't want. My father knows that. However, he still continues to hold out hope that I will change my mind."

Heather reached for a pack of coffee filters in the cabinet. "Will you?"

Grant put his knife down on the cutting board and came up to her, letting his eyes linger on her features. "What do you think?" he finally asked.

Heather dropped the pack of filters in her hand on the counter. "I think you and I could have a lot of fun together, but neither one of us wants a relationship."

He folded his arms across his chest, scrutinizing her. "What makes you say that?"

"You never struck me as the kind of man who wanted any ties with a woman and I ... well, I'm not good at relationships. So let's just keep things simple."

"Is that your usual line with men?"

"It's not a line." She stretched for the coffeemaker, avoiding his eyes. "It's what we both need right now."

"We'll see about that." He went back to his cutting board.

A sting of regret cut through her. Heather knew of his reputation, and reason told her not to expect much from the man. Besides, she had no interest in becoming emotionally invested in something that would never last. Past encounters in the show ring had taught her that Grant was a cold and calculating man you did not cross. Such men were only good for one thing ... sex. That was the only thing Heather wanted from him ... at least, that's what she kept telling herself.

Chapter 10

Empty dishes were scattered about the pine breakfast table as Heather sat back in her chair nursing her second cup of coffee. Grant was seated next to her, waving his hands about as he told her the story of his encounter with a big bad bull named Goliath.

"I swear I was too terrified to move. Here I was in the middle of the field with this snarling, gigantic Black Angus staring me down. I kept hoping someone would come along and see me, distracting the son of a bitch so I could run away. I knew he would kill me if I took off running."

Heather put her coffee down, resting her elbow on the edge of the table. "What happened?"

Grant rocked back in his chair. "My father happened. He was driving to the house and coming back from the city when he saw me in the pasture. He got out of his car and came straight into the pasture. I was looking at him as if he was nuts. Then Old Goliath started charging. I knew I was a goner." He shook his head. "Then my dad pulled a gun from his pocket and shot straight into the air. Damn bull took off running."

"So he saved you." Heather chuckled.

"He beat my ass," Grant confessed. "He had always warned me to stay away from Goliath. That bull had a nasty reputation. But me being me, I didn't listen. That was the way of it when I was growing up ... anything my father told me not to do, I did."

Heather ran her fingers along the rim of her mug. "You're still chasing Goliaths, aren't you?"

He lifted his white coffee mug to his lips. "Yeah, I guess I am."

"It doesn't have to be like this, Grant. You should make peace with your dad. You never know when...." Her voice grew quiet.

He sighed as he put his coffee on the table. "I know how hard it must have been for you when your father was sent away."

"Sent away? That's a nice way of putting it."

Grant angled closer to her. "How long was he sentenced for?"

"Twenty years for involuntary manslaughter."

His blond eyebrows went up. "I didn't realize it was that long. How much did he serve?"

She rubbed her hands together as a rush of unhappy memories came back. "Six, before the heart attack. They found him in his cell the next morning."

"I'm sorry." He placed his hand over her forearm. "Was that when your mother took the overdose?"

"No, before. She was a mess when Dad was convicted of murdering his patient. It was a short time after he went to prison that she died." She shook her head. "How can a physician trying to save his patient's life be accused of murder?"

"What exactly happened? Can you tell me about it?"

She gazed into his eyes, trying to discover if he was just another curiosity seeker out to hear a sensational account of her tragic life, or if he was one of the rare few who genuinely cared about her past. She shook off his hand and stretched for her coffee cup, sensing that familiar wall of distrust building inside of her.

"Perhaps another day."

A light tapping on the front door startled Heather, making the coffee cup in her hand wobble.

"That might be one of the hands, asking for instructions on some herds," Grant reasoned while he stood from his chair.

Heather sipped her coffee as he went to the living room door. After a few seconds, she heard the distinct sound of two men arguing. Standing from her chair, she carried her mug into the living room. When she was able to see who was at the front door, she cringed.

"Ms. Phillips." Tad Crowley's angry eyes were fixated on Heather. "Gigi told me I would find Grant here, but I didn't expect to see you."

"We were having breakfast," Grant explained. "Then I was going to school Heather over some fences on one of the show horses."

Tad Crowley glared at his son. "That will have to wait. I have a new shipment of bulls coming from Oklahoma today and I need you to go over them with me."

Grant glanced back at Heather over his shoulder. "Why not have Phil do it?"

"Because he's the ranch manager and not the owner, Grant. We need to stay on top of the breeding program, you know that. Phil will just stick those bulls in with any of the breeding heifers."

"Dad, I wasn't planning—"

"Go on, Grant," Heather interrupted. "I'll head over to the stables and have Gigi find me a horse."

"She can't help you in the ring like I can," he insisted.

Heather motioned to Tad Crowley. "It's okay. Your father needs you. Go help him."

Reading the reassurance in her eyes, Grant nodded his head. He turned to his father. "Okay, Dad. I'll meet you at the breeding shed after I've finished having breakfast with Heather."

"We need to go now." His father's voice was peppered with impatience. "I already have the four-wheelers downstairs and waiting."

Grant's shoulders sagged. "Fine." When he shifted his gaze to Heather, his lips were pressed tightly together. "I have to go on and take care of this."

"Don't worry, Grant. I'll clean up here and then head to the barn."

Grant's weak smile did little to hide his anger. "Just leave the dishes. I can get them later." Without another word, he stepped through the front door. The last thing Heather saw before the door closed was Tad Crowley's stormy eyes glaring back at her.

* * *

After Heather had put the last of the dishes in Grant's fancy Bosch dishwasher, she walked from the kitchen and surveyed the living room. She was intrigued that the man could opt to live in such a cozy apartment as opposed to the sprawling mansion. It was just another little insight into the psyche of Grant Crowley. Fascinated by the possibility of what else she could learn about the man, Heather decided to take advantage of the opportunity and get a quick peek at his apartment.

"I can't believe I'm considering this," she muttered. "I'm like some deranged girlfriend."

First, she inspected his pantry and freezer. He had an inordinate amount of boxes of macaroni and cheese in his pantry, along with several rib eye steaks in his freezer. The music in the CD player next to his big screen television contained a lot of jazz and some classic rock. The Britney Spears CDs, she decided, had to belong to Vanessa. Grant just didn't seem like the Britney Spears type.

Moving to the bedroom, she was surprised by the size of it. Two wide windows on either side of the king-sized sleigh bed had a great view of the kidney-shaped pool in back of the main house. Heather went to his dresser and smelled the woodsy fragrance of his cologne, and then fingered the selection of suits and casual dress shirts he had hanging in his closet. Emboldened by her need to learn more, she went to the round nightstand next to his bed and checked out a small drawer. Inside, she found several packages of condoms and two pairs of handcuffs.

"Mr. Crowley." She lifted the handcuffs from the drawer. "There is a whole other side to you."

The handcuffs made Heather feel guilty, as if she had gone a bit too far with her snooping. She quickly replaced the cuffs in the drawer, and decided that it was time to get to the stables.

Strolling along the gravel road that led from the house to the stables, her thoughts kept returning to the silver handcuffs in his nightstand drawer. Images of Grant securing her hands and then having his way with her, made her break out in a sweat on the short jaunt to the barn. By the time she stepped below the shaded shed row, Heather was completely undone. She had never thought of Grant as being the type of man who was into such games, but now that she had discovered his secret, Heather was aroused by it.

After making sure Tyke had been returned to his stall, she roamed the aisles, petting the horses and watching a few riders who were warming up in the jumping ring. Occasionally, her eyes would drift back to the red tack room door and she would remember how his lips tasted. Then, those damned handcuffs would return to the forefront of her thoughts.

"I need to stop this. You've never been into that sort of thing, Heather."

None of the men she had been with in the past had ever offered to handcuff or tie her up. They had all been a lot like Ben: polite, attentive, sweet, but none of them had ever really turned her on. So why was the fantasy of Grant handcuffing her to a bed awakening such compelling feelings?

Edgy and wanting to put that red tack room door out of her mind, she hiked back to the house. Climbing the front porch steps, she worried about Grant. He wasn't a hundred percent yet, and if he pushed too hard....

"Stop it. He's a grown man and can decide when he has done too much."

Back in her bedroom, Heather was desperate for a distraction. Checking her cell phone, she wasn't too surprised to find that Ben had left her three messages, along with one from her brother.

Immediately, little alarm bells went off. Stewart never called unless something was wrong.

It took three rings for him to pick up the line, and when she heard his deep, rumbling voice her grip on the black iPhone tightened.

"Where are you?" he barked into the speaker of her phone.

"What's your problem?"

"Christ, Heather. I go by your house last night and you're not home. I call your cell phone all morning and get no answer. I've been worried."

"Worried? You? Please, Stew. One call every few months to see if I'm alive is not giving a shit about me."

"Jesus, you're always such a hard ass. Of course I care. I'm your brother and all you've got, baby girl."

Baby girl. It was the only nickname her older brother had ever given her growing up. Her father had hated it, but the endearment had always made her feel special.

"Why did you go to my house, Stew? You never go up to Lewisville. You hate driving out of Dallas." She thought she heard him chewing on something, but wasn't sure.

111

"I found some old shit of Dad's in my closet and wondered if you wanted it. I don't have room anymore at my place. Lynda's crap is taking up everything."

Heather picked at a mud stain on her jeans. "You still plan on marrying her?"

"Yes," he grumbled. "You know I am. I'm thirty-seven and have put off marriage long enough. Lynda's good for me."

"But you don't love her."

"It's not about love anymore, Heather. It's about having someone around. You're no spring chicken, either. You need to think about finding a guy and popping out a niece or nephew for me."

"I don't want kids."

His deep laughter boomed through the speaker. "Liar. You always talked about having kids and being a mom before Dad went away."

"Yeah, well, after everything that happened to Mom and Dad, I decided kids were a bad idea."

"Whatever happened to that ER guy you were seeing? He sounded nice."

Heather rubbed her hand over her face, wanting to tell her brother all the crappy details of her life, but knowing he wouldn't listen. He never listened to her.

"He's still ... around."

"Then don't act like you usually do when you get scared and blow it with him."

Her mouth fell open. "I don't get scared."

"Yes, you do. When a guy gets too close, you get scared and run away. You think they're all going to dump you because your father was a convicted felon."

"Don't call him that, Stew," she snapped into the phone. "He wasn't that, at least not to me ... or you."

"He embarrassed us, Heather. He was a sadistic drunk and a liar, who had no business taking care of patients. It's taken me years to get over the stain of what he did at this hospital. I've had to work harder to prove myself because of him. We both have."

An uneasy silence passed as Heather bit down on her lower lip, determined not to let one tear fall.

"So where are you?" Stewart finally questioned.

"In Denton. Doing private duty."

"Do you need money again for Murphy? I told you I would give you whatever you needed."

"No, it's not like that. I'm at Crowley Ranch."

He let a low whistle escape his lips. "Wow, that's big money. That family donates a lot of bucks to Baylor Hospital every year."

"Yeah, they donate to Lewisville Medical Center, too. That's why I'm here. Grant Crowley got kicked by a cow and his father insisted I watch him for a few days at the ranch."

"Why you?"

"We ride together ... well, not together, but against each other at the local shows. His father thought Grant would be more comfortable with someone he knows."

"Cushy job." His boisterous chuckle filled the speaker. "You get to live the high life at that big old ranch while I sit in the shitty doctors' lounge stuffing a stale ham sandwich in my mouth before heading back to the cath lab for another four hours."

"You shouldn't eat ham. Pigs are sweet."

"Coming from a vegetarian who is staying at the biggest cattle ranch in the state, that doesn't make a whole lot of sense, Heather." She heard his beeper going off in the background. "When are you going to be home?"

"In a few days."

"That's the cath lab. I've got to go, baby girl. Call me when you get home and I'll bring Dad's stuff by."

"Listen, Stew, I don't want—"

The line went dead before she could finish telling him she didn't want any more reminders of their father. Her attic was full of them. Sighing, she tossed the phone to the bed.

"I think that's the longest conversation we've had in three years."

Sitting on her bed, Heather's back and hips began to ache. She wondered if she had taken a harder tumble than she realized in the jumping ring. Toying with the idea of soaking in a hot bath, she went to the bathroom, and inspected the Jacuzzi tub in the corner set against a picture window. Turning the tub faucet, she tested the water until she was satisfied, and then began removing her clothes. Easing the jeans from around her hips, she winced when the fabric rubbed against her right hip bone. When she finally wrestled the fabric from about her hips, she inspected the tender area. Already a dark shade of red, her right hip and around to her butt was going to have a very nasty bruise.

"It didn't hurt that much after I fell." Raising her hip a little higher, she viewed the entire bruise in the vanity mirror. "Shit."

She recalled falling and then the abject humiliation she had felt being thrown in front of Grant. Shaking her head, Heather figured the pain of the fall had been overshadowed by the dent to her ego.

Stepping into the hot water, she eased back in the tub and then became distracted by the array of buttons to the side. Pressing a few of the buttons, she happened on the one that started the jets situated along the bottom of the tub. As the water massaged her battered body, she closed her eyes.

It did not take long for the veil of sleep to tempt her. After the long night with Grant and the events of the day, she was suddenly very tired. Assured that the warm water had done its therapeutic job on her sore hip, she climbed from the tub and wrapped her body in a thick white towel that had been left on a shelf beside the walnut-stained vanity. With a long, loud yawn, Heather shuffled into the bedroom and climbed beneath the green comforter on her four-poster bed. For just a little while, she wanted to sleep and forget about her brother, her father, and all the silly fantasies she had entertained about sleeping with the alluring Grant Crowley.

Chapter 11

When her eyes popped open, the bedroom was engulfed in darkness. Fumbling for the lamp on the night table, Heather finally found the switch and the room was soon bathed in a warm glow. Sitting up, she felt the sore muscles in her body instantly rebel. Not only was her hip achy, but her back and right thigh hurt as well. Slowly standing from the bed, Heather tried to stretch the sore muscles as best she could. She checked the alarm clock on the night table next to her bed. It was already after seven in the evening.

She rubbed her face, coming out of her fog. "I must have been more tired than I realized."

Cursing that she had already missed most of dinner in the formal dining room, Heather dashed to her closet and grabbed a pair of black jeans that she had packed in her overnight bag, along with a fresh white blouse. Rushing to the bathroom, she ran her fingers through her hair and then pulled the long brown locks back in her usual ponytail. Heather was still putting on her shoes when she opened the bedroom door and peeked out into the hall. Tucking her shirt into her jeans, she hurried to the spiral staircase.

She was halfway down the steps when she spotted Tad Crowley coming toward her.

"I was beginning to worry, Ms. Phillips. You weren't at dinner."

Heather noted the casual jeans, pressed blue dress shirt, and black cowboy boots he had worn earlier that day. Briefly, she marveled at how his clothes stayed so pristine on a cattle ranch. "I, ah, fell asleep. I'm very sorry, Mr. Crowley. I didn't mean to miss dinner."

"Not to worry. I'm sure Lola still has some of the vegetable dishes she made for you in the kitchen."

Heather rubbed her hand over her brow, fighting a yawn. "I guess the lack of sleep got the better of me today."

He came up to her step, towering over her. "Lucky for us, it appears Grant is back to normal. He spent the afternoon with me checking on herds, and did not seem the least bit bothered by what happened."

Heather's irritation bristled. "Excuse me, Mr. Crowley, but I think if your son was suffering any discomfort from his injury he wouldn't say a word to you."

Tad Crowley calmly eased his hands behind his back. "What makes you think you know my son better than I do, Ms. Phillips?"

"I just know what I see, Mr. Crowley. I think your son is afraid of letting you think he is weak, and very afraid of disappointing you."

The older man chuckled, accentuating the deep lines about his eyes. "Then you truly don't know Grant. He's impervious to any suggestions or comments I make. Many a time, I think he does the opposite of what I want to spite me."

"Even so, he is going to marry Vanessa to please you."

He took in a frustrated breath and unclasped his hands. "Marrying Vanessa is not about me, it's about what is best for the ranch. If she were to be married off to another cattle rancher, a competitor, then Crowley Ranch would suffer. Marrying Vanessa guarantees the ranch stays the biggest and the best."

"Is that what all of this is about? The ranch staying the biggest? Isn't your son's happiness worth more than that?"

Tad Crowley cracked a pained smile. "No. Grant understands, Ms. Phillips, more than you." Reaching into his pocket, he pulled out a folded slip of paper. "I was coming to give you this."

Heather took the folded paper from his extended hand. "What is it?"

"A check for your services. I added a little more in there than we agreed on. Your job is done and your services are no longer needed."

Heather opened the check and her eyes almost popped out of her head when she saw the amount. It was equivalent to three month's salary for her. She held up the check to him. "Why are you doing this?"

"I think we can be frank, Ms. Phillips. You're a distraction to my son; a distraction he doesn't need." He pointed to the check. "That is payment for your services as we agreed on ... and more to stay away."

She wanted to laugh out loud. This wasn't the kind of thing that happened to her. Being bought off was something that tempting mistresses in cheesy television mini-dramas experienced, not boring nurses from Dallas.

She was about to give the check back when he raised his hands, stopping her. "Take the check, Ms. Phillips. We both know you need it."

Heather wanted to rip up the check in front of him and then toss the pieces over his beautiful staircase, but she didn't. He was right; she needed the money for Murphy. Visions of her beloved horse made her put the check in the front pocket of her jeans and head back up the stairs.

Inside her bedroom, she swallowed her pride and went to the closet, eager to retrieve her overnight bag, pack, and get the hell out of there. After tossing the overnight bag on her bed, she was about to go back to the closet for her clothes when she heard the low howl of a dog outside her bedroom window. Pausing, Heather glimpsed the window, and then heard the same noise once more. She remembered what Grant had told her about the packs of dogs roaming the grounds at night, and suddenly curious to see what kind of creature could make such a sad and haunting sound, she went to the french doors that led to the balcony.

At the window, she pushed the thick green curtain aside and shoved the doors open. The coolness of the night air made her skin prickle. Rubbing her hands up and down her arms, Heather snuck closer to the black iron railing that ran the length of the balcony. There was a half-moon out and the grounds below were bathed in a faint gray light. As she squinted into the distance, Heather caught the shadow of a large dog running across the grassy lawn.

"They roam about the pastures guarding the cattle at night," a voice said beside her.

Her heart flew to her throat when she saw Grant standing outside of his balcony door just a few feet away.

"They're called Russian Ovcharka. My father had ten of the dogs flown here from Russia as puppies. They are bred to live in the fields with livestock and protect them from predators. The downside is they can get pretty aggressive with their owners."

"What are you doing here? I thought you would be back at your apartment."

He hooked his right forefinger through the belt loop of his jeans as he walked up to her. "I wanted to check on you. I got concerned when you didn't come down to dinner."

"I fell asleep. When I was heading down to the dining room, I ran into your father on the stairs."

He stopped right before her, gazing into her eyes. "Let me guess. He wants you to go."

She turned away. "You don't need me anymore."

"I could relapse."

Heather stretched for the handle of her balcony door. "I need to get back to Ben, and you need to get back to Vanessa."

The loud boom of laughter that came from him stunned her. She had never heard him laugh like that. Actually, she had never heard any genuine emotion from him before. Spinning around, Heather took in his amused countenance.

"You really don't believe that, do you?" He came up to her. "I told you, I have no intention of marrying Vanessa, and you're about as interested in Ben Eisenberg as my sister would be."

The notion of Ben and Gigi getting together made Heather cover her mouth, stifling her giggle.

His eyes twinkled as he watched her. "I'm glad to see you can laugh."

She lowered her hand from her mouth. "Of course I can laugh. I just don't do it around you."

He was inching closer and Heather could see his muscular chest beneath his half-opened white shirt. "What did my father say to you?"

"He asked me to leave and gave me this." She tugged the check from her front pocket and held it up to him.

His eyes went from the check to her face. "You're going, just like that?"

She nodded, slipping the check back into her pocket. "Why not?"

His blond brows scrunched together. "I was hoping we could continue our discussion. The one we started in the tack room earlier today."

Her insides melted into a ball of white fire. "Your father said I was distraction for you. Perhaps he is right. I should go."

He tilted over her, letting his face hover above hers. "You can't go. I haven't shown you my bedroom."

"If I stay, things could get complicated."

"I certainly hope so." His lips moved closer. "Since the day I first laid eyes on you in the ring, I've wanted to get to know how you...." His lips grazed her cheek. "Know how you would feel beneath me."

When his lips finally met hers, the intensity of his kiss was catastrophic. Heather had never known a man to make her forget herself in a kiss, but Grant had that mastery over her. She wanted to curl into his body and lose herself completely in him. His tongue teased her as his hands pressed her body closer to him. The cool breeze whipped around them as the heat from his body warmed her. Her loins grew hot as his kiss deepened. When she realized she was kissing him back, entreating him with her tongue to take more, she pulled away.

"We shouldn't be doing this."

He lifted her head, gazing down into her eyes. "Did you like kissing me?"

She wanted to lie to him, to tell him it didn't matter, but she couldn't. Instead, she nodded her head, afraid to say the words.

"Grant?" a woman's voice called from his bedroom door.

They both turned to see a worried Gigi coming toward them. Grant let her go and took a step closer to his sister.

"What is it?"

"I went to check on Maximillian after dinner and he's not doing well." Her dark eyes veered to Heather. "I've called the vet, but I think you should come to the stables."

He turned to Heather, gripping her arm. "I'll come back later."

"No, I should go with you. I can help."

"Please, Heather," he begged in a strained voice. "Stay here."

Leaving her on the balcony, he took off with Gigi, heading back to his bedroom. Once they had disappeared inside, Heather went to the iron railing and gripped the cold metal. She waited, hoping to see their shadows passing before the house on the gravel road that led to the stables. When a whir of engines came from down below, Heather spotted the dim headlights of two four-wheelers speeding toward the stables.

She thought of the magnificent black horse and questioned what could have happened. Earlier in the day, he had seemed so strong and healthy. Even so, that was the way of it with such skittish creatures. In an instant, they could crumble before your eyes.

Back in her room, Heather tried to return to her packing, but she soon became consumed with worry for Maximillian. Deciding that three heads would be better than two to help the horse, she went to her bedroom door, resolved to make her way to the stables and offer some assistance.

After stepping through the front door, she was surprised at how dark everything appeared. The view from her balcony above had not been so black. Wishing she had at least brought a flashlight, Heather waited several minutes for her eyes to adjust. Slowly, she was able to make out shapes and patterns on the gravel road. Breaking into a brisk jog, she rushed toward the stables.

About halfway to the stables, Heather began to reconsider her decision to venture into the dark night. Sounds of owls hooting, mosquitos buzzing, and other noises she could not identify seemed to grow louder with her every step. Then, rising above all the other noises of the night, a dog's lone howl cut through the chilly air. Heather remembered what Grant had told her about the big dogs that roamed the ranch at night.

This was a very bad idea.

Just as the lights from the stables were coming into view, a strange sensation came over her. Heather felt as if she were being followed. Looking over her shoulder, she tried to make out shapes in the darkness, but could not detect a thing. Finally, when she could not stand the crawling sensation on the back of her neck any longer, she stopped and took a detailed survey of the land around her. Then she heard another low howl, but this time it sounded close ... very close.

"Oh shit." She took off running.

Heather did not get far before she heard the thud of feet on the gravel road around her. She was pumping her legs as fast as they would go, but running on the gravel was akin to running on sand. The harder Heather tried, the slower she felt she was going. A sudden whoosh of air flew by her right hand and she saw a large dark shadow cross her path. Panicking, Heather knew she was being tracked by the massive dogs. She just hoped they would realize she was a human and not some predator out to decimate the herds. The lights of the stables were getting closer and she estimated she was almost to safety when a shadow cut across her path. She stumbled to the right, wanting to avoid a collision, and ended up tumbling to the soft grass on the side of the road.

She sat up and gaped around, listening for the slightest sound. Then, her heart surged to her throat when she detected the faint rumble. At first, it was like a roll of thunder getting closer, but the growl grew in strength until it seemed as if it was right on top of her.

Heather didn't know what to do. She didn't have a lot of experience with dogs, and wasn't sure if confronting them or cowering to them would matter. Slowly rising to her feet, the bitter taste of terror crept up the back of her throat. Her instincts kicked in and she balled her hands into fists, ready to fight to save her life. It was the smell that hit her first, that stink of mud, rot, and wet dog, that let her know her tormentors were closing in. With her heart racing, she took on a warrior's stance.

"Come on, you bastards," she shouted into the darkness.

The seconds ticked by and she didn't hear a thing. It was as if they were toying with her. In the distance she thought she heard the whine of an engine, but decided her mind was playing tricks on her. Another deep growl immediately to her left let her know where one of her tormentors was positioned. Swinging around, she blindly kicked into the darkness and felt her foot connect with something solid. A soft grunt followed by a yelp filled the air. Empowered that she had hit something, she waited to see if the animal would come back for more. The sound of the engine suddenly grew louder. Then, a beam of light illuminated the area around her.

She swallowed back her scream when she saw that she was surrounded by three hulking, dirty dogs that resembled wolves more than friendly Fido's.

"Heather. Don't move."

The pitch of the engine picked up, and within seconds the light grew brighter. The dogs began to look to one another, unsure of what to do next, but when the four-wheeler was almost on them, they took off running into the darkness.

Heather sank to her knees. Breathing hard, she bent over and fought back the urge to vomit.

"Are you all right?" Grant came running up to her. He threw his arms around her and pulled her to him.

Relieved, she nestled against his chest, fighting back the tears.

"What in the hell are you doing out here? You knew about the dogs." He stood back, checking her over in the beam of light coming from his four-wheeler.

After catching her breath, she looked up at him. "I'm all right. I forgot about the dogs until I was on the road. I wanted to come to the stables and help with Maximillian."

He slipped his arm around her waist. "He's fine. Gigi and the vet are with him. It's nothing, just a cold. Let's get you back to the house."

After helping her onto the back of the four-wheeler, he paused and ran his hand over her hair. "Are you sure you are all right?"

She let out a long breath and then began shivering. "Just shaken up a little."

"I know just the thing for that." He climbed on the front of the four-wheeler and tucked her arms around his waist. "Hold on to me. I'm going to take you home."

Alexandrea Weis

Chapter 12

He said nothing as he helped her from the four-wheeler and wrapped his arm around her shoulders. Walking behind the garage, they climbed the straight wooden steps together to his apartment. When he pushed the door open, Heather felt a sudden twinge of excitement mixed with trepidation.

"Let me get you something to help calm you," he told her while closing the front door.

She waited in the living room, still shivering, as he went to the kitchen and retrieved an old-fashioned glass from a cabinet.

"So what on earth possessed you to wander into the pitch black night and head to the stables?" he demanded, returning to the living room with the glass and a bottle of whiskey in his hands.

"I told you. I wanted to see if I could help with Maximillian."

He twisted the cap from the whiskey bottle and filled the glass. "You could have been hurt."

He held out the glass to her. The dark brown liquid looked so enticing. "I know, but I guess I was so distracted by … everything."

He put the bottle down on a glass coffee table. "Distracted by what?"

Gripping her glass with both hands, she peered into her drink. "You."

He pointed to her glass. "Drink it down."

She frowned at him. "I don't think I should. I need to drive home tonight."

"You're not going anywhere, Heather."

Too tired to fight him, she raised the glass to her lips and grimacing, gulped back a good portion of the whiskey. When she lowered the glass, she coughed as the alcohol burned the back of her throat.

Grant took the glass from her hand and put it on the coffee table. "We had better resolve this dilemma before one of us gets hurt."

"What dilemma?"

He took her hand. "Come with me."

She did not protest as he led her into his bedroom. The slight buzz from the alcohol combined with the prospect of what was to come removed the last traces of shaking from her limbs. When he stood by the nightstand, Heather's eyes darted about the bedroom. He quickly slipped off his white shirt and dropped it to the floor. She saw the red, ugly stitches on the left side of his chest and wanted to chastise him for not having a bandage covering the site, but her voice failed her when he sat down on the bed.

"Take off your clothes," he ordered.

"What ... no seduction, no moves?"

"Do you really want to waste time with that?"

She shrugged. "It might help."

He stood from the bed and came up to her. "Nervous?"

She shook her head. "No, just not used to being so up front about ... all of this."

He edged closer, his lips next to her ear. "This isn't a game, Heather. It's not about dating or getting to know each other. It's sex. I want you, and I don't want to wait any longer to have you."

The crude comment should have made her angry, but instead it turned her on. Her skin tingled, her cheeks flushed, and her heart raced with excitement.

"Now do as you're told and take off your clothes." His voice was sprinkled with need.

Keeping her eyes on his, she raised her fingers to the buttons on the front of her blouse. Taking her time, she undid each button one by one, hoping to tease him. When her shirt fell to the floor, she went to unzip her black jeans until he stopped her.

"No, the bra first."

Doing as he directed, she unsnapped the clasp of her bra, letting her full breasts fall free. She liked the way his eyes became a little rounder when he saw her naked breasts. He licked his lips and Heather imagined his mouth on her nipples. She could feel her wetness seeping through to her panties.

When she finally stepped out of her black jeans, he went around her, circling her like a predator deciding where to bite first. As she slid her lacy beige underwear to the floor, he cupped her buttocks with his hands, causing her to suck in a quick breath.

"Is this from the fall today?" He gently fingered the purple bruise on her hip and thigh.

She nodded, but did not turn to face him.

"Does it hurt?"

"Not too much."

His fingers lightly traced up her back along her spine. The sensation sent a ripple of electricity coursing throughout her body. "How many lovers have you had?"

She was taken aback by the question. "What difference does—?"

"Answer the question," he interrupted.

She had to take a moment to add up her experiences. "Ah, three … I think."

"You think?" He came around in front of her. "That doesn't say much for the men you've been with."

Tilting her head to the side, she smirked at him. "Maybe they weren't that memorable."

"I promise you won't forget me."

"I wouldn't get too cocky, Grant. You haven't done anything yet."

"I see my pit bull is back." He raised his hand to her right nipple and lightly drew circles around her pink flesh. "I think I'm going to like breaking you in."

She thought of the handcuffs in the drawer of his nightstand. "Is that what you do, break women in?"

His hand went to the valley between her legs. He slipped his fingers into her folds. "Not women, just you. It's what I like to do to determined pit bulls." His face came within inches of hers. "You would like that, wouldn't you?" His fingers stroked her.

She gasped, fighting to stay focused. "I—I'm not sure."

"You're flustered by the question. That's good. It means I'm right." His fingers moved in and out, rubbing her sensitive flesh. "Now, tell me what you want from me."

Her eyes stayed on him and she felt an overwhelming desire to say that was exactly what she wanted. Then, she stifled her words. Glaring into his eyes, she felt his fingers continue to move teasingly over her clit.

When she said nothing, he pinched her clit, hard. Her knees give way. "Tell me what you want, Heather."

She stood up straight, keeping her eyes on him. She had never said such a thing to a man before, but with Grant she wanted to tell him exactly what she needed. It was what she had always wanted from a man, but kept locked away.

"I want … don't be gentle. I don't like gentle."

Grant's amber eyes sparkled with interest. "I knew we had a lot in common."

He removed his hand from between her legs and stood back from her. When he stepped behind her, Heather anxiously waited.

For several seconds nothing happened. The anticipation slicing through her body was seductively addicting. Then, she felt his hand on the side of her neck. He squeezed into her flesh and quickly shoved her toward the bed. Heather's knees butted up against the edge of the sleigh bed. When he pushed her onto the bed, she wasn't sure what to do or how to act. No man had ever been this way with her. She flopped down on the bed before him, planting her face into the thick ash gray comforter. As he climbed up behind her, lifting her hips in the air, the desire in her belly consumed her. Not knowing what he was going to do and submitting to him felt absolutely wonderful.

She groaned when he slapped her backside, relishing the sting of his hand on her flesh. He reached between her legs and drove three fingers inside her, making Heather gasp.

"You're so tight. I can't wait to fuck you."

He rhythmically moved in and out, stroking her flesh and making Heather moan with need. She began rocking against his hand as he quickened his pace. The first indication of the orgasm to come began in her gut as a maddening tingle, but then the tingle grew into a burning. By the time her climax hit, she was panting and gripping the comforter in her hands.

Her insides were still pulsating when Grant's arm went around her waist, lifting her from the bed and setting her on all fours. Before she could catch her breath, he entered her with one brutal thrust. She cried out and he did it again, harder than before. He said nothing but held on to her, ramming into her and ignoring her whimpers.

This wasn't the gentle kind of lovemaking Heather had known with Ben and the others. It was primal, and satisfied some inner desire she had to be taken completely by a man. She clutched the gray bedspread, her body rocking forward with every penetration. Despite the initial discomfort, Heather's body responded to him. She moaned as the second orgasm shot upward from her groin, more powerful than the first. Bucking beneath him when the first waves hit her, every fiber of her being exploded and then she screamed.

Overcome, she wanted to fall on to the bed and close her eyes, reveling in the satisfaction streaming through her, but Grant kept on. He roughly held her closer to him, shifted his hips and went even deeper. Heather wanted him to stop; she was getting too sensitive and it was becoming painful. When she tried to wiggle out of his grip, his arms clamped tighter around her.

"No, this is what you want. I promise it will be memorable."

She felt a jolt of alarm at his words and struggled harder against him. Grant held on to her, resisting her efforts to break free. As she squirmed, he pounded into her. Heather wanted to cry out, but then she felt that tingle rising once more. This time the climax was as relentless as Grant. It came over her faster than the previous two and made her body quiver as it gained strength. When it finally overtook her, Heather lost all sense of time and place. Her body was embraced with a searing heat, and she screamed with every ounce of energy she possessed when he slammed into her for the last time. She did not hear him groan or feel his body curling into her as he came. All she could do was let the overwhelming tide of passion carry her away.

"Jesus," she commented a few minutes later with her face scrunched against the bedspread.

"Yes, but was it memorable?" Grant bit her shoulder.

As they lay on top of his bedspread, he spooned against her back. Heather wasn't sure when they had come to rest on the bed; everything after her last orgasm was still a blur.

She sat up on her elbows and removed the stray strands of hair from her damp face. Instantly, she was exhausted. Between her legs throbbed, her arms felt weak from clutching the bedspread, and the bruise on her hip was beginning to ache.

"I think you broke something." She ran her hand over the bruise.

His arms came around her. "You said don't be gentle." He bit her earlobe. "I aim to please."

She rolled over to face him. "That you did. I may not be able to walk for a day or so, but you did make it … memorable." She rubbed her hand over her hip, wincing slightly.

"What is it?" He inspected her hip. "Is it bothering you?"

She looked down his naked body, wondering when it was during their encounter that he had slipped off his jeans and put on a condom. The stitches on his chest were very red, and as her eyes dropped lower, she admired the cut of his firm stomach muscles and the size of his….

"Let me take a look," he offered, sitting up.

She moved her hip around to give him a better look. Fascinated at how his golden eyes examined her large bruise, Heather found it a little hard to believe that just a few days ago she had despised the man.

His fingers delicately caressed her bruise. "We need to take care of this."

She touched his laceration. "We need to put a bandage on this."

He removed her hand from his chest. "I'm fine." Grant stood from the bed. "Stay right there."

As he walked out of the bedroom, she admired his firm, round ass, making a mental note to get her hands on it before their evening was over.

And after that?

She choked back the thought. There could be no more after tonight. Despite growing closer over the past two days, sleeping with him would change nothing. Eventually, their time together would drive a wedge between them. Initially, chance encounters would be uncomfortable, but with time Heather was convinced the sting of regret would recede. She firmly believed former lovers could never succeed as friends; no one wanted to be reminded of their mistakes.

"Here, this will help." He returned to the bed carrying a bottle of olive oil.

"What's that for?"

He kneeled down on the bed. "Roll over on your stomach."

After giving him a dubious glance, she did as he requested.

He dripped a few drops of the oil on her hip and lower back. When his fingers pressed into her sore hip, she sucked in a sharp breath.

"Oww. That's tender."

He began massaging the area. "Don't tense up. You'll make it worse."

"Well, what am I supposed to do?" she argued as he kept prodding. "It hurts."

"Talk to me about something to get your mind off it." His fingers rounded her butt and squeezed hard.

She clenched her fists. "Talk about what?"

"How about riding? When did you know you wanted to compete?"

She took in a deep breath, trying not to think about the pain his fingers were inflicting. "My dad was the one who wanted me to compete. He taught me how to ride and do the basics, but then he hired a trainer for me when he felt it was time to start entering shows. That's when the fun began."

His hands slid along her hip to her back. "What do you mean?"

"My dad was always insisting I move ahead to the next level with my riding. When I started learning how to jump, my father wasn't happy with my progress over the small fences. So, he would take me into the jumping ring and make me jump the big fences."

"That must have been scary for a little girl."

His fingers worked on her lower back, and she relaxed as he kneaded a tight knot. "I was terrified. I was pretty terrified of my father, too. I think the biggest thing I remember about being a little girl was my father always yelling at me. I don't think I actually had a conversation with the man until I was twelve."

"So he is the one who pushed you to show."

"Yeah. He pushed me to show, pushed me at shows, and wasn't happy if I didn't win. My mother used to swear he was going to have a heart attack every time I went into the show ring. I even gave up riding for a while because I got so tired of him yelling at me."

Grant stopped rubbing her back. "When was this?"

"When I turned eighteen. I wanted to go away to college. Mostly to get away from my father, but he wouldn't let me go out of state, so I stopped riding. I sold my horse and thought I had gotten the better of him. I stayed away for two years, and then I missed it so much I had to go back. By then I was in nursing school, and Dad…." She grew quiet as a myriad of unhappy memories came back to her.

"What happened?" He stretched out next to her.

She stayed on her stomach, keeping her eyes focused on the gray comforter. "Everything just got bad."

"Do you want to talk about it?"

She turned to him. "There's no point."

"There's a point, Heather. We're friends and friends talk about what's troubling them."

"I don't think we can say we're friends anymore after tonight."

He ran his hand down to her round butt. "Why not?"

She heaved with longing as he kneaded her ass. "We should talk about this in the morning when we are both thinking clearly."

He nuzzled her neck. "There is no clear thinking when it comes to sex, Heather."

"Perhaps we just need to get this out of our systems and then we can go back to being competitors," she reasoned. "I think it would be better to just keep this simple and not let it get complicated."

"By complicated do you mean emotional?"

"I mean complicated," she slyly replied.

He wrapped her in his arms. "You're sure you want it that way?"

Her hands went to his cock, suddenly eager to have him once more "Yes, I think we both do."

When he kissed her again, Heather pushed the possibilities of what they were doing out of her head. As far as she was concerned, it was all going to end come morning. Grant was a man who could get dangerously close to her heart, and Heather could not allow that to happen. Opening up meant letting go. Her past had taught her to never lose her heart. Hardened hearts could never be broken, and a life untouched by love was better than a lifetime filled with regrets.

Chapter 13

The next morning Heather awoke in Grant's arms. She blinked with confusion as she looked around his bedroom, trying to remember the events of the previous night. Wiggling free of his embrace while trying not to wake him, she slowly rose from the bed. Watching him as he slept, Heather studied every detail of his face, storing away the memory for when she was old and gray. She wanted to be able to look back and say, "Yeah, I had that one night."

After scooping up her clothes from the bedroom floor, she quickly dressed in the living room, eager to make a hasty exit. Creeping toward the front door, she grimaced as she opened it, praying the noise didn't wake him. The cold morning air hit her skin, making her shiver. Tiptoeing down the wooden steps, she blew out a relieved sigh when her feet hit the walkway. Glancing at the sky and taking in the early morning sun, she took off at a slight jog for the front of the house, wincing as her body ached with every movement.

At the front door of the mansion, she tried the handle and cursed when she found it locked. As the burning in her cheeks began—knowing that she would have some explaining to do—she rang the doorbell.

"Hey, Ms. Phillips," Lola said after answering the door. "You're up mighty early."

Heather silently thanked the gods of serendipity that she had not been discovered by Tad Crowley.

"You want me to make you anything special for dinner?" Lola inquired as Heather darted in the door.

Heather turned to the round-faced woman and smiled. "No, Lola. I'll be leaving this morning."

"You want me to tell Mr. Crowley?" Lola asked, her lovely brown eyes shrouded with concern.

"He already knows, Lola. Thanks for everything."

Leaving Lola, Heather scurried to the spiral staircase and hurried to her room. It was time to put Crowley Ranch behind her, and tuck her adventures away for remembering on a cold, rainy day when she needed to smile.

* * *

After the hour drive from Crowley Ranch, the only place Heather could think to go was Southland Stables. Leaving her purse and overnight bag in her Pathfinder, she rushed to the stable entrance. When she rounded the edge of the shed row, Murphy spotted her and began whinnying with joy. Seeing her beloved horse made all the events of the past few days disappear from her mind … well, almost all of them. Images of her time with Grant were still pretty hard to push away.

As she stood before Murphy, rubbing his long face and telling him how much she had missed him, she thought of Grant and what he had made of her early departure. Had he cared? He wasn't the kind of man to care; motivation enough for leaving the way she did. No point in ruining the night before with memories of the morning after.

"You're back," a smoky voice called to her from further down the shed row.

Heather peeked over Murphy's head to see Trent coming toward her. Wearing jeans and a long-sleeved T-shirt, he strutted up to her. His confident swagger reminded her of Grant, making her insides heat up.

Stop it! It's over and done with.

"Rebecca said you would be at Crowley Ranch for a few days, at least."

"My patient healed quickly."

"I'll bet." He stepped closer to Murphy's stall door. "You've lost three days in the ring and you've got Riverdale in less than two weeks. Are you ready to get back in the saddle?"

Heather met his gray eyes. "I'm ready."

Trent leaned against the stall door. "When Rebecca told me you would be taking care of Crowley, I was rather shocked. I thought you hated the guy."

She shrugged and tucked her thumbs into the front pockets of her jeans. "I did, but his father offered me a ton of money to take care of him. I've got bills to pay."

Keeping his skeptical eyes on her, he folded his arms over his wide chest. "Why you?"

"Grant came into my ER and his father apparently knew who I was. Gigi had told him about me." She peered down and kicked at the shavings on the ground. "He said he wanted someone who knew his son to care for him. When he offered to pay me a month's salary for a few days of babysitting, what was I supposed to say?"

"Heather, you've never been one to be motivated by money," he pointed out in a worried tone. "I know you struggle sometimes, but you've never put your principles aside for your finances."

"I'm not noble, Trent. I'd do anything to keep Murph." She rubbed the horse's head. "If that means sitting with the arrogant Grant Crowley, then so be it."

He pushed away from the door. "Get tacked up and meet me in the back ring in fifteen minutes. We have a lot of ground to cover."

"Don't you have to go to work?" she questioned. "It's the middle of the week."

"We're going to the OB today at one, so I took the day off. I've got a little time to kill before I need to pick up Rayne."

She gave him a half-smile. "Are you two getting excited about the baby?"

His laughter was melodious and heartwarming, the kind a happy father made when tossing his child into the air.

"I think I'm more excited than Rayne right now. She's miserable with her big belly and swollen feet. Personally, I think she looks beautiful."

A pang of jealousy ran through Heather. Would she ever have a man love her like that? Seeing her as beautiful when she was at her worst? Then Heather remembered Ben and his offer. Perhaps it was time to seriously consider the good doctor as a partner. She had lived her one night of passion with Grant, and could now settle down and accept the inevitability of her life. She may not have that torrid desire with Ben, but she would have comfort.

"You need to have one of those soon," Trent said, snapping her back from her thoughts.

She gave him a blank stare. "One of what?"

He chuckled at her reaction. "A baby. You would be a great mom."

The comment made Heather shift nervously on her feet, uncomfortable with the idea of being anyone's mother. "What makes you say that? I think I would be a lousy mother."

Trent took a step closer to her, squeezing her arm with encouragement. "Hey, you'll be a great mom. You love that horse of yours like he was your child. If you can open your heart to him, you'll do the same with your baby."

Her maternal desires roared to life at the thought of a baby, but for the past few years she had dismissed the possibility of ever being anyone's mother. Brushing off his comment, she turned to Murphy. "Let me get him tacked up and I'll meet you in the jumping ring."

Weighing her features, Trent squinted his eyes. "You all right?"

She squared her shoulders as she lifted Murphy's halter from the side of the stall door. "Don't I look all right?"

"No. You're troubled. I've known you too long, Heather. You've got the same sad look in your eyes like you did after your Dad went to prison."

She slipped the halter over Murphy's head. "It's nothing, Trent."

"I'm not going to fight it out of you. I learned not to do that a long time ago. If you ever need a friend, you know how to find me."

Friend. The word tore through her heart like a bullet finding its mark.

With one hand on Murphy's halter, she dropped the chain in front of his stall door and clucked for him to move forward. "I appreciate the offer, Trent," she remarked, leading the tall bay into the shed row. "But I'm fine. Everything is just the way it should be."

* * *

In the back jumping ring, behind the red and white stables, Heather warmed up Murphy along the white railing, pushing him to perform some simple flat exercise while Trent set up a combination of fences in the center of the ring. Occasionally, she would watch him out of the corner of her eye as he counted off strides in between fences and lifted the heavy poles into the cups mounted on the side stands.

Of all the people she had associated with through the years, the one person who had always stayed a part of her life was Trent. She found it odd that she had never wanted to date the good-looking man, and despite his desire to pursue a relationship when they had first met, something about him had felt wrong. In many ways, Trent had reminded her of Stewart. Both men had that ruthless drive to get ahead and a sense of taking whatever they wanted without regret. She had once thought Grant was cut from the same mold, but her time at Crowley Ranch had changed her opinion of him. Hell, it had decimated it. To her, Grant was no longer ruthless, but troubled. He was a man trying to please everyone, while showing his emotions to no one.

"Sounds like me," she mumbled as she cantered Murphy around the ring.

Deciding her horse was ready to take a few jumps, Heather rode to the center of the ring to confer with Trent.

"Let's take him over the triple combination to start," he suggested. "Get him to move out on the second portion of the combo. He gets lazy on the back end and likes to tip the last fence. He always looks like he falls asleep toward the end."

Heather tightened the chin strap on her riding helmet. "I know, Trent."

"If you know, then wake him up, push him," he asserted in a raised voice.

"Jesus, you're such an asshole." Grasping her reins, she pointed Murphy toward the rail.

"Me being an asshole is better than having your boyfriend beat you in the ring again," he shouted behind her.

She turned in her saddle and glared back at him over Murphy's rump. "Don't even go there. You know Grant is my rival and not my ... whatever."

"Then stop letting him win." He pointed to the fences lined up along the side of the ring. "Take the combo and remember to push him at the end."

"No wonder I never dated you," she muttered. "Rayne can have you, you contentious self-centered son of a—"

"What was that?" he cut in.

She smirked back at him. "I was talking to Murphy."

He scowled at her. "Sure you were. Now jump the goddamned fences."

Picturing a selection of sharp instruments she would have loved to have driven into Trent's flesh, she asked Murphy to canter, made a small circle, and then made her way toward the first fence in the combination; a blue and white triple oxer that was as wide as it was high.

Tightly gripping the reins, she squeezed her legs into the leather saddle and directed Murphy to the fence. The cool air whipped against her face as she felt the thud of his hooves hitting the hard ground. She concentrated on the fence ahead, counting his stride, looking for the best spot to take off. When Murphy was right before the high blue and white poles, he pulled against the reins, wanting his head, but she resisted.

Wait, Murphy, hold on.

Then she felt the rhythm ... the rhythm a rider gets when they feel the stride of the horse and are judging the distance to a fence. Like a metronome clicking inside of her head, she could time the approach to the fence.

Murphy listened to the cues she gave him with her hands and legs, and just at the right moment, he took off over the hurdle. She rocked forward, resting her hands on his neck and arching to help carry him over, and when he landed on the other side, she popped up in the saddle, dug in with her legs, and held him back once more. The second fence was just two strides away, and she waited again, counting his steps before urging him over the next jump.

When he landed, she felt Murphy begin to slow down. With only one stride to go, she dug her heels into his sides, making him use all of his strength to clear the last fence; a wide red monstrosity built to resemble a smaller version of Southland Stables.

"Good, you got him to listen to you, but he still looks asleep over the fences," Trent shouted from the side of the last fence. "Now do it again, but cut the approach this time. Pretend this is a jump off. Let's really test him."

She remembered what Grant had taught her, and then she smiled. Before going to Crowley Ranch, she would have been nervous about now. Worrying about cutting her approach too short and messing up Murphy, but that anxiety was gone. It had been replaced by an undeniable hankering to see just how close she could cut it.

Cantering Murphy to the rail, she made a sharp turn and guided the horse toward the beginning of the combination. As the first fence loomed, she doused her inkling of fear and held on.

After she cleared the last fence, she laughed and patted Murphy's neck. He must have felt her exuberance because he hadn't plodded through the final fence this time, he'd flown over it.

Trent's calculating gray eyes watched as she rode Murphy up to him. He stared at her as she dropped her reins and gleefully patted Murphy's neck once more.

"When did you start doing that?"

"You told me to cut the approach. Why? What did I do wrong?"

His eyebrows went up as he considered the question. "You didn't do anything wrong. In fact, for the first time, you got it right." He ran his hand over his chin, his thin lips pressing together. "I can't put my finger on it, but there is something different with your riding. It's like you're suddenly adventurous in the saddle."

"Maybe I was just having fun with it."

"Fun?" He gazed up at her, letting go a throaty chortle. "That was never you. This was never 'fun' for you. You've always been a cautious rider, Heather."

"You can't be cautious and show jump horses, Trent." She collected Murphy's reins, about to head back to the rail, when he put his hand on Murphy's snaffle bit.

"You've never beaten Grant Crowley before because you weren't willing to take risks, but what I just saw … if you do that in the show ring, you will win. You have to risk everything in order to win." He let go of the bit. "Now take the touch and go, and let's see if you can do it again."

Heather secured the reins in her hands and tapped Murphy with her heels. Taking a posting trot to the side of the ring, she spied the touch and go combination across from the white gate. As her horse began an easygoing canter, she remembered the touch and go she had jumped the day before with Grant. Smiling, she flashed back to her embarrassing fall and how he had rubbed her still tender bruise with olive oil in bed that night. Kicking Murphy to move faster, she made her tight turn and instantly all the words Grant had said to incite her anger came back as the green and white poles of the first fence drew closer. When Murphy sailed over the first fence and then was on his way to the second, a thrill of confidence uplifted her. She had what it took to win, she knew it now, and nothing was going to keep her from the blue ribbon anymore. Not even Grant.

"Now that's more like it," Trent declared as she rode to the middle of the ring. His eyes beamed with pride, his smile was contagious, and the lilt of his voice made Heather want to giggle with happiness. "I don't know what happened at Crowley Ranch, but it sure improved your riding."

Heather was snapping off the chin strap from her riding helmet when Trent's cell phone rang out a snappy jazz tune from the front pocket of his jeans. The sudden look of panic that came over the riding master made Heather grin. She could not remember how many times she had seen the same wide-eyed fright grip many an expectant father.

"What is it?" he almost shouted into the phone.

He listened intently for a few seconds and then he glanced up at Heather, rolling his eyes. "No I'm not stopping for pizza on the way home, Rayne. Yes, I'm on my way now. I'll be there in ten minutes." He paused and mouthed to Heather, "I've got to go."

As he walked toward the gate, Heather eyed the touch and go once more, reliving the feeling she had experienced soaring over the fences. With another happy pat on Murphy's neck, she kicked her feet out of the stirrups and sagged in her saddle. They had done enough for today.

Back beneath the long shadows of the stable's metal roof, she was giving Murphy a good brushing before putting him up for the night when her cell phone on the shelf just inside her tack room door rang out with a musical tone, indicating a text message was coming in.

Leaving Murphy tied to his hitching post, she went to her tack room and checked her iPhone.

We need to talk. Why haven't you called me? I'm worried about you.

She wanted to throw her phone to the ground when she read the text from Ben. "I can't talk to him right now."

Heather was about to put the phone back on the shelf when another text came through.

You shouldn't have left. I wasn't done with you.

The quiver of surprise that came over her was unexpected. How had Grant gotten her cell phone number? As her shock abated and reason took over once again, she realized a man like Grant probably had many ways of getting her phone number, including calling her boss. That Ben had given the number to Grant she found harder to digest. The attractive ER physician would ask a lot of questions and she would....

"It doesn't matter," she whispered into the dimly lit tack room. "I'm done."

She deleted the text, replaced the phone back on the shelf next to a black curry comb, and returned to Murphy. She had enjoyed their night—actually, she had more than enjoyed it—but it was time to put Grant aside. Ben was going to be her future, and there could be no turning back. "Some things were never meant to be," her mother had once told her. "So just make sure you grab on to those things that are meant to be and never let go."

Chapter 14

By the time Heather parked her black Pathfinder in the single car garage of her modest stone-covered ranch home, she was exhausted. The long night with Grant and the afternoon with Murphy had worn her out. Removing her overnight bag from her front seat, she trudged across her garage to the back door. Pounding her feet on the cement floor, she tried to knock the last remnants of mud from her short brown riding boots before tracking the dirt into her house.

Pushing the white metal door open, she went to the alarm panel located just inside the back entrance and punched in her code. After slamming the door shut and setting the deadbolt, she reactivated the alarm. Kicking off her riding boots inside the small hallway that led to her kitchen, she listened to the stillness of the house. The past two days had been filled with activity and people. Now she was suddenly alone, and she didn't like the feeling. Heather had never felt isolated or lonely before, and that disturbed her.

"Maybe I should consider getting a dog."

Dropping the overnight bag on her kitchen counter, she went to the stainless refrigerator and retrieved her favorite bottle of Asti sparkling wine. By the sink, she struggled with the stubborn cork, and after several attempts freed it and poured an iced tea glass full of the fruity, bubbly wine. Yeah, it was one of those of nights.

Taking her drink, she crossed the living room done in oak-paneled walls and a light beige Berber carpet. Along the walls were posters of cities she had always longed to travel to: Paris, Athens, London, and Madrid. The centerpiece of the room was a stone fireplace with a thick beam of unfinished wood set into the mantle. Along the mantle, family pictures had been lovingly preserved in silver frames. Passing her plush white sofa, she made a mental note to tidy up the array of horse magazines she had left there a few days before. Her life being what it was, housekeeping was far from a priority.

Down the yellow-painted hall that led to the three bedrooms, she ducked into the first open door and flipped on the lights. A warm glow from the ceiling fan fixture illuminated the oblong room. Set in the center, and surrounded by two long windows, was a king-sized trundle bed with a throw blanket covered with horses running across an ocean shoreline. The furniture was simple, the one painting on the wall was of the Eiffel Tower, and the floor was covered in the same beige Berber that was in the living room. Putting her drink down on the round oak table by her bed, she went to the bathroom and turned on the water for her bath.

Done all in white with a white double vanity, white-tiled floors, and white-painted walls, she eyed the silver towel racks and trim about the vanity mirror and reminded herself to one day change the décor in her bathroom. It was one of the numerous things on her to do list that she had kept vowing to fulfill since moving into the home three years ago. Unfortunately, like most of her best made plans, they had been sidelined due to time and budget constraints. Remembering the check Tad Crowley had given her, she considered finally making those needed changes around the house. The extra money would come in handy. Then she thought of things she could buy for Murphy—new brushes, a new winter blanket—and again the house plans were put out of her mind.

Stripping down, she checked the bruise on her hip in the mirror and smiled as she recalled Grant rubbing olive oil on it. His fingers on her skin had made her feel so….

"Enough of that," she scolded, climbing into the hot bath.

Finally settled in her bath, her wine in hand and her head resting on a rolled up towel, she relaxed against the tub and closed her eyes. Visions of Grant enveloped her. Instantly, her body was revived with a quickening of desire. Letting her mind linger over their night together, she had no regrets. It had been just what she needed; some really great sex.

Lost in her fantasies of him, the peel of her irritating doorbell cut through the air. The high-pitched chirping always reminded her of a songbird on meth. It was another one of those pesky changes she had promised to make around the house.

Sighing at the thought of interrupting her comforting bath, she climbed from the water and reached for her fluffy white robe. Cursing her nosy neighbor, Ms. Timmerick—who had a propensity for dropping by at odd hours—she barreled toward the door while tying off her robe and wrapping her long hair about her right shoulder.

Scurrying down the short entrance hall done in brown stone and decorative plaster inlay, she placed her hand on the brass door handle, punched in the alarm code on the panel to her left, and put a saccharin smile on her face. But when she yanked the heavy door open, it was not her elderly neighbor standing there with yet another casserole, it was Grant.

His long arms were stretched out, gripping either side of the doorframe around the entrance. His blue button-down shirt was open halfway, and his gray slacks looked a little wrinkled. His amber eyes were drawn together, and his thin lips were pulled back in a displeased scowl.

"Why did you leave?" His voice was saturated with anger.

Heather tugged at the collar of her robe. "I thought it was better this way."

He furrowed his brow. "Better for whom? Because it sure wasn't better for me. I didn't like waking up to find you gone." He bounded in the door. "Don't do it again."

"Hey, wait a minute," she fussed as he rushed past her.

He stood in the hallway, analyzing the decor. "We're going to have a little chat."

"A chat?" The loud whack of the front door closing resonated around them. "How did you get my address, and my cell phone number for that matter? What are you, some kind of stalker?"

"It's in your employment record at Lewisville Medical."

She came up to him, fuming. "You talked to Ben, didn't you?"

His eyes traveled the curves of her robe. "Of course not. I called your hospital administrator, Tim Wellborn. I told him I wanted to thank you for all the personal care you gave me."

"You manipulative bastard."

He inched closer. "Why did you leave this morning?"

She marched past him and into her living room, trying to formulate an answer that would appease him and sound somewhat reasonable. At the white sofa, she stopped and faced him, shoving her damp hair aside. "You know why I left. You have Vanessa and I—I have Ben. Last night was just one of those things that can never be repeated."

He barreled up to her, glaring into her eyes. "Bullshit. You know last night was a hell of a lot more than that."

She tossed her hand in the air. "You're practically engaged, Grant."

"Do you honestly think I can marry her after last night?"

"That's what your father wants, right? Don't you always do what he wants?"

The fire in his eyes scared the crap out of her. She knew he was capable of real rage, she had seen it in the show ring, but never had she expected to be in the line of fire. His hands gripped her arms, pulling her against him. His fingers were squeezing into her robe, crushing her flesh.

"Don't ever speak to me like that again," he snarled. "You have no idea what…." He went quiet. His face was inches from hers. She could feel his hot breath on her lips. "Tell me to go away and I will."

She mustered the strength to ask him to leave, but could not form the words. Having him so close was setting off a firestorm of desire. She ached for him … she longed for one more night naked in his arms.

He pushed her away. "That's what I figured." He untied the belt of her robe and slowly slipped it through the loops as Heather held on to the lapels.

Wrapping the thick piece of terrycloth about his right hand, he then lowered her hands from the robe.

"You can't push me away, not without consequences, Heather."

Her stomach balled into a knot. "What consequences?"

Ripping the robe from her body with one swift movement, he spun her around and grabbed her hands. Heather almost cried out as he wrenched her arms behind her and then secured them tightly at the wrists with the belt. He then pressed on the back of her neck, pushing her thighs into the white sofa.

"I'm a man who likes to maintain control over my horses and my women. There is a system of punishment and reward with me. Be good and you will reap the rewards, but be bad...." His hand slipped between her legs and his fingers shoved hard into her.

She arched her back and gasped as he probed her. Heather knew she should protest, scream, and insist he leave her home, but she couldn't. She was excited by his rough handling of her. It was erotic, it was exhilarating ... it was exactly what she had always wanted.

"You're already wet for me," he whispered in her ear. "Have you been thinking about me ... about us?" His fingers moved in and out. "Do you want more of me?" He withdrew his fingers and pinched her clit, causing her to cry out. "Tell me to stop, and I will." He squeezed her sensitive nub between his thumb and forefinger, making Heather curl with need. "I'm waiting for your answer," he breathed in her hair.

"Yes," she replied in a raspy voice. "I want more of you."

He removed his fingers from her wet flesh. "Why did you leave?"

Pinned by his body to the back of the sofa, she showed him her profile. "If I had stayed ... we won't work, Grant."

His fingers gently found their way back to her tender folds. "We're working now, Heather."

When he entered her again, Heather gave in to him completely. She backed up against him, rubbing her butt against the fly of his trousers. She wanted to feel his cock inside of her, and as he worked her clit, pinching and rubbing it with his fingertips, the desperate tingle of her orgasm began its steady assault up her spine. She was swaying back and forth, butting against him, eager to come. Just as she could feel the last wave of tension climbing higher, about to take over her senses, he stopped and removed his hand.

"No," she cried out, almost falling against the sofa. "Don't stop."

"Spread your legs apart," he insisted behind her.

Anxious for him to finish, she spread her feet apart, trying to maintain her balance with her hands still tied behind her. Waiting, she was once again enthralled with the quiet of her home, and then she heard him lowering his zipper and the faint crinkle of what sounded like a foil wrapper being opened. She clenched her fists with anticipation.

He plunged into her, making her grunt against the discomfort. Rutting into her, he forced her flesh apart, going as deep as he could and sending her bucking forward into the back of the sofa.

"Tell me you like this," he hissed. "Tell me you like being fucked this way."

She bent her head back, gasping for air as he pushed deep into her once more. "Yes … yes, I want you this way."

His thrusts sent exquisite jolts of searing heat throughout her body. The hard, brutal pounding was taking Heather over the edge. She was spiraling closer to her release. She was groaning loudly as he slammed into her again and again. Then, when she was about to plummet into that chasm of ecstasy, he pulled out of her.

Heather almost dropped to the floor. "What? What are you doing?"

His arms encircled her as he bent her over the back of the sofa. "I told you there would be consequences for your leaving." He rubbed his hands over her exposed bottom. "Now you will pay the price."

The first slap on her behind shocked her and her eyes flew open. She was about to wiggle around and shout at him when the second slap hit her. Harder than the first, the sting of his hand against her tender skin brought tears to her eyes.

"Grant, stop it." She squirmed, but could not push her body up from the sofa.

"Once you have been punished and promise never to leave me like that again, then I will give you what you desire."

"I'm not some spoiled child," she protested. "You're hurting me."

He slapped her again and this time she yelped in pain, struggling against the tie on her wrists. "I require discipline of my mounts. I don't take bad behavior from my horses and I'm not going to take it from you." He spanked her again, and Heather cried out. "Now tell me what I want to hear and I will stop."

"What do you want to hear?" she begged.

His fingers slipped between the round cheeks of her butt and teasingly traced the outline of her wet folds. "Tell me you will never leave me like that again." He dipped his fingers into her.

Heather bit down on her lip as he rubbed his fingers lightly over her clit. "I'll do whatever, please...." Her voice dimmed as her body yearned for more.

"Please what? What do you want?" he seductively taunted.

His fingers became more insistent, pressing into her flesh and arousing her desire. Heather caved.

"Just fuck me, Grant. I'll never leave you again, all right? Just ... finish me."

He wrapped her long hair around his hand and arched her head back. "From now on, no one else can have you, baby," he murmured into her cheek. "You're mine. Say it."

Heather hesitated, not sure if she could say such a thing. Then, she opened her mouth and whispered, "I'm—I'm yours."

She felt conquered by the words, as if she had been the unbroken horse he had finally tamed.

Spreading her folds apart he rammed into her, pinning her thighs painfully to the back of the sofa, but she didn't care. All that mattered was that he was inside of her. Heather reveled in his arms hugging her, heard the sound of his hips slapping against her butt, and savored the smell of sex in the air mixed with his woodsy cologne. Everything seemed to move in slow motion as she gave in completely to him. It did not take long for the addictive heat to erupt in her belly, adding to her pleasure at being ravaged by him. She figured at this point analyzing why submitting to Grant sparked her desire was pointless. She was his and wanted to go on being his for as long as possible. When the powerful orgasm finally rocked her body, her piercing scream cut through the quiet of her home.

    He had pulled her to the plush carpet and untied her hands. After tossing the robe belt to the side, she was cuddled against him. Her bruised bottom was aching and the flesh between her legs was throbbing, but she didn't want to move, too afraid his embrace would fall away.

    "When I woke up and you weren't there, I ran to the house looking for you." His soft voice reverberated against her right cheek. "I confronted my father about paying you off and sending you home. He told me to forget about you." He rolled slightly to the side and kissed her chin.

    "He's right. You need to forget about me."

    "I told him that I wasn't going to marry Vanessa."

    She sat up. "What did he say?"

    He rolled over on his back. "He yelled, I yelled back, and then he went to the lower forty to inspect the cattle." He brushed the long brown locks from her face. "I want you in my life, so no more running away."

    She scooted up, wincing slightly. "I wasn't running. I was avoiding the hassles we'll eventually encounter." She examined her thighs, noting the ugly red mark across them.

    "What hassles?"

    She gazed down at him. His shirt was still half-opened and his pants were hanging loosely about his hips. "The fights, the lies, the regrets; what else is there in relationships?"

    Grant sat up. "I don't know … there's the laughter, good times, and great sex." He smiled, dipping his head to her. "It's not all bad, Heather."

    She stood from the floor. "You don't want me, Grant."

    He deftly removed the condom he had slipped on. "I've got you, Heather. You're mine now." He dropped the condom next to the terrycloth belt.

    She pointed to the sofa. "What was that? Are you into that shit? Spanking women and tying them up." She picked up her robe. "I found the handcuffs in your apartment, so I'm sure this is nothing new for you."

"You snooped around my apartment?" He snatched the robe away from her and threw it out of reach. "Did that turn you on?"

She gaped at him. "Of course not."

In one swift movement, he lifted her naked body and swung it over his shoulder. "Wrong answer."

"Grant, put me down." She slapped his back.

He slapped her bare bottom.

"Ow, dammit, Grant."

"Hit me again, and I will spank you even harder." She settled against his shoulder. "That's better." He pointed to the hallway on his right. "Is this the way to your bedroom?"

"Yes, why?" His shoulder was cutting off her air.

"Because I'm going to continue my lessons." He ducked beneath the archway that led to her bedroom hallway.

"Lessons? What lessons?" she demanded, swinging from his shoulder.

"It's all part of the plan, Heather. Just do as I say and I promise you'll love it."

"Literally, do as you say? Like I'm some kind of slave?" She tried to push herself up from his back, but he had her so wedged into his shoulder that she could barely move. "I'll never do that, Grant."

He carried her to the first door along the hallway and peered inside. "You'll do as I say, Heather." He plopped her down on her trundle bed. "You'll do as I say because the rewards will be so much better than the punishments."

She sat up on the bed. "Reward, punishment ... next you'll be ringing a dinner bell and expecting me to sit up and beg for my food."

He pulled his shirt over his head and dropped it on her carpet. "Dogs are easier to train than horses and women. You're going to take some effort, but I can see we are already making progress."

She stood from the bed. "You're crazy. Get out." She was about to take a step toward her bathroom door when he held her arm.

"Did you like what we did in the living room?"

She smirked up at him. "No, I don't like being spanked. I hated it when I was a kid and I hate it now."

He came up to her, putting his arm around her waist. "Who spanked you as a child?"

Her eyes veered away from his face. "My father. He always spanked me and Stewart."

"I'm sorry, but you needed to heed me."

She glared at him. "My ass still stings."

"That was my punishment." He kissed her lips. "This is my reward." He pushed her back to the bed and climbed on top of her.

Kissing the recesses of her neck and the clavicle of her right shoulder, he pushed the pants down his hips and then kicked them away. Finally free to get her hands on his round, ripe butt, Heather laughed.

"I've always adored your ass," she told him. "I've spent hours watching it. Rayne said watching a man's butt is a sign of interest in him."

"I'll tell you a little secret." He nipped the nape of her neck. "I knew you were watching me and I loved it."

She curled her arms behind his back. "I guess I should be embarrassed, but I'm not."

"Now I get to kiss my favorite part of you." His lips wandered down her chest, kissing her left breast.

"So you're a breast man." She chuckled.

"No," he refuted as his lips moved further down her stomach. "Not quite."

His hands manipulated her legs wide apart as he kneeled between them. Spreading her folds, his mouth clamped down on her sensitive flesh, making Heather arch and reach for the blanket on her bed.

His mouth was relentless. He repeatedly kept nipping and licking her clit. She had never experienced anything like it before. His mouth was making her entire body quake. When the powerful climax finally overpowered her, Heather's upper body rose from the bed and then she screamed.

She fell back against the bed, gasping for breath, but Grant was not finished. He continued on, torturing her with his tongue and teeth until she cried out once again.

When he climbed up her body, kissing her skin along the way, she felt completely drained until his fingers slipped into her very wet flesh.

"How many times have you come with a man in one night?"

Heather slapped her hand over her face, forcing her mind to focus. "You've already surpassed that, Grant."

He brutally drove his fingers into her, causing her to gasp. "How many? I want to know."

"Just once." Her hips were moving against his hand.

"Only once?" He pinched her sensitive nub. "Then we have a lot of work to do tonight."

"You're killing me," she called, trembling, on the verge of another orgasm.

"Baby," he bit down hard on her right nipple, "I've only just begun."

Chapter 15

Heather awoke to discover the faint light of the moon filtering through her bedroom windows. The unfamiliar sound of someone breathing made her sit up in the bed. When she saw Grant sleeping comfortably next to her, she smiled.

He was on his back with one hand behind his pillow, the sheets wrapped about his waist, leaving his naked chest exposed to the chilly air in the bedroom. She spied his blond curls and let her eyes travel down his sinewy chest to the stitches on his left side. She found it hard to believe that less than three days ago he had been injured and under her care. Now it was as if he were taking care of her. Not wanting him to get cold, she pulled the covers around his shoulders.

What was she doing? Here was her bitter rival in her bed after a night of … well, she had no words to describe it. No man had made her feel so vulnerable and yet so safe. It was as if he knew how to break down her barriers one by one and open her heart.

Open my heart?

Heather wanted to giggle at the concept. Since when had her heart come into this?

Tossing the covers aside, she carefully rose from the bed, not wanting to wake Grant. Creeping out of her bedroom, she quietly closed the door behind her. In the living room, she found her robe on the floor and slipped it on. After retrieving the belt, she secured it around her waist and headed to the kitchen.

She flipped on the recessed lights and opened the refrigerator, desperate for something to eat. The night's excursions had left her famished. She was rummaging through the paltry offerings in her refrigerator, debating between cereal and a cheese sandwich, when the living room lights flickered on behind her.

"I woke up and you were gone again," he commented, walking into the kitchen.

She stood from the refrigerator and glanced back at him. "I was getting something to eat, not running out on you. Besides, it's my house."

He had put on his gray trousers, but nothing else. "True, but you still weren't there and I got worried. I can never tell where I stand with you."

"Where you stand?" She went back to examining the contents of her refrigerator. "After everything we did tonight, you should have no more reservations."

"I never had reservations about you. What I was asking is where I stand with you, Heather. How do you feel about you and me?"

She closed her eyes for a second, dreading the conversation about to come. The last thing they needed to discuss were feelings; that was usually when things turned ugly.

"What do you want me to say? I love you? I need you? You know better than that, Grant."

"No, but for starters I do need to hear that it's only me. There will be no one else. No Ben Eisenberg, no one. I don't share what I possess."

That made her stand up and look back at him again. "Possess? You don't possess me."

He came up to the refrigerator door. "I believe I do. Tonight when I said you were mine, I meant it."

"I thought you were just caught up in the heat of the moment. I didn't think you were actually serious."

He cupped her chin, directing her eyes to his. "I was very serious, Heather. Once I make a woman mine, there can be no other men."

She pushed his hand away. "What about you, Grant? Will I have to compete with a long line of women to keep your interest?"

His eyes moved past her, checking out the inside of her refrigerator. "What are you talking about?"

"You have a reputation where women are concerned. You usually go through them like most people go through toilet paper."

He folded his arms over his wide chest, glowering at her. "Where did you hear that?"

She returned her attention to the refrigerator, avoiding his dissecting gaze. "Around the show circuit."

"For your information, Heather, I'm a one woman man. People have always assumed I played the field because I dated a lot of different woman, but it was usually one at a time."

She spun around to face him. "Usually?"

Grinning, he rubbed his hand over his chin. "I may have juggled seeing more than one woman at a time when I was younger, but that was when I had a lot more free time and energy. Those days are far behind me."

She rested her arm on the refrigerator door, assessing his cocky smirk. "Why don't I believe you?"

"You need to trust me, Heather."

Her eyebrows shot up. "Trust you? I'm still trying to figure out how I feel about us, remember?" She shook her head, suddenly exasperated. "Perhaps it would be wise if we didn't tell anybody about our seeing each other."

His playful demeanor cooled. "Why not? Are you ashamed of being with me?"

"No. I simply don't want to have to explain to Trent or Rayne, or anyone, why or how we happened to get together. Questions make me nervous."

"When you get nervous you run, right?" The tone of his voice was slightly menacing, giving Heather pause.

She went back to the refrigerator. "I don't run."

"So what is it? Will your reputation be ruined if you are seen with a meat-eater like me?"

The uneasy sensation in her gut eased a little and she turned to him, smiling. "No, of course not. It's just that when you grow tired of me and move on, I don't want to deal with the questions and funny looks people will give me. I've learned over the years to keep my relationships to myself, so when they come to an end—like they inevitably do—I won't be embarrassed that I…." She abruptly shut her mouth.

He put his hands on her shoulders, shaking her slightly and pressing her to speak her mind. "That you what, Heather?"

"That I failed, all right," she blurted out. "I'm tired of failing. I fail at everything. Relationships most of all."

The concern in his eyes appeared genuine. "Hey, where is this coming from? You're the most successful woman I know. You have a career, are a champion rider, and now you have me." He stared into her eyes as if trying to absorb the impact of her disclosure. "We won't fail, Heather. We are the same, you and I. We can't fail."

Heather didn't bother to tell him that she believed they were doomed from the moment he had kissed her. With his family business, his father, and her father's sordid past, they would never find the kind of happiness Rayne and Trent had discovered. That was what she had always craved in a relationship; that endearing form of love that could survive all obstacles. In her experiences, it was the obstacles that usually started tearing relationships apart. No man had been willing to stay with her when things turned ugly, and she doubted Grant was much different. She should appreciate the time they had together and when things took a turn toward hell, she could cut her losses and run.

* * *

Later that afternoon, Heather arrived at Southland Stables, eager for a workout with Murphy. Dressed in her brown riding pants and short brown boots, she was saddling up Murphy outside of her tack room door when a throaty voice called to her.

"So, you got the hots yet for your rival, Grant Crowley?"

Heather slumped against Murphy when she heard that distinctive voice. There was only one person at the stables who would ever speak to her like that.

"Jesus, Rebecca. You want to announce that to the whole damn barn?"

A brassy blonde with an ample bosom and round figure strolled toward her.

"Why not? 'Bout time you got laid," Rebecca uttered in her forthright style. "I would go after him if I was twenty years younger. Man's got an ass like warm buttermilk biscuits. The kind I want to sink my teeth into."

Heather stared into the older woman's long, tanned, but wrinkle-free face. "I really did not need to hear that, Rebecca, and

I'm not going after Grant Crowley. He was injured and I took care of him. That's all. Anyway, he's my arch rival in the ring and he's—"

"Available," Rebecca injected. "Which means he's ripe for the picking ... like his ass."

Heather honed her blue eyes on Rebecca. "Would you stop talking about his ass? And he's not available; he's got a girlfriend."

"Had a girlfriend. It's in the Twittersphere that he dumped Vanessa Luke yesterday."

Heather finished tightening the girth on her saddle, anxious not to let Rebecca see the surprise in her face. "Since when are you on Twitter?"

Rebecca came up to her. "Since I bought this stable, I'm on all the social media sites. Have to be for business nowadays." She patted Murphy's rump. "Seems Vanessa was so pissed about Grant dumping her that she took to Twitter. In one hundred and forty characters or less, she wrote a scathing critique of his lovemaking skills."

"She would." Heather snorted. "Woman's so damned vain I'm surprised she knew there was someone else in bed with her."

Rebecca got in front of Heather's face. "She also commented that he had dumped her for someone else. I was hoping it was you."

"Me? Are you completely deranged?"

"I don't know. Men get turned on when women take care of them. What do they call that ... the Nightbird Complex?"

"It's called the Florence Nightingale Effect, and it's when nurses form attachments to their patients." Heather unfastened Murphy's shiny new red halter.

"Did that happen to you?"

Heather snatched up her everyday bridle with the rubber grips in the reins. "No, it didn't. Now, if you're finished with the interrogation, I have to get Murphy to the ring. "

Rebecca fingered the red halter. "New halter, new saddle pad." She motioned to the bright white fleece pad under Heather's

English saddle. "You're already spending the windfall you got from taking care of Grant."

Infuriated, Heather whirled around. "How do you know about that?"

Rebecca shrugged her broad shoulders. "Gigi told me when she called to tell me you would be taking care of Grant after his accident. She let it slip her father was paying you a boatload. Tad Crowley even sent me a check for taking care of Murphy."

Heather's anger subsided when she remembered Tad Crowley mentioning Gigi contacting Rebecca. "Yeah, old man Crowley is very generous."

"I hope you're not putting all that money you made toward Murphy," Rebecca commented. "You should do something nice for yourself. Buy a new dress, or get your hair done."

Heather finished slipping Murphy's bit into his mouth and pushed the top of the bridle over his black-tipped ears. "I am doing something for myself. The extra money is letting me take time off from work to get Murphy ready for Riverdale. I need to train extra hard for this show."

"So you can beat Grant?"

Heather nodded as she gathered up the reins. "That's right. I've only got Riverdale left before competing against him in the state championships in November."

Rebecca followed her as she led Murphy away from the tack room door. "You're the only one who can beat him, Heather. I would sure love a blue ribbon from the state show on my wall. I'm sick of Crowley Stables always beating us every year."

"This will be our year, Rebecca."

"Lord knows, I would love to rub Gigi's nose in it this year." Rebecca patted Murphy's rump as Heather turned the horse toward the shed row. "Damn woman's been trying to steal away all my riders and my riding master. Someone needs to put those Crowleys in their place."

"That's the plan." Heather halted with Murphy to run down her stirrups. "I'm gonna beat Grant Crowley this time, no matter what."

Rebecca careened her head around Murphy's neck, taking in Heather with her curious brown eyes. She studied her for a moment and then the older woman's features lifted and she smiled. "Something happened between the two of you, didn't it?"

Heather clucked to Murphy. "Nothing happened. We just found out we ... have a lot in common."

Rebecca's throaty chuckle followed Heather to the barn entrance. "That's how it starts, Heather. First you find common ground, and then you're ripping off each other's clothes."

"Ain't gonna happen, Rebecca," Heather called back.

Leading Murphy into the bright afternoon October sun, Heather's hands were shaking as she climbed atop her horse. It was getting harder to keep lying to all the people she knew about Grant. How much longer could she smile at their comments and maintain that she had no interest in the man? Turning Murphy in the direction of the jumping ring, she got comfortable in the saddle, adjusting her stirrups and pulling in her reins. Murphy pranced, excited about their afternoon of jumping.

"Yeah, you love it don't you, man." She patted his thick neck as a swell of pride came over her.

No matter how many times she mounted his back, Heather still felt a sense of accomplishment knowing that she had saved such a beautiful and loving creature from the clutches of death. Her heart broke every time she thought of the tens of thousands of other Murphys out there being senselessly killed because they could not win a race around a stupid oval track.

As a nurse, Heather had witnessed too many atrocities to remember, always amazed at how little regard people gave to the lives of others. But when it came to the voiceless victims of mankind's lust for greed and excitement, she wished just once that those who inflicted the crop and cruelty to the racehorses on the track would one day know the misery they had caused.

As the white gate of the jumping ring came into view, Heather's cell phone vibrated in the back pocket of her pants. After a few seconds of tugging and juggling Murphy's reins, she pulled the phone free.

On the screen she found a text message waiting from Grant.

I'll be at your place at seven.

She blushed as she thought of another night with him. Pulling Murphy to a stop—because it was impossible to text and ride—she answered back.

What if I don't want you to come over?

Just be naked and in bed when I get there.

She laughed, deciding to play along. *I'll be in the kitchen cooking dinner.*

Perfect ... what are we having?

Good question. Bring wine. I'm out, she texted back.

I'll bring whiskey and the handcuffs.

Tucking her phone back in her pants, she calmed her rising libido. She needed to focus on Murphy and their upcoming show. Despite her relationship with him, she had to defeat Grant. Her competitive nature wouldn't let anyone beat her, no matter their relationship outside of the show ring. Entering the gate, she looked over the jumps she had set up earlier.

"'You're a winner, so win,' Dad used to always say." She clucked to Murphy to move ahead. "I was taught never to settle for second-best."

Chapter 16

It was a few minutes after seven that evening and Heather was rushing around her kitchen, frantically putting the finishing touches on the vegetarian meatballs she had prepared. Checking the spaghetti boiling in the pot, she was about to set the small breakfast table she had tucked to the side of the kitchen when her cell phone rang out it's musical tone from the green-granite countertop.

Cringing when she saw the incoming number, she debated about picking up the call. Shifting her eyes from the dinner cooking on the stovetop to the phone, she let out a long, heaving sigh.

"Shit." She took the call. "Hello, Ben."

"I've been calling and texting for almost three days. What's going on? Why haven't you called me back? Are you still at Crowley Ranch?"

"No. I'm home. Got home yesterday, but I've been busy with Murphy."

"Too busy to call me and tell me how you are?" He sounded hurt and though she wanted to appease him, Heather held back.

"Yes," she flatly conceded. "Look, Ben. I said I would consider your offer to start seeing each other again. I never—"

"I thought we were going to discuss our living together, not seeing each other," he interrupted. "There's a difference, Heather."

She picked up a wooden spoon from the side of the stovetop and stirred her boiling spaghetti. "I've been thinking."

"Which is usually bad news for me," he griped. "Last time you said that, you ran out my front door and avoided speaking to me for damn near a month."

"Ben, please don't make this harder for me than it is."

"Harder for you? Do you have any idea how this is killing me, Heather? I care about you. I want to be with you, start a life together, but you keep running from me. Why is that?"

She dropped the spoon on the stovetop with a clang just as the doorbell let out an irritating chirp. "I can't talk about this now. Just don't push me, Ben."

"Or you'll what? Run away again? Somebody needs to push you, Heather. You're so damned terrified of making the wrong choice that you'll pass up the right man when he comes your way. I'm the best man for you, and you know it."

The doorbell rang again.

"I've got to go. I'll be back at work Monday. We can talk then." She hung up before Ben could get another word in.

Still holding her phone in her hand, she trotted to the door. When she pulled the heavy door open, Grant was standing there. His navy blue suit appeared wrinkled, like it had seen a long, taxing day. The dark circles under his amber eyes accentuated the fatigue in his gaunt features, and his curly hair was a disheveled mess. However, the grin on his lips dispelled all of her worry. In one hand he was holding up a pair of silver handcuffs, in the other a bottle of whiskey.

"I said wine," she admonished with a deep frown.

"I'm not big a wine drinker," he confessed, and stepped inside the doorway.

Coming right up to her, he planted a long, passionate kiss on her lips. "Now that was worth the wait," he whispered, coming up for air. "I would relive this entire crappy day if I knew I had that waiting for me at the end of it."

She shut her front door. "Why was your day crappy?"

"You want an itemized report or the highlights?"

She took the whiskey from his hand and turned her nose up at the handcuffs. "Highlights."

He followed her down the short entrance hall to the living room. "My father delighted in telling me that Vanessa announced our break up all over Twitter. Basically slandering my name and my family's."

Heather entered the kitchen and put the bottle of whiskey down on the countertop by the sink. "I also heard she ripped you apart in the bedroom department."

He shrugged his suit jacket from around his shoulders. "You saw it?"

She checked the spaghetti again. "No ... Rebecca Harmon, the owner of Southland, told me about it. She made it sound pretty bad."

He draped his jacket over the back of her white plush sofa. "It was. My father is livid, and blames me for the entire humiliation."

"It's not your fault she's bitter. Unfortunately, today people like to announce their feelings to the public instead of keeping them quiet."

He strolled into the kitchen. "You would never announce your feelings to the world, would you?"

She turned off the flame below the spaghetti pot. "Of course not. I've been where you are. I know what it's like to have your name dragged through the mud."

He rolled up the sleeves on his yellow dress shirt. "Are you talking about what happened to your father?"

She snatched up a pot warmer and lifted the boiling spaghetti to the sink. "My brother and I have spent years trying to show the world that we are not ... criminals."

"Your father's mistakes aren't yours, Heather. No one blames you for what he did."

She emptied the spaghetti into a colander in the sink. "Stewart and I don't think that way. We both became so sensitive to every story or innuendo about our father that after a while, his sins became ours."

"Hey." He took the pot from her hand and set it in the sink. "You're not your father. I know that, everyone knows that. What happened is in the past."

"The past is never forgotten, Grant, it just gets blurry with time." She negotiated around him and went to her stove. "I hope you like meatless meatballs."

He chuckled, coming up behind her. "Isn't that an oxymoron?"

"No, it's vegetarian."

His arms went around her, nibbling on her neck. "Perhaps you could put some meat in my meatballs."

"Don't have any meat in the house, I'm afraid."

He looked over her shoulder to the pot of dark red sauce simmering on the stove. "What does it taste like? Cardboard?"

"No, they're pretty good." She removed a fork from the drawer to her left and stabbed one of the meatballs sitting in the thick sauce. She held the meatball up to him while Grant furrowed his brow with serious trepidation.

He arched away from the meatball. "I think I'd rather drink the whiskey."

"It's good for you … better than eating a dead cow."

"Dead cows are how I make my livelihood, Heather."

"Well, if you cook dinner for me one night, then you can serve dead cow. In my house, there is no animal flesh."

"Not even tuna?" he questioned, a little surprised.

"No." She blew on the meatball. "This is a cruelty-free house."

A lurid smile snaked its way across his wide mouth. "Okay, let me taste this pseudo-food of yours."

He took her hand holding the fork and brought it to his mouth. After he took a small bite of the meatball, he covered his mouth and his eyes came together in absolute disgust.

"Oh God, that's the worst thing I've ever eaten. What's in it, sawdust?"

He spit the meatball pieces into his hand. "You're not actually going to eat that, are you?"

Stewing with indignation, Heather's blue eyes bore into him. She wrenched the fork away and popped the half-eaten meatball into her mouth. "You have no couth, Grant Crowley," she garbled, while munching on the meatball. "You're never supposed to insult a woman's cooking."

Heather was about to drop the fork on the countertop when he caught her in his arms. "Perhaps I'm a little rough around the edges, but your meatball was terrible." He bit her earlobe. "Let me make amends."

She wiggled in his arms. "Too late."

His hand went to the crotch of her jeans. "It's never too late, baby."

He rubbed along the seam of her jeans, making Heather moan. It was as if he knew just how to touch her to make her body bend over with need. Her hands clutched the edge of the counter as his fingers pressed into her, causing her blood to boil with yearning.

"I think I have something else in mind for dinner." Unzipping her jeans, he slipped his hand inside her pants and stroked her folds. "God, you're so wet. You're making me crazy."

"Then do something about it," she begged, grinding her hips into his growing erection.

Grant spun her around, lifting her on to the countertop, and then he peeled the snug jeans from around her hips. Once he had maneuvered the thick fabric and her silky panties down her legs, he discarded them on the kitchen floor. Pulling her hips to him, he pushed her head back on the hard countertop.

"What are you doing?"

"Having dinner," he murmured against her thigh.

Heather closed her eyes as his lips traveled lower to the valley between her legs. When he opened her folds and licked her aching clit, she whimpered. First his tongue drew circles, then his teeth nipped at her, and when he started sucking mercilessly on her nub, she cried out and reached for the base of the cabinet above her head.

Her body was on fire. When that relentless kick of electricity shot up from her groin, her body bucked wildly against the countertop.

Limp, she felt as done as the wet spaghetti in her sink. When she opened her eyes, Grant was standing back from the counter, dropping his navy blue pants around his ankles. She did not even have time to speak before he grabbed her and flipped her on her stomach, letting her toes just touch the floor. She watched over her shoulder as he hurriedly slipped on a condom. With one hand, he spread her folds open and then dove into her.

"Christ, you're relentless," she said breathlessly as he pushed into the depths of her.

"I want you," he groaned in her ear. "I'm going to fuck you until you beg me to stop."

She gripped the edge of the counter, holding on as her body rocked back and forth with his every penetration. "I never beg, Grant."

He mercilessly stabbed into her, making her grunt. "We'll see about that."

Grant slammed into her flesh and Heather thrilled at the way he felt inside of her. This was what she had wanted from a man; to hell with being made love to in the quiet darkness of some cozy bedroom. She needed raw, rough, and passionate sex that made her feel alive.

When her body tingled all over and her muscles tightened, she closed her eyes and waited. Panting and writhing with pleasure, her orgasm let go in one unforgiving rush. She was clinging to the countertop, and swore she wasn't going to be able to walk for days. When his hands dug into her shoulders, Grant groaned loudly like a wild animal, thrust into her one last time, and then went still.

Sweat was dampening her brow as the edge of the countertop dug into her hipbones. She tried to shift from beneath his dead weight on her back when his hands held her hips, forcing her to stay as she was.

"I never said you could move," he whispered in her hair, sounding more cruel than gentle.

"This isn't comfortable."

"So…," he cooed behind her.

Heather was attempting to sit up from the countertop when his elbow went into her back, driving her into the hard granite. His fingers roughly shoved into her, causing her to struggle.

"When I say you can move, you will move. Until then, you will take everything from me."

He forcefully manipulated her folds. With his weight holding her down, she had no choice but to submit to him. His fingers were demanding and showed no regard for her. When he pinched her clit, she squealed with protest, which only made him pinch even harder. Instead of wanting to run from him, his harsh handling of her seemed to bind her to him. When she climaxed, the emotional intensity of her release matched the physical pleasure.

Raw and burning between her legs, she was covered with sweat when she roused from the fog of her orgasm.

He kissed her back. "You're getting sore, aren't you?"

"I'm okay," she insisted.

"So stubborn. I swear, you're the most difficult woman I've ever known," he reprimanded, pressing his hips into her. "If I fuck you hard again, it will hurt."

"I'm not going to beg you to stop." She held up her head … her muscles were cramping from being wedged against the countertop. Her hip bones were getting tender from being banged into the edge of the counter.

He let up on her back. "Wouldn't dream of it." Stepping away from her, he went to the open pantry door in the corner of her kitchen and searched the shelves.

She climbed down from the counter.

"Did I say move?" he voiced from the pantry.

"No," she admitted, admiring his long legs.

He pointed to the counter. "As you were."

She ignored his command. "What are you doing?"

He came back from the pantry holding a bottle of extra virgin olive oil in his hand. "Getting something to make you comfortable." He glimpsed the bottle, raising his blond brows. "Olive Girl olive oil?"

"Hey, don't knock it. It was on sale." She pointed to the bottle. "You're not supposed to use that with condoms. It can cause them to break."

He poured a few drops on his fingers. "I've done this before. It works fine." He kissed her forehead. "Back against the counter."

She showed him her butt and leaned forward on the counter. After putting the bottle of olive oil down next to her, he slid his fingers between her legs and massaged the oil around her folds. When his fingers moved inside of her, she reflexively flinched.

"See, you're sore." He removed his fingers and reached for the olive oil.

"You play rough."

He pressed his erection into her backside. "Want me to stop?"

She spread her legs wider apart, resting her head on the counter. "No, I want more."

His fingers went deep inside her. "Are you sure? I won't be gentle."

She rubbed her ass against his groin. "Again."

He did not hesitate and immediately thrust all the way inside of her. The oil helped, but she was sore as hell and winced as he pulled out and plunged into her again.

"Beg me to stop," he urged in her cheek.

She shoved her hips back into his. "Harder."

"You're incredible." He rammed into her with such force, he lifted her feet off the floor and Heather cried out with surprise and pleasure. The rougher he got, the more she liked it. The slight pain was nothing compared to the intense vibration that coursed through her with his every brutal penetration. Heather held on as his hips sent her slamming into the counter, sending her to climax almost instantly. She was so tender that the slightest nudge from his cock was creating shockwaves throughout her body. The deep guttural scream that erupted from her at the height of her orgasm sounded foreign.

With one last thrust, Grant grunted and then bit down on her back. They were resting against her counter when Heather thought she heard knocking.

"What was that?" She pulled up on her elbows.

He chuckled against her shoulder. "Nice try, but I told you—"

"Grant, let me up. It's coming from my front door."

He held her down, refusing to let her up from the countertop. "Pretend you're not home."

She pushed him away. "You ass, I can't. I've got an elderly neighbor who might need me and … oh, for Christ's sake, help me up and find your pants."

Grant stood back, lifting her from the counter just as the knocking turned into a loud banging. Scurrying across her living room, she stood before the short hallway that led to her front door. "Who is it?" she called out.

"Baby girl, it's me," a man's muffled voice came through the door.

"Just a second." Heather mouthed, "Shit!" into the air. She then scrambled to collect her jeans and panties from the kitchen floor.

Grant grabbed her arm, his eyes burning with jealousy. "Who in the hell is that?"

She shirked off his arm and gestured for him to finish dressing. "It's my brother, you idiot."

His wide mouth curled into a malicious grin. "Your brother ... now?"

She was tugging up the fly of her jeans while heading out of the kitchen. "Just hurry up and get dressed. The last thing I need is for Stewart to start asking a lot of questions. When he gets started interrogating the men in my life...." She left the words hanging, hoping he got the message.

Grant stepped into his pants, narrowing his eyes on her. "So what if he asks questions? You're a grown woman, Heather."

She quickly ran her fingers through her hair and straightened the blue top she had spent ten minutes deciding on before he arrived. "According to my brother, I'm still sixteen and a virgin."

He snickered under his breath. "This should be fun."

She rushed toward the front door, ignoring his comment. Fun wasn't the word that came to mind. For Heather, this was a disaster in the making.

"What took you so long?" The towering man with the deep blue eyes and long black lashes asked as he stood on her doorstep. "What are you up to?"

"Stew, what are you doing here?" She tried like hell to keep the panic from her voice and swore it wasn't working.

He held up the box in his arms. "Dad's stuff. I told you about it on the phone the other day."

"Yeah," she mumbled, rubbing her forehead. "I forgot about that." She waved him in the door. "Come in."

He smiled for her, and Heather was struck by the memory of her father. Stewart had his tall, sinewy body, long, wide nose, square jaw, full lips, and rounded chin, but his blue eyes, and wavy brown hair belonged to their mother, Marissa.

A demure French teacher who had given up her students to raise a family, all the kindness, patience, and love that Heather had inside of her she attributed to her mother. It was the short temper, stalwart stubbornness, and strong distrusting nature that had belonged to Carl Phillips.

When Stewart casually ambled into her entrance hall, Grant appeared in the living room. He had, thankfully, dressed, and despite appearing a bit rumpled, looked surprisingly appealing.

"Ah, so I did interrupt something?" Stewart muttered in his deep velvet voice.

Heather had always loved his voice. Growing up, she had teased him about his high girly voice until puberty had taken over, and his squeaky vocalizations turned charming and very pleasing to the ear.

"Ah, Stewart, this is a friend from riding." She motioned to Grant as he came toward them. "Grant—"

"Grant Crowley," Stewart jumped in. "Yes, I know." Stewart dumped the box on the stone floor and held out his hand to Grant. "Ben Eisenberg introduced us."

Heather closed her eyes and suppressed an urge to scream.

Grant took her brother's large hand, giving it a firm shake. "Good to see you again, Dr. Phillips."

"Stewart, please." Stewart released his hand and hoisted the cardboard box from the floor. "I can hardly have one of the hospital's major contributors calling me Dr. Phillips."

Heather's belly knotted up. "So, ah, Stew, are you coming from work?" She looked over his loose-fitting blue scrubs with Baylor University Hospital printed down the front right leg.

Stewart moved past Grant and into the living room. "I left the cath lab about an hour ago, so I could drop this off to you." He went to the sofa and dumped the box on the plush white cushion. When he turned back to the hallway, Heather and Grant were standing next to each other.

"So, are you two seeing each other?"

Heather wanted to curl in a ball and die. Stewart had always been a relentless teaser, and when she had started dating, his taunting had turned maddening.

Heather squared her shoulders. "Ah, actually, we—"

"We're seeing each other," Grant edged in. He put a possessive arm around Heather. "It just recently happened."

Stewart folded his arms over his thick chest and glowered at his sister. The uncanny resemblance to their father made Heather shift her weight nervously from one foot to the other.

"Isn't this the guy you told me was your arch rival?" he probed, cocking one dark brow at her.

"Was being the key word here," Grant hinted.

"I guess we found we have a lot in common," she explained.

Her brother didn't look convinced. "Uh huh."

"What's in the box?" she questioned, moving away from Grant.

"I have no idea. It's the last of Dad's things from my attic." Stewart raised his long nose in the air. "Are you cooking?" He stared at his sister in amazement. "You never cook."

"I cook," she indignantly replied. "I just never cook for you."

He gazed up at Grant. "Don't eat it. Whatever it is, don't touch it. Her cooking is better suited for bug repellent than consumption."

"Stew, shut up!" She charged toward her brother, eager to punch him in the arm.

At the sofa, she was about to pummel her fist into him when he grabbed her and held her to him. "Mom couldn't teach her any culinary skills and, trust me, she tried." Heather fought against his arms. "Baby girl didn't learn to boil water until she was fifteen."

Heather broke free and landed a hard punch on his right shoulder, but her hand bounced off him. "Jerk."

He smiled lovingly at her. "But she sure could ride a horse. Dad said she was the best rider he had ever seen."

Heather stood back from him, gawking. "When did Dad say that?"

Stewart shrugged. "Plenty of times."

"I never heard it."

His smile fell and his eyes sobered. "I heard it. You know how he was. We never heard the good stuff from him, only the bad." He lifted his eyes to Grant. "How's your father?"

Grant slowly walked into the living room. "Doing well."

Stewart knitted his dark brows together. "He missed his last two appointments with me. You know that, don't you?"

Heather glanced back at Grant. She spotted the hint of worry in his cool eyes.

"Yes, I, ah, know that. I've been urging him to go back, but you know how stubborn he can be."

Stewart nodded. "Yeah, I do, but it can't be ignored forever. Make sure he comes to see me as soon as possible." Stewart's blue eyes veered back to his sister. "I'd better go. I didn't mean to interrupt your date."

"It's not a date," she insisted.

He came up to her and kissed her brow. "Yes, it is." He stood back from her, furrowing his brow. "You smell like olive oil."

Heather turned three shades of red. "I was cooking with it."

He went around her. "Smells like you were bathing in it." He stopped and held out his hand. "Good to see you, Grant."

Grant shook his hand. "We'll talk again, Stewart."

"You have my number." Stewart stopped and looked at Grant anew. "You smell like olive oil, too. What were you guys cooking?"

Grant grinned, turning to Heather. "We were just experimenting in the kitchen."

Stewart tossed his head to the side. "Just don't let her cook those weird vegetarian dishes she's into. You'll be sick for a week."

"Not funny, Stewart," Heather exclaimed.

Stewart grinned like a happy little boy, glad he had gotten a rise out of his little sister. "When you two want to make a trip into the city, let me know. We can double date. I'm sure Lynda, my fiancée, would love to meet you, Grant."

Grant smirked at Heather. "I would like that, Stewart."

Feeling the eyes of both men on her, Heather wished she owned a gun. It was at times like this that she really needed one.

"I've got to run." Stewart turned for the front door. "I've got to get back to the hospital. Long night ahead." He waved good-bye over his shoulder. "Call me, baby girl," was the last thing he said before shutting the heavy front door with a loud thud.

Standing in her living room, Heather's eyes were all over Grant. "You know my brother?"

He nodded, coming toward her. "I told you my family contributes to Baylor Hospital. We've met a few times at several fundraisers."

"And your father? He's one of Stew's patients?"

His arm went around her waist. "Dad's been seeing your brother for a while. He has bouts of angina and high blood pressure, but making my father stick to a medicine regimen has proven to be difficult. He still thinks he's twenty and impervious to disease."

A light bulb went off in her head. "Is that why you let him dictate so much of your life? You don't want to upset him."

His other arm went around her. "A few years back we had a terrible fight over my future, and he collapsed on the floor with chest pain. He spent three days in the hospital and when he got out, I swore I wouldn't piss him off anymore. I'd rather do as he wishes than be the cause of something terrible happening to him."

"You can't go on like that forever, Grant. You have your own life."

He shrugged and let her go, directing his attention to the box. "You above all people should understand why I am the way I am with him." He motioned to the box. "Weren't you the same way with your old man?"

"Sure, when I was younger."

He went to the sofa. "If your father were still here, you would be no different than me. We try to protect those we love as best we can, but circumstances change ... people change. We know we should let go, but old habits die hard."

"Sometimes not letting go can be a bad thing, Grant." Heather stared at the box. "I've got an attic full of memories that I should get rid of, but can't. I feel like if I throw out one box, toss away one trinket, I'm betraying my past. Lately I've been feeling like I need a hoarding intervention."

He sat down next to the box. "May I?"

Nodding, she had a seat on the sofa. "Go ahead. It's just what's left of my father's things from our old house. All the stuff Stewart and I boxed up before we sold the place."

He lifted the flaps of the cardboard box and peeked inside. The first thing that caught the light was a silver picture frame.

The picture was slightly faded, but still sharp with emotion for Heather. She was young—maybe fourteen—frowning and sitting her old horse, Heathcliff, while holding a blue ribbon in her hand. Dressed in her show regalia, her father stood by the stout jumper, beaming with pride.

"When was this?" Grant prodded.

"One of the hundreds of horse shows I attended when I was young. My father went to every show. He liked to school me over the fences before I went into the ring."

"Did he ever ride?"

She shook her head, feeling that old burn of bitterness in her stomach. "He knew a little about riding, but what he was good at was yelling. He always yelled at me at horse shows. 'Do better, Heather. Don't slouch. Keep your heels down, push your horse....'" She let go a long sigh. "When I was about fifteen the yelling got worse, and he became obsessed with my winning blue ribbons."

Grant put the picture back in the box. "Any idea why?"

"I think it was about the time he first started getting into trouble at the hospital. He always drank. I grew up with him drinking, but he never drank before going to take care of his patients. It was just two or three glasses of scotch when he came home at night."

"What do you think changed?"

She sank back on the sofa. "I don't know. One day he came home and announced that he was under investigation with the state medical board and was no longer allowed to perform surgery at the hospital. A month later, Stewart and I learned about the patients who had died under his care. A few nurses who worked with him reported that he had been drunk when he performed those operations. I never did believe it. He always loved being a doctor." She clasped her hands tightly together. "Two years of hearings and trials about bankrupted my parents. I had finished nursing school and was working at a hospital in Dallas. Stewart was still in medical school. I think all the publicity was harder on Stew. I mean, he could never get away from it." She shrugged. "At least I had my riding."

"Your mother? What happened to her?"

Heather flopped her head back against the plush fabric. "She was always a rock of strength for all of us. After Dad was convicted, Stew and I pulled away. I moved to Lewisville, got on at the medical center, and took a job teaching at Wescott Stables on the weekends. The day after he was taken to prison, I called Mom to see how she was holding up. She sounded fine. A week later Stew called me with the news." She closed her eyes against the pain. "I don't know where she got the pills. Maybe from Dad, maybe she had collected them during the trial ... who knows? By the time Stewart found her, she had been dead for three days. She had enough narcotics in her system to kill three people and then some. I think she knew she was going to kill herself from the day Dad was indicted."

He put the box on a glass coffee table in front of the sofa and scooted closer to her. Wrapping her in his arms, he held her close. "That must have been hell for you."

She snuggled against his chest. "It was a long time ago."

"The passage of time doesn't reduce the pain of memories, Heather. Only happy memories can lessen the sting of the past. Maybe it's time you make some of those happy memories."

She held her head up from his chest. "How do you suggest I do that?"

He kissed her on the forehead. "Why don't we go to Dallas next weekend? Have dinner at some fancy restaurant in town. Let me wine you and dine you. We can spend the night at my house in Highland Park. It might be a nice break for both of us."

She peered into his soulful eyes. "Is this going to be a date?"

He kissed her lips. "Absolutely. I think it's time we take this relationship to the next level, don't you?"

Relationship? There was that dreaded word. She hesitated, not sure of how to respond, and then just nodded. Perhaps it was time to give this relationship thing a try.

"Good, that's settled." He patted her thigh. "How about we eat the dinner you prepared, and then we can crack open that bottle of whiskey, get drunk, and fool around?"

She offered him a genuine smile. "I like the sound of that."

He stood from the sofa and held out his hand. "Come with me. Let's brave those meatballs together."

Heather giggled while taking his hand. "They're not that bad."

He tugged her to her feet. "I'll be the judge of that."

While Grant escorted her to the kitchen with one arm around her waist, Heather felt a strange sense of rejuvenation. It was as if Grant had pushed aside all of her apprehensions with a wave of his supple hand. She knew he wasn't a magician, but for the first time since she had seen him on his massive black horse, she was beginning to believe that he did have a special kind of magic; one that was working its way beneath her skin and chipping away at the thick walls around her heart.

Chapter 17

Saturday afternoon—following a long morning session over fences with Murphy—Heather was packing an overnight bag for her date with Grant. She was rushing about her bedroom, debating on whether or not to pack the black negligée she had purchased a few years back, hoping for such a weekend getaway. Figuring she had nothing to lose, Heather stuffed the lacy number into her black bag, along with the expensive perfume Stewart had given her one Christmas. While she shoved the toiletries from the bathroom and a pair of jeans and T-shirt into the bag, she thought ahead to their evening.

Heather had been nervous all day. Well, not nervous ... more excited than nervous, but also a little apprehensive. What was she doing? Was this getting serious, or was she hoping it was getting serious? And if she did hope it was getting serious, did that mean she was developing feelings for the man? This was new territory for her. Usually she was walking away from relationships, but she eagerly wanted to embrace this one.

Heather had never allowed herself the luxury of wanting a man ... maybe because most men had bored her, or at least fallen short of her expectations. However, Grant was different. He had not been polite or played by a certain code of conduct. He had taken what he wanted and in the process given her what she had always craved. That terrified her. When you finally discover what it is you've been searching for, then what? How long would it take before they both grew bored? Like radioactive waste, relationships had a very short half-life as far as Heather was concerned. What started out as a big bang with time always ended up as a lifeless pile of ash.

"Christ, listen to me," she muttered, exiting her bedroom. "Just enjoy it, and if ... when it's over, move on."

In the living room, she set the overnight bag next to her black leather purse on her sofa. She quickly ran through her mental checklist of things she needed to do before leaving. Satisfied that she had locked the back door, unplugged the coffee maker, and taken out the trash, she checked the clock on her microwave.

The sound of her unnerving door chime almost made her jump out of her skin. "I have got to get that thing changed," she voiced, stumbling toward her front door on her high black heels.

He was standing on her short porch, wearing a casual pair of black slacks, a white shirt, and a gray tie. His hair appeared neatly combed and the woodsy fragrance of his cologne wafted through her open door.

"You look nice," she commented, liking the way his trousers clung to his lean legs.

His eyes swept up and down the black cocktail dress she had pulled from the back of her closet. Fitted about the bust and waist and with slender straps at the shoulder and a flared skirt, she knew it flattered her curves.

"I approve," he purred, letting his eyes linger on the line of cleavage peeking out over the black satin bodice.

She moved away from the door. "I thought you weren't a boob man."

"I'm a man," he admitted, rushing in the door. "Boobs, butt, legs, it all turns me on. But with you in that dress…." He shut her front door. "I'm definitely a boob man."

She walked down the short hall, her black heels clicking on the stone floor as she went.

"Then again," he went on, following behind her. "I could be an ass man, too."

She picked up her overnight bag, and Grant came jogging up to her. "Allow me." He took the bag and swung it over his shoulder. "You all set?"

She picked up her purse. "Yes," she answered in an unsteady voice.

"What's wrong?"

She pensively peered up at him. "Are you sure we should do this? Maybe we shouldn't date."

"It's just dinner. Nothing contractually binding." He leaned in closer to her. "Want to cancel? We can stay here and explore the various uses of olive oil."

She shook her head. "Hell no. I packed something special in there for tonight."

He raised his eyebrows. "Want to show me?"

"I'm hungry. Dinner first and then the show." She flipped off the lights in the living room.

"How about a dinner show? We could have pizza delivered to my house while you show me what you've got in here." He patted her black overnight bag.

She motioned to her dress. "I put on this thing expecting to be wined and dined on fancy food."

He stood in front of her. "I can get pineapple put on the pizza. Is that fancy enough for you?"

She studied his angular features, trying to make up her mind. "Are you being funny?"

He grinned at her, accentuating a glint of mischief in his eyes. "How am I doing?"

"I've never seen this side of you before. I've always thought of you as very serious."

He started for her front door. "I think it's time you got to know the real me."

"I thought I already knew the real you," she asserted, behind him.

Grant opened the door and flourished his hand through the threshold to her porch. "I still have a few secrets up my sleeve."

She stopped just short of stepping outside and frowned into his face. "Like what? An ex-wife in Cleveland?"

He slid his hand behind her back and urged her outside. "Now who's being funny?"

* * *

The drive to Dallas took about an hour in the Saturday evening traffic. Humming along the freeway in his black Mercedes S550 Sedan, Grant updated her on Maximillian's health—his cold was not improving—and Gigi's latest antics back at Crowley Ranch.

"She's insisting my father allow her to oversee the books. She claims his current manager is clueless about proper feed and supplies for the livestock. My father then told her he couldn't think of a woman telling his ranch hands how to care for his cattle. He claims the men would feel threatened."

"What did Gigi say?"

Grant slowed the car as he went down an exit ramp. "You know Gigi ... she had a tantrum. Proceeded to call my father every name in the book, and I was left spending the next hour trying to keep both of them from killing each other."

"Were you always the peacemaker growing up?"

He nodded, pulling the car up to a red light. "Always. They won't admit it, but they're exactly the same."

"You must take after your mother."

His face changed in the light from the street lamps along Walnut Hill Lane, and Heather could not tell if he was angered or saddened by the comment.

"I have no idea what Maureen is like." His deep voice sounded touched with a bit of sadness. "Last time I spoke to her was the day she left. After she married Gus Stevens, she had another son, Paul. She didn't need to see me anymore ... she had found my replacement."

The light changed and Heather tilted across the fancy leather divider to him. "You don't really believe that, do you?"

His hands gripped the wood-trimmed steering wheel while the car moved ahead. "I was eleven when she left. Thirteen when she had her other son. I got over it a long time ago."

"But you never saw her again. Weren't you the least bit curious to see what she was like?"

"No," he grumbled.

The tone of his voice made Heather decide to drop the subject. No point in starting their evening on a sour note.

The car slowed in front of a wide one-story building made of stone with large arched windows along the façade. There was an exotic garden with wide ponds that meandered along a cobbled walkway. At the end of the walkway were massive arched wooden doors with brass slats cutting across the center.

"It's called Ya Amar," Grant said over her shoulder as she peered through her car window at the romantic entrance. "It's supposed to be one of the best vegetarian restaurants in town."

She swung around in her seat. "You picked a vegetarian restaurant?"

He turned the car into the parking lot in front of the restaurant. "Where else was I going to take you for dinner? A steak place?"

The interior of the restaurant was rustic, with unfinished beams crisscrossing the white plaster ceiling. Heavy dark wood tables with red leather chairs were set with colorful plates in different shades of red, gold, and yellow. Above, chandeliers made of tapered lights set in round brass plates cast a yellow glow on the diners. Along a wall made of stone was a long bar made of polished brass and inlaid with panels of dark walnut. At a podium, just inside the massive doors, a pretty woman in a long black dress with black eyes, and short black hair greeted them with a smile.

"Welcome to Ya Amar. Do you have a reservation?"

"Two for Crowley," Grant told her while adjusting the sleeves on his black suit jacket.

The round-eyed woman checked the name on the iPad on the podium in front of her.

"Of course, Mr. Crowley. This way, please." She beckoned for Grant and Heather to follow.

Heather smelled the exotic spices lingering in the air, and heard the strains of strange music coming from the speakers in the ceiling above.

"What kind of restaurant is this?" she asked as they weaved between tables to the back part of the long dining room.

"It's Egyptian."

Seated at a table set for two with a single candle set in a yellow sconce in the center, Grant unbuttoned the front of his jacket as he helped Heather to her seat. After he took his chair, their hostess handed them black menus and smiled as she backed away.

"Have you ever eaten Egyptian food?" Heather inquired, opening her menu.

"I was hoping you would be able to help me with that," Grant professed as he gleaned the menu.

"You're sure you're ready for this?"

He put his menu down on the table. "I'm in your capable hands. I'll leave the ordering to you."

A young, tanned waiter all in black with a red sash around his waist and a white turban on his head glided up to their table. He bowed slightly and made a sweeping gesture across the table with his right hand. "Good evenin'," he said in a Texas drawl. "I'm Matt. I'll be waitin' on your table tonight."

After Heather ordered Tahini salad, stuffed grape leaves appetizer—the vegetarian version and a beef version—and fried calamari for Grant, Matt recommended the eggplant moussaka for Heather. Covered with a red sauce made from tomato paste and Egyptian spices, he claimed that it was one of the best dishes in the house.

"If you don't love it, dessert's on me," Matt promised as he jotted down their order. "And whatchya gonna be havin' to drink tonight? We got a great selection of wine."

"Do you have any sparkling wine?" Grant asked, motioning to Heather. "She's partial to sparkling wine."

"We sure do." Matt stuck his pen under his turban and scratched his head. "I'll get y'all a bottle of our Aida wine to start, and then get them salads right out to ya."

After Matt was gone, Heather rested her elbows on the table and gazed over at Grant. "How did you know I liked sparkling wine?"

He removed the red napkin folded into a flower from his plate. "I saw the two bottles you had in the bottom of your pantry." He shook out the napkin and then slid it onto his lap.

"What sharp little eyes you've got."

"I always pay attention to what a woman drinks." He lifted his chunky goblet of water. "It can tell you a lot about a woman."

Intrigued, Heather sat back in her chair. "Such as?"

He took a sip of water and set the goblet on the table. "Well, for instance, you like sparkling wine, which means you're not serious about drinking, drink for taste and not effect, and are probably distrusting of people who do drink hard liquor."

She nodded slightly, impressed with his assessment. "What if I had stored bourbon in my pantry?"

He ran his hand along the edge of his brightly colored plate. "That's easy. You would have been loud, obnoxious, and drank to get more attention than you already cultivated. You would have been more focused on your needs, as opposed to those of the people around you."

"Wow. I'm glad I don't drink bourbon then."

He smiled apologetically. "Sorry, but Vanessa drank bourbon, a lot of it. It was one of those irritating idiosyncrasies of hers that drove me to whiskey."

"I guess her love of bourbon explains why she posted your break up all over the Internet. Must have been her need for attention."

"Vanessa was an attention whore. Ever since she almost won Miss Dallas, she has been yearning to get back into the spotlight. Everywhere we went, she needed to be catered to and made to feel important. It got to be very exhausting feeding her ego all the time."

"Yes, but you stayed with her for—"

"I stayed with her until that first night with you." He angled closer to her. "Now will you tell me why you left that morning?"

Heather removed the napkin folded to resemble a rose from her plate and stuffed it into her lap. "You know why I left."

"I may know, but I still need to hear it from you."

Feeling that there was no way out of discussing it, she rolled her eyes. "I was scared, all right? Scared of how we were together, scared of it...." She patted her hand on the table. "Scared of it turning into this."

"And now that it has, how do you feel?"

"I'm still scared, but for a whole different set of reasons."

"That's good." He sat back in his chair, seemingly pleased. "Being scared means you're afraid of losing something. It's when you're not afraid that you have nothing to lose."

Heather wanted to question his reasoning, but Matt returned to their table carrying a bottle of wine in his hands.

"Y'all are gonna love this wine," Matt announced. "You've never tasted nothin' like it."

* * *

Matt was right. They had never tasted anything quite like the wine. As they sat, the barely touched salad and appetizer dishes scattered about the table, Grant examined the light golden wine with the very fine bubbles through his heavy crystal glass.

"Was it me or did this stuff taste like I just chewed on a plastic toy?"

Heather covered her mouth, almost spitting out the gulp of water she had just taken to offset the astringent taste of the wine. "More like licking the floor of a department store."

He plunked his wineglass on the table. "Now there's a bit of imagery I could have done without." Picking up his fork he stabbed at the grape leaves stuffed with ground meat before him. "What was this again?"

Heather picked at her grape leaves stuffed with vegetables. "I'm not sure. I've had stuffed grape leaves before," she pointed her fork at her plate, "but I've never had anything like this."

Grant sat back, spying the other diners. "I'm beginning to think that pineapple pizza may have been a better dinner selection."

"We still have the main course to go. Maybe it will get better."

Grant arched one blond brow at her. "How close is the nearest emergency room?"

Heather giggled, unable to hide her amusement. "I have to admit that pineapple pizza is sounding awfully good about now."

Grant tossed his red napkin on the table. "That's it." He stood from his chair.

Heather became alarmed. "What are you doing?"

Grant adjusted his coat jacket and his eyes circled the wide dining room. "I'm going to find Matt and get the bill. We can pick up a pizza on the way back to my place."

"Grant, no." She clasped his forearm when he came by her chair. "It's all right, really. I don't want to spoil the nice dinner you had planned."

He kissed her forehead. "The dinner is irrelevant. Anyway, I still have the entire night to make it up to you."

As he walked away from the table, Heather snuck a peek at his firm ass beneath the fabric of his suit. "Yeah, I can think of a few things you can do to make it up to me, Mr. Crowley." Curtailing her sudden giddiness, Heather stopped for a moment, surprised at her behavior. When was the last time she felt like this with a man?

"Never," she softly confessed.

Gathering up her purse, a flash of red appeared out of the corner of her eye. Looking up, Heather almost fell out of her chair. Draped in a tight-fitting red silk dress with a gathered waist and thigh high skirt, she saw Vanessa standing next to her table. Beside her was a swarthy plump man with a black beard, coal-black eyes, and a pronounced double chin.

"I thought that was you," Vanessa squawked, scorching Heather's ears. "I told Khalil that it was you." Vanessa's overly made-up face looked more clown-like than belonging to a former beauty queen. Her thick lips were painted a hard shade of red, her black lashes were caked with too much mascara, and her creamy cheeks were glowing beneath an unattractive orange blush.

"Vanessa, what are you doing here?" Heather anxiously scanned the dining room for Grant. This was all the two of them needed.

"I'm with Khalil." She tugged on the arm of the stout man next to her, towering over him in her spiky red-leather high heels. "Khalil and the owners of this place are great friends. I just adore the food." She patted her hand over her ample bosom while the gentleman next to her sighed with apparent boredom. "So are you here on a date?" Vanessa's eyes lingered on the unoccupied chair across from Heather. "Anyone I know?"

"I've taken care of everything. We can go now," Grant declared, coming up to the table. His eyes fell on Vanessa just as he came alongside Heather.

The tension around the table was palpable. Heather eagerly searched for something to say, but words eluded her as Vanessa's blue eyes narrowed to two furious slits.

"Well, Vanessa." Grant's voice was rife with contempt, taking Heather by surprise. She had forgotten how he used to speak to his former girlfriend. "What are you doing in Dallas?" he probed, eyeing her date.

Vanessa stuck out her chest and put on her best beauty queen smile. "I'm here with Khalil Ahmed. He owns an oil company in the panhandle."

Grant dipped his head politely to the man. "Mr. Ahmed."

"Khalil, this is Grant Crowley." Vanessa motioned to Grant with a diamond clad hand. "He's my ex. The one I told you about."

Khalil said nothing, but turned his eyes toward the bar of the restaurant. Then he called out something unintelligible and waved to a man behind the bar. "Excuse me, I must go and say hello," Khalil told the group in a heavy Middle Eastern accent.

Grant waited as the man waddled away. "Your newest conquest?"

"He's worth more than you," Vanessa shot back.

Grant cupped his hands behind him, grinning at her comment. "How do you know what I'm worth, Vanessa? I don't recall discussing my financial matters with you. Every conversation we ever had always ended up being about you."

Vanessa tugged at the rhinestone inlaid strap on her shiny gold handbag. With an indifferent toss of her head, she sneered at Grant. "That's rich coming from a man who wouldn't know how to please a woman in bed if he tried."

Heather held her breath, not sure if she wanted to burst out in laughter or gasp in shock that Vanessa would be stupid enough to challenge Grant.

Grant showed not the slightest bit of concern as he took Heather's elbow. "I think there is a pizza with our name on it."

Giving Vanessa a fake smile, he nodded politely to her. "I hope you and Khalil are very happy together."

Guiding her through the restaurant entrance, Grant kept the placid smile on his lips, but Heather could have sworn there was real fury burning in his eyes. The only hint she had to his emotions was his firm grip on her elbow, making her believe he was angrier with the encounter than he let on.

Her suspicions were quickly dispelled when they reached his car and he let loose a resounding belly laugh. Seeing Grant Crowley take part in such an overwhelmingly human and endearing gesture surprised Heather. Here was a man she had seen at his cruelest in the show ring, at his most demanding in the bedroom, but tonight he had finally shown her the most intimate part of himself, his genuine laughter.

"Where have you been hiding that?" she asked, enjoying the way his eyes glistened in the streetlights.

"Hiding what?" He wiped his right eye as he opened her car door.

"I never thought you could laugh like that."

"It's been a long time since I felt like laughing." He leaned against the roof of his black car. "The past few months with Vanessa were especially trying for me."

"I thought you would have loved being with a woman like that. All beauty and no substance. Isn't she what most men want?"

He shrugged, contemplating her question. "Beauty only goes so far with a man. Vanessa was very predictable and pretty boring to be around. Conversations tended to be one-sided, we fought a lot, and the rest of our time together wasn't ... memorable."

"I find it hard to believe she didn't please you in bed," she blurted out, feeling a twinge of jealousy.

His eyebrows went up. "She was very ... vanilla."

Heather tilted her head inquisitively to the side. "Which means what exactly?"

"She wasn't adventurous." He waved inside the open car. "And she was nothing like you."

Heather climbed into the car and waited as he shut her door. Watching as his long legs carried him around to his driver's side door, she pondered what he had meant by adventurous. All of her life she had thought her desire for rough sex to be a deviant flaw in her character, but Grant was changing that viewpoint. She found it odd how it took the wrong kind of man to make her feel the right kind of way about herself. For years, she had struggled through relationships, hiding her true nature. Now she had met a man who embraced her eccentricities and made her feel almost normal … and sometimes even special.

Inside the car, he fastened his seatbelt and then retrieved his cell phone from his jacket pocket. "There's a pizza place not far from my house. We can pick up dinner and take it home." He scrolled through the numbers on his phone. "Anything special you want on your pizza?"

She smiled at him. "Why don't you surprise me? I'm suddenly feeling adventurous."

He hit a button on his phone. "Now that's what I like to hear."

Chapter 18

Nestled in the quiet wooded area of Highland Park, not far from Southern Methodist University, the home Grant parked in front of was nothing like Heather had expected. Mediterranean in design with a wall of white stucco topped orange brick on either side of an all-glass entrance, the split two-story home sat beneath sprawling oak trees with a dense garden of green shrubbery along the front. The walkway was done in a light orange stone, and when Grant hit a button on his car remote, outdoor lights bathed the house in a warm orange glow.

Heather stood from the car, carrying her overnight bag. "How long have you lived here?"

"I went to UT in Arlington for my undergraduate degree and bought this place during my senior year. I got sick of living in apartments and knew I was going to go on to grad school, so I decided to make an investment." He juggled the pizza box in his hands as he went to a stylish black iron gate with intricate swirls in the center.

They entered a small, asymmetrical courtyard with etched cement made to resemble stone, and round terra cotta planters placed on either side of a smoky glass doorway. Built out of thick beams of wood, the entrance was covered with a slanted portico of red terra cotta tiles that stretched over the patio.

"I had the entire place renovated about three years ago by a good friend from college, Hayden Parr." He handed Heather the pizza box and went to a panel on the side of the arched glass door. "He's a well-known architect in town. He made the whole house keyless for me." He punched in a code and the front door popped open. "Makes things so much easier."

Inside, Heather was greeted by clay patina on the walls and rich, dark wood floors. The ceiling was done in the same clay color with recessed soft lights and a central rustic two-tiered chandelier made of polished iron rings. Along the wall, a straight thick staircase done in the same dark wood as the floor rose to the second story.

He took the pizza box from her and brought it to a round stone and iron table in the center of the foyer. He removed the black overnight bag and purse from around her shoulders and set them on the table while Heather peered up the stairs.

"How many bedrooms do you have?"

"Five. With three and a half baths. There's a gourmet kitchen, three limestone fireplaces, including one in the master suite, a pool, sauna, and the den can be converted into a screening room."

She went to the stairs and fingered the thick, cool wood on the bannister. "Quite a house."

He came up to her. "It's my sanctuary from Crowley Ranch. I come here to get some peace from Gigi and my father." He took her hand. "Let me show you the best room."

Her stomach rumbled as the aroma of pepperoni and melted cheese wafted by her nose. "What about our dinner show?" she questioned, recalling her surprise in her overnight bag.

He squeezed her hand. "I have something else in mind."

There was no hesitation, no second-guessing from Heather's always working mind as they climbed the steps to the second floor. On the landing, he led her to the right along a balcony that overlooked a wide room below. The wall across from her was done in the same smoky glass windows she had seen at the entrance, but this wall was covered with glass from floor to ceiling. Beyond the windows, a rectangular pool, lit by blue lights beneath the water, beckoned.

When he reached a pair of dark double doors, he pushed them open. It wasn't as grand as she expected. With a wall of windows to the right that overlooked the pool, the room glowed with the ethereal blue light from below. Set in the corner was a limestone hearth without a mantle or any decoration. The bed was king-sized with a leather headboard and fluffy white comforter. Dark wood floors contrasted against the clay-covered walls, with a single brass ceiling fan in the center of the room. The furniture was minimal: a dark chest of drawers and thick dresser hugged one wall, with only a simple glass table next to the bed. In one corner was an open entrance to the master bath.

"I expected more." She turned to him.

"I'm not like my father. I don't like grand designs."

He eased his jacket from around his shoulders and took it to a bench at the foot of the bed. Mesmerized by his movements, Heather was fascinated with the way he slowly slid the tie from his neck and then wrapped it around his hands.

"Do you trust me?" he asked, his voice barely above a whisper.

Desire like molten lava swirled in her belly. "Yes."

"Then turn around."

Heather faced the bed and felt him come up behind her. He lowered the tie over her eyes and secured it behind her head. She could see nothing, and raised her hands to touch the blindfold when he held them.

"You are to submit to me tonight, do whatever I desire, and feel whatever I want you to feel." His voice was inches away from her ear. His breath was teasing her cheek. "You will take everything from me, and you are never to utter one single sound."

"What if—?"

His hand covered her mouth. "Not a word. You must endure in complete silence. If you do not, there will be consequences." He paused and heat swarmed between her legs. "Do you understand? Nod for yes."

She nodded her head, the excitement building in her muscles. His hands were on her back, lowering the zipper on her cocktail dress. She could hear the crush of the fabric on the bench in front of her after he helped her out of the clothing. He asked her to kick off her shoes, and when his hands caressed her shoulders, inching along her back to her bra, she held her breath. Once the bra was free, she anxiously waited for his touch on her flesh, but there was nothing.

She turned her head to the right and the left, listening for the slightest sound from him. Her senses were heightened, she was breathing faster, and her heartbeat was like a distant drum pounding in her ears.

Cool fingertips raked down her back to the waistband of her panties. She had worn her fancy black lace ones, hoping they would end up being removed by him
at some point in the evening. Inching the panties down her thighs, he helped her step out of them. Naked before him, she shivered at the chill in the room.

"Are you cold?" His voice was deep and seductive.

Remembering not to speak, she simply nodded.

"You'll warm up soon enough."

Footsteps could be heard walking away. His black leather shoes cut across the hardwood floor and then sounded as if they had entered another room to the left. The bathroom? She remembered the master bathroom was to the left. Waiting, she ran through a possible list of possible items he could be gathering in the bathroom, but all she could think of was condoms.

It did not take long for his heavy footfalls to return to her side.

"I have something special for you." She heard the sound of something being turned on, like an electrical device that whirred. "Something I have wanted to try on you since the moment I first saw you in the ring."

The shock of the cool device against her behind made her jump, and then his hand went to her shoulder to steady her. The object vibrated against her skin and he pressed it into her right butt cheek. She knew then what it was.

"There is a bench before you. Lean over and place your hands on it. Palms down, and spread your legs for me."

Heather's mind reasoned she should be concerned about what he was going to do, but another part of her was thrilled by the prospect of being at his mercy. She was at a loss for why such a game appealed to her, but it did.

Placing her hands palm down on the cool leather bench, she shifted her legs wider apart. The vulnerable position only added to her excitement.

"No matter what you feel you cannot utter a sound. Cannot move from that position. Otherwise, I will be forced to discipline you for disobeying me."

The vibration continued along her butt as he pressed the device between her thighs. When the vibration rubbed against her folds, she realized what torture he had planned for her. Her knees almost gave way and she opened her mouth to scream when he pressed the vibrator against her clit. The shock to her body was instantaneous. She wanted to cry out from the overload of stimulation.

"Oh God!" Then, she contemplated what she had done.

The vibrator was yanked away and went quiet. A slap came down on her right butt cheek.

"I said you must endure in silence."

For several seconds there was no noise. The vibrator started up again, and when it touched her folds, she prepared for the avalanche to come. He pressed it hard into her clit, but she did not flinch or gasp. Closing her eyes, Heather opened her mouth to release a silent scream.

The intense waves shooting up and down her body were incredible. Heather thought she would never be able to endure his game.

"You must take it. I know it is too much. Many women cannot stand so much stimulation." He pressed his body into her back. "But you can. I know it."

Her nails dug into the leather of the bench as the muscles in her thighs quivered uncontrollably. She was fighting to stay upright, forcing herself to give into the tidal wave of sensations barreling through her. Biting her lip, she pressed her eyes closed to keep from crying out. And then, a surge of tension made her tuck her head into her chest. A rising flow of heat rushed to her face, making her break out in a film of sweat.

"You're doing it; good girl. I promise this will be like nothing you've ever experienced."

When her insides started twitching, she knew what he said was true. A bolt of fire tore through her gut, and she tossed her head back, wincing. Her loins were convulsing with such ferocity she could barely stay on her feet. When the climax reached its height, everything about her went away. When the world came back into focus, Heather realized he had removed the vibrator and was rubbing his hands along her back.

"Very good. You did better than I expected."

Panting hard, she reached up to remove the tie from her sweaty face. Heather careened her head around to glare at him and was greeted by his infuriating grin. Slowly, he unzipped his pants and shoved them over his hips.

His cock popped up as he dropped his briefs to his ankles with his pants. She eyed his smooth, hard member and ached to take it in her mouth. She wanted to torture him just like he had tortured her.

Reaching for his swollen cock, her hands teased him, her fingers stroking up and down his shaft. His eyes followed her movements as she began to stimulate him. Before he could stop her, she knelt before him and lowered her lips over his tip.

The groan of pleasure he gave was far more satisfying to her than the best orgasm … well, almost. Lowering her mouth over him, she gently eased him into her until she could feel his tip hit the back of her throat. Moving him in and out, she used her tongue to tantalize him.

"Christ, you never cease to amaze me," he muttered.

Never being one to shy away from blow jobs, Heather had spent years perfecting her technique, and she was determined to show Grant that she could be in charge, too. He started pumping his hips in time with her. Wanting to heighten his pleasure, her fingers began to gently caress his scrotum. Grant moaned as her fingers deftly worked his balls. She could feel him getting more excited, sense his mounting tension, and just before she felt he was ready to come, he pulled his cock from her mouth.

"Tonight, I'm only coming inside of you, baby."

Grant gripped her shoulders and spun her around to the bench. Before she could stop him, he shoved her hips in front of his, forcing her hands back on the bench.   He spread her folds apart and entered her deep from behind. Heather was so sensitive from the vibrator that his slightest push almost had her collapsing on the bench.

"I'll go slow," he stated, kissing her back. "Slow and deep, so you can enjoy it."

With his every penetration, her body hummed. It did not take long for him to make her come again. He pushed all the way into her and she grunted as the rush of electricity took her. It was not as intense as the first, but still overwhelming and she longed to cry out, but remembered his warning. Her nails clawed the leather when the waves hit her. She rocked against the bench as he continued to push her forward with his thrusting.

By the time her third orgasm came over her she was covered in sweat, and aching all over. Grant held her close and quickly pounded into her, grunting into the air, and she knew he was close. With a last groan, he came inside of her. Resting against her back, he took a few seconds before he patted her behind.

"Get on the bed," he breathlessly directed.

Climbing over the bench, Heather was grateful to collapse on the plush white comforter. Standing beside the bed, he quickly kicked away his pants and wrestled his shirt from his shoulders. Naked, he came alongside her, wrapping her in his arms.

"I didn't use anything this time. Did you know that?"

For a moment, Heather was shocked. She was a nurse and fully aware of the diseases out there—not to mention the chance of pregnancy.

"What are you thinking?" he whispered.

"What I should ask you first. When was your last AIDS test, or how do you feel about becoming a father?"

He laughed into her hair. It was a warm kind of rumble that touched her heart. "Baby, you're the first woman I haven't used a condom on since I was twenty." He paused and his arms tightened around her. "As for the other ... would it be so bad?"

She smiled at his attempt to appease her. "Don't worry. We're safe ... this time. Just don't do it again." She turned to him, rubbing her hand along his muscular chest. "Where did you learn to do that? Torture a woman like that?"

"I hung out with a group of guys in college who were into such games. They taught me some things about pleasure and pain."

"Have you always been this way with women?"

"Yes, but what I do depends on the woman. You have to get to know a woman. Study her; see how she reacts to the world. I watched you in the show ring for a very long time. The way you strived to beat me, and how you were always so focused. I got the feeling you would like my games … like being controlled by a man."

She sighed against him, luxuriating in the warmth of his skin. "I always wanted something more, but I never met a man … no one has ever done to me the things that you've done."

"There's nothing to be ashamed of, Heather. It's natural … it's normal."

"Normal?" She chuckled and rolled over on her back. "I don't know what normal is. I've lived so far outside of normal for so long. Ever since the trial, I've been afraid of people, afraid of what they would think of me, so I withdrew. I pulled away and have been very self-conscious about my every action, every word I utter. Terrified of what people might think of me." A heavy sigh escaped her lips. "You should be concerned about that, too. Vanessa knows about us. When she tells everyone, it could cause problems for you."

He sat up. "What problems?"

She avoided his eyes by locking her gaze on her hands. "People will think you're crazy for being with me."

Grant reached for her. "Heather, I don't give a damn what people think."

"You say that now, but you've never been in the spotlight like me. You've never had every aspect of your life dissected and ridiculed by strangers. There will be guilt by association for being with me. Are you ready to face that?"

His hand ran up and down her hip. "You're exaggerating."

"No, I'm not. Being with me could be bad for you … bad for your business."

"Is that why you push people away, because you think you'll be bad for them? Because of what your father did?" He lifted her face to his. "What your father did has nothing to do with you."

She sat up, pushing his hand away. "The family of a serial killer is just as tainted as the killer. Everyone thinks I have something in me like my father."

"Heather, no one blames you for your father's missteps."

"They may not say they blame me, but they're thinking it. The crimes of the parents are often passed down to the children, Grant. I just want you to remember that. I may not be good for you."

"All right." He pulled her into his arms. "Enough of this kind of talk. You are good for me. You're better for me than any other woman I've ever known, because you're just like me: hard, competitive, and driven."

He kissed her lips, and as his kiss grew more ardent, Heather's stomach rumbled.

Grant chuckled against her lips. "I think I should go and get that pizza."

She patted her stomach. "Definitely. I'm starving."

He climbed from the bed and went to the bedroom door. "I'll bring up some beer to go with our pizza. In the meantime, don't get dressed."

After he left, she flopped back on the bed. When had everything in her life gone from being so wrong to being so right? Maybe this was one of those flukes of fate that would soon be corrected and vanish in the blink of an eye.

And if it is meant to be?

The question hovered in her thoughts like a thick mist on a desolate road. She decided she would enjoy what they had and when the time came, she'd move on. After all, the best things in life never lasted, but at least they existed, forever fostering the hope of their eventual return.

Alexandrea Weis

Chapter 19

The following Monday, Heather returned to the ER at Lewisville Medical Center. Wearing her usual blue scrubs and strutting through the front glass doors, she was eager to begin working again. The week before had been more than eventful, with her days occupied by Murphy and preparations for the upcoming show, and her nights filled with Grant's pleasurable games.

Grinning as she passed the signs that directed the way to the emergency room, she reminisced over her time with Grant. Things were heating up with him. He was spending every night at her house, sharing her bed, and in the morning would head back to Crowley Ranch. He had never wanted her to return to his apartment, claiming he enjoyed her home and the freedom from the prying eyes of his father and Gigi. Heather had been relieved by the comment. She had no intention of returning to the ranch, knowing that the pressures of his family and work would take him away from her soon enough. Even though she may not have liked the idea of it ending, Heather was resolved to accept it.

"Hey, you're back," Cali voiced from behind her curved sign-in desk.

"Yes I am, Cali. I needed the break."

Cali's bright brown eyes dimmed a little. "Well, get ready. Dr. Eisenberg's been asking for you every ten minutes since he got here an hour ago. You've been warned."

Heather pensively inspected the wide double doors to the side of the desk. She had forgotten about Ben. Several of his calls and texts to her phone were still unanswered.

"Son of a bitch," she mumbled, and slapped the round metal button on the side of the wall.

"My sentiments exactly," Cali vented behind her.

Marching through the doors, Heather surveyed the area beyond. It looked quiet, but then again this was an ER and the calm usually came before the storm.

Sneaking down the corridor, she kept her sights on the nurses' station ahead. Just when she thought she was about to reach the station undetected, a deep voice called to her from one of the rooms.

"Where in the hell have you been?"

Wishing for that hole in the floor to open up and swallow her, Heather turned to greet the owner of that surly voice.

Ben was standing in an exam room doorway to her right, holding a blue binder in his hand. Behind him an elderly woman was sitting up on the gurney, her eyes glistening with bewilderment.

Ben hastily shut the exam room door and clutched the binder to his chest. He took two steps forward, coming right up to her, his scowl as scary as his eyes.

"I've sent fifteen texts, left dozens of voice mails, and you never got back to me. I was about to call the police when I finally decided to drive past that stable of yours and see if you were there. When I saw you riding your horse, I figured you weren't dead."

"You were spying on me?"

"Of course not," he affirmed, raising his voice. "I was making sure you were still alive. You don't have anyone to check on you, Heather. I feel responsible for you."

Her leather backpack suddenly felt like it weighed a ton. She shifted the bulky pack from one shoulder to the other, buying time to come up with a reasonable excuse for ignoring his messages.

"I've been busy preparing for this show, Ben. I told you I needed time to think, and talking to you on the phone or answering your texts isn't giving me that time. I felt like you were hounding me."

He stood back from her. Heather noticed his fingers were white as they tightly gripped the edge of the binder. For several seconds, Ben said nothing. The look in his blue eyes worried Heather. Something was wrong.

"I never realized you were thinking and seeing Grant Crowley at the same time."

Uh oh! Her stomach dropped to the floor. "What makes you say that I'm—?"

"Come on, Heather! It's all over the Internet about the two of you." He tossed the binder to a cart outside the door.

"What's on the Internet?"

His hand sliced indignantly through the air. "Vanessa Luke put it all over her website and on Twitter that she ran into you and Grant in Dallas last weekend. She claims you're a gold digger after his money."

Heather's anger erupted. "That lying, manipulative, back-stabbing—"

"The least you could have done was warn me that you were seeing someone else," he cut in. Heather was about to say something, but he held up his hands. "I know ... you were just getting it out of your system. Crowley can be an intriguing guy, but he's no good for you, Heather. He's no good for any woman. I hope you eventually see that. When you are done fooling around with him, I'll be waiting. My offer still stands. I want to be with you, to build a life—"

"Ben, enough!" she shouted.

He glared at her, as if no one had ever spoken to him like that in his life.

"I can't do this with you. I can't pretend that we have something when I—I just don't feel it. I don't want to live with you." She ran her hand over her forehead, shocked that she was just deciding to turn him down. "I can't lie to myself anymore about us." She paused and took in a deep breath. "You're a great guy; you're just not the guy for me."

His blue eyes were on fire. "I suppose Crowley is the right guy."

She shook her head, blistering with frustration. How in the hell could she tell Ben what Grant meant to her when she didn't even know?

"Grant Crowley and I are just ... having fun. It's not serious, and I'm not a fool about him, but he isn't the man you make him out to be. He's better than that, Ben."

His scowl deepened. "Jesus Christ, you're falling for him." He pointed at her face. "I can see it in your eyes. You really care for this guy. It's not a fling, at least not for you."

Her heart came to a standstill. Was he right? She searched the deepest regions of her being to find an answer. Her head protested loudly that Ben was wrong; Grant was nothing to her except some great sex. However, as she delved deeper into her emotions, she felt it. That stirring in the pit of her gut that there was more, that she felt more. It had been there all along, but until that moment she had not been willing to accept it.

She wanted to shout back that Ben was wrong, that he didn't know what was in her heart, but she couldn't. She couldn't find the words. So instead of confronting him, she walked away—actually, she jogged—desperate to find some place to hide from his prying gaze.

Inside of the nurses' lounge, she dropped her backpack on the ground in front of her locker and took off for the restroom. Locking herself in a stall, she put the lid down on the toilet and had a seat. Images of Grant and their time together overwhelmed her, and as the pictures came and went, the spark of emotions in her chest grew into a raging inferno. This was bad, very bad. Not only had she failed in keeping Grant out of her heart, she had probably jeopardized her job. Stomping her foot on the ground, she was about to stand when the cell phone in her tunic pocket blared its musical ringtone.

Seeing Grant's number on her caller ID, she eagerly answered her phone.

"Hey, Grant," she said, trying to sound upbeat.

"I realize you're at work, but I think there is something you need to know." He sounded grave.

She pushed a loose strand of hair from her eyes. "Let me guess, Vanessa outed us all over the Internet."

He chuckled, sounding relieved. "You saw it."

"No, I heard about it from Ben Eisenberg."

"You okay? You want me to come and get you?"

The question made her smile. She was touched that he would make such an offer. "No, I'm fine. I just had it out with Ben."

"Let me guess," his soothing voice poured over her phone speaker. "He said I was bad news for you and you should steer clear of me because I will only hurt you."

She lightly chuckled. "Something like that."

"He's always hated me."

"Why is that?"

"Who knows?" He sighed into the phone. "A lot of people have preconceived opinions about me because of my family, our wealth, my father, my sister ... take your pick. I think I've spent more time dispelling rumors than proving them true."

She kicked the floor with the toe of her tennis shoe. "Sounds like my life."

"See? I told you we were just alike. I understand you, Heather. Better than you think."

Before that instant, she would never have believed Grant, but now she understood that what he said was true. They had both been fighting the misconceptions of others all of their lives.

"I guess your family history in many ways is as murky as mine," she told him, feeling closer to him than ever.

"It's not what you've gone through, it's how you've fought to overcome it that matters. You and I are born fighters."

"Thank you, Grant. But I wonder sometimes if I can keep on fighting."

"You're not a quitter, Heather. I've seen it in your eyes. I believe in you, remember that." He paused, sounding as if he wanted to say more. "Call me if you need me to come and punch out your boss for you."

That comment made her laugh out loud. "I would pay to see that."

"I like it when you laugh. Let me know what time you'll be home tonight, and I'll meet you."

Emboldened by the confidence he was instilling in her, she said, "Perhaps I should get you a key to my place, so you don't have to wait for me to come home."

Silence greeted her and as she held her breath, waiting to see if she had gone too far, someone entered the restroom.

"I never thought you'd offer," he finally murmured.

"Heather?" a woman's voice called from outside of her stall door.

"I've got to go," she whispered into the phone.

"Have a good day, baby." Then the line went dead.

She was still running his endearment over in her head when a knock came on her stall door.

"Heather, it's Babs. We've got an MVA on route. Dr. Ben needs you to get room two ready."

Heather stood from the toilet, tucking the phone in her tunic pocket. It was time to get back to work.

* * *

Ben wasn't the only one who had seen Vanessa's announcement on the Internet. When Heather arrived at Southland Stables after her eight hour shift in the ER, Trent was there. She could tell by his angry stride as he came up to Murphy's stall that he had heard about her and Grant. His thin mouth was turned downward in a cruel frown and his gray eyes were as cold as ice.

"Are you insane?" he roared as she was tacking up Murphy outside of his stall. "Grant Crowley?"

Tightening the buckles on the girth, she rolled her eyes at him. "I don't need to hear it from you of all people, Trent."

"You do know he has a reputation, Heather."

She chuckled, putting down the side flap on her English saddle. "So did you as I recall, and Rayne still took a chance on you."

He stopped for a moment, stumped for a comeback. "I'm not Crowley."

Heather reached for her bridle on a hook by the stall door. "Trent, you're just like Grant. You're both hard men who like to push the people in your life to be the best they can be."

"I don't push anyone," he insisted, raising his voice.

"You push me," Heather hurled back with equal volume.

"You're my rider. You ride for this stable and it's my job to push you." He patted Murphy's round rump. "How else are you going to win?"

"It's not about winning, Trent." She urged Murphy to take the bit. "You've been pushing Rayne to do natural childbirth and she wants to use drugs ... all the drugs she can get."

Trent's gray eyes shifted away from her. "It's healthier for the baby."

She slipped the bridle over Murphy's ears. "Are you having the baby?"

Trent came around the horse. "Rayne is tough. She can handle it."

"Rayne is terrified." She clucked to Murphy and led him away from the stall. "She doesn't want you to think she is weak, but she's scared of childbirth, every woman is." She waited as Trent jogged slightly to keep alongside her. "No one wants to suffer pain, and there isn't anything much more painful than having a baby."

Trent tugged on her arm, stopping her. "If you were having a baby, wouldn't you want to go natural?"

Heather was amused by the hopeful light she saw in his face. "Hell no! You forget, I work in an ER. Do you know how many babies I've seen delivered naturally?" She shook her head, tittering. "If you want your wife to speak to you after the baby is born, let her decide how she wants to have it, and keep your mouth shut."

He stood for a moment, considering her suggestion. Heather was intrigued at the way his brow knitted. She had seen many sides to Trent through the years, and could read his moods pretty well, but for the first time she saw real anguish in his sharp features. Heather had never seen him so in love with anyone as his wife, and it warmed her heart. She had always wanted to be loved like that.

"All right, you win." Trent tossed his hand in the air. "I'll keep my mouth shut and let her decide."

"I know how hard that is for you to do, but it's for the best, Trent, I promise."

Heather took Murphy the rest of the way to the barn entrance as Trent followed them. When she stepped out into the glowing afternoon sunlight, Trent was still behind her.

"I still think you need to be careful with Crowley, Heather."

Heather stood at Murphy's shoulder, put her left foot in the stirrup, and then pulled her body into the saddle. Gathering up her reins, she peered down at Trent.

"He's my concern, not yours."

"It'll be my concern if he throws you off your game at Riverdale this weekend, or worse … causes you to screw up at the state finals." He came up to her side and patted Murphy's thick shoulder. "He could be out to hurt you, to see you fail in the last show of the season."

Heather was incensed. "I can't believe you would even say something like that, Trent. You know Grant may be many things, but he is not devious like that. He would want to beat me fair and square. I, at least, know that much about him."

Trent held up his hands in supplication. "It was just a suggestion. I honestly don't know what you see in the guy."

She tapped Murphy's sides. "Obviously, a lot more than you."

"Fine, I won't bring it up again."

Murphy walked ahead and she glared back over the horse's rump at Trent. "Good. Don't."

"Work on that touch and go in the ring," he called as she moved further away. "I'll check in after I finish teaching the beginner's class."

Riding Murphy toward the back jumping ring, Heather concentrated on controlling her outrage. Never before had she encountered such opposition when dating a man. Then again, she had never had her dating life spilled all over the Internet. The entire incident reminded her of all the upheavals her family had endured before, during, and after her father's trial. The pain was not as deep, but the intrusion into her private life bothered her more than when her father's face and crimes had been splashed all over the front page of *The Dallas Morning News*. She did not want to repeat that horrible time in her life, but it would seem dating a man like Grant Crowley was going to create a whole new set of problems for her.

"Jesus, I hope this doesn't continue." She watched as Murphy's black-tipped ears swung to and fro, listening to her every word. "What would you do, Murph? Would you keep seeing someone everyone tells you is wrong for you?"

Of course, Murphy had no answer for her, but Heather pretended he did. She often did that, giving him a deep masculine voice in her head as she would ponder important decisions in her life ... and a few unimportant ones, as well.

"At the end of the day, all that matters is that you love me, my man." She patted Murphy's thick neck. "You make me better. You make me whole."

And Grant? How does he make you feel?

The voice in her head was deep, smooth, and assertive, as she had always imagined Murphy's voice to be, but she knew it wasn't Murphy. An insistent nudge from her conscious begged the question to be answered.

She had changed since being with Grant. That her confidence had soared was a given, but there were other things he had done for her; things she could not describe. With Grant, her past had become ... well, her past. Thoughts of her father and the misery her family had endured seemed to dim when she was with him. Something the other men in her life had never been able to accomplish. Still, Heather was afraid of entertaining any hope of a future with Grant. She had vowed to keep it friendly and flirtatious from the first kiss, but now her heart was insisting on another outcome.

"I think I'd rather go through natural childbirth," she whispered, and then she clucked for Murphy to break into a trot, eager to get to the ring and put her growing apprehensions behind her.

Chapter 20

The day of the Riverdale Farms Horse Show was unusually chilly for late October, causing riders to fret but making the horses very happy. All about the freshly mowed green pastures that surrounded the grand show ring with its solid white-railed fence and round gazebo in the center, horses were neighing, prancing, and being generally frisky.

Heather was even having a difficult time handling Murphy. The excitement of the other horses made him put a little more strut in his step as she rode him to the warm-up area outside of the show ring. Her hands were getting stiff in the nippy air as she tightly gripped the reins, anxious to keep Murphy from acting up.

"You should have worn your gloves," Trent scolded as he walked beside Murphy to the warm-up area.

Heather eyed the two fences in the center of a roped-off section just ahead. A few other riders were waiting in line to take a turn at the jumps. Some of the horses she recognized from previous shows in the season. Her eyes kept scanning the warm-up area, ignoring Trent's scowl.

"You're not paying attention to me." Trent slapped her boot. "Let me guess ... you're looking for Grant."

"I haven't seen him." She glanced down at Trent. "He was hung up in Dallas last night on business and phoned to say he was trailering Maximillian in this morning, but I've been so busy helping Rebecca get the other riders from Southland ready that I've never had a chance to look for him."

"I take it you two have been spending most of your nights together then."

"Don't even go there, Trent." She cast her eyes to the warm-up area.

"Damn it, Heather! This is what I was afraid of ... you're not concentrating."

"I am concentrating," she shouted at him.

"You two should keep it down." The soothing voice was immediately familiar to Heather. She spun around in her saddle.

Coming up to them, dressed casually in jeans and a long-sleeved white T-shirt, was Grant. Instantly, Heather was alarmed.

"What's wrong? Why aren't you dressed for our class?"

"Maximillian got sick late last night. The vet advised me to hold off on the show." Grant patted Murphy's rear. "Looks like you will have to go ahead without me."

When he came up to her saddle, she leaned over to him. "Why didn't you call me?"

He kissed her lips. "Didn't have a chance."

A little embarrassed by the public display, Heather twisted her head around to see if anyone had noticed their kiss. When her eyes landed on Trent's brooding countenance, she sat upright in her saddle.

"What's wrong with Maximillian?" Trent asked, his gray eyes still glaring at Heather.

"It's a cold, nothing more. He's been fighting something all season, and the vet felt it better not to tax him." Grant hooked his finger through the belt loop of his jeans as he eyed Trent. "I've got enough points to qualify for the state show, so there is no need to push my horse if it isn't warranted."

Trent folded his arms and nodded ahead to the warm-up area. "Heather, get Murphy ready."

"I saw Rayne coming in the front gate," Heather heard Grant say to Trent when she rode off, leaving the two men to talk.

With one eye on Trent and Grant and the other on the riders darting about the warm-up area, Heather found it hard to concentrate on anything Murphy was doing. She could see Trent frowning at her—a sure sign that she was screwing up—but she was too interested in trying to figure out what the two men were saying to each other. Seconds later, she spotted a slow moving Rayne coming across the paddock area.

Assured that Rayne could keep the two men from throttling each other, Heather turned her attention to Murphy. She worked him at a trot, and then asked him to canter, making sure she didn't run into the other riders also trying to warm up their horses.

Off to the side of the grassy area, an older man with gray hair was yelling at a slender girl on a fat palomino gelding with blue ribbons braided into his mane. The young woman's face was hidden by the brim of her black helmet, but Heather could guess what she was feeling. It was the same way she had felt at shows when her father would yell at her before a class.

The rush of a thousand agonizing memories stabbed at her heart. It never failed to amaze her that at any given horse show she attended there was at least one parent shouting at their child. Every time Heather saw such heartbreaking encounters, it took everything she had not to punch the offending parent right in the nose.

"Heather, I want you to take a fence."

It wasn't Trent ordering her to the center of the ring. It was Grant.

Astounded, she trotted Murphy up to him as he adjusted the cups on either side of the fence, raising it higher.

"What are you doing?" she demanded, keeping her voice low.

"Schooling you." He adjusted the last cup. "You need to take Murphy over a few fences before you go in."

She searched the warm-up area. "Where's Trent?"

"With Rayne. She said she needed him."

Heather's eyes went to the entrance of the warm-up area. "Is everything all right? She's due any day now."

Grant stepped up to Murphy's neck. "She's fine. Trent asked me to see you over a few fences."

Her gaze dropped to him. "You?"

Grant grinned at the shocked look on her face. "He seemed to think I could get you to focus better than he could." Grant moved in closer to her. "I could probably even get you to listen to me if I took you over my knee and spanked that fine ass of yours, but since we're in public...." He moved away and pointed to the jump set up next to him. "Take the fence."

Heather took to the outside of the make-shift ring and asked Murphy to canter. Keeping her eyes on the fence—well, partially on the fence and partially on Grant—she proceeded to the single red and white pole he had set rather high.

Murphy tugged against the reins, eager to fly at the fence, but she held him back.

"Get him under control, Heather. He's getting away from you," Grant shouted.

Murphy took off too soon over the fence and knocked the pole to the ground with his back foot. Coming around, she returned to Grant's side as he placed the red and white pole back in the cups. For a brief moment, she admired how his strong arms made an easy lift of the heavy wooden pole. She always had to struggle with the blasted things when she set up jumps.

"Take it again, only this time, get him to tuck his head more. It will slow him down and get him closer to the fence." His amber eyes stared up at her. "Lower your hands on his neck and sit further back in the saddle. You're getting ahead of the jump."

Heather wanted to make a smart remark, but she knew he was right. She had not been positioned correctly in the saddle before taking the fence.

"Do it right this time," he added in a frosty tone, "or I will take you over my knee."

Part of her wanted to laugh at his statement, and part of her was disturbed by an image of her father saying the exact same thing to her when she was a girl riding in her first show. An uncomfortable knot twisted in her stomach.

After taking Murphy over the fence again, with much better results than their first attempt, she circled back to Grant.

"Do it again," he growled. "You can do better. I've seen you jump better. You can do this, I know it."

This time the burn in her stomach was unmistakable. It was how she used to feel when her father yelled at her as a child.

After her third attempt over the fence, she warily went back to his side, afraid she had done it wrong yet again. But when he grinned up at her, the burning in her stomach ceased.

"Now that is what I know you can do. You placed him perfectly before the fence and maintained control of his head right up until takeoff. Jump every fence like that in the ring and you'll get the blue ribbon."

She shifted the reins to her left hand and pressed on her stomach as if pushing the uncomfortable feeling away.

"What is it?" Grant inquired, eyeing her movements.

"Nerves," she lied.

"Nerves ... you?" He inched up to her horse. "What is it?"

She gazed into his eyes, ashamed to say anything. It was a childhood insecurity that she had thought long forgotten. Did he really need to know?

She adjusted the reins in her hands, deciding it better not to share all of her past. "Nothing. Like I said, just nerves."

He rubbed his hand along her thigh, sending a tingling sensation up her spine. "I've watched you long enough to know that you don't get nervous before you go into the ring, you get angry. Now what is going on with you?"

The loudspeaker set up at the show ring announced her class, saving Heather from admitting her true feelings. "I've got to check in," she said while turning Murphy away.

"Fine." He came alongside the horse as they made their way toward the show ring. "We'll talk about it tonight at your place."

Heather surveyed the horses and people scattered about the grounds. "There's nothing to discuss."

"Don't bullshit me, baby, especially about what you're feeling."

She pulled Murphy to an abrupt halt. "Why in the hell are you suddenly so fascinated with what I'm feeling, Grant? You never wanted to know before."

His eyes widened with surprise at her reaction, and then they became like the dangerous orbs she had always seen in the show ring. "Something is bothering you ... that's obvious. We'll talk about this after the show." He took Murphy's reins and started leading the horse to the show ring. At the gate, he patted her leg. "I'll be waiting when you come out." Then he turned away.

Feeling like an ass, she reprimanded herself for the outburst. "Get it under control, Heather."

After checking in with the steward, Heather discovered that she was fifteenth in a class of twenty. That was good. It gave her time to learn the required sequence of fences. Parking Murphy in front of the bulletin board to the side of the gate, she studied the diagram outlining the course. Every now and then she would glance up at the ring and observe the horse and rider currently tackling the jumps. By the time the fifth horse had completed the course, it became obvious that the touch and go at the very end was the fence that would be every horse's biggest challenge.

When the last horse to take to the course before her also knocked a pole off the confounding touch and go, Heather's nerves sparked to life.

"You can do it," a sultry voice said beside her. "I've seen you take command of the fences. Do it in there."

She looked down at Grant, standing next to Murphy. "I know I can do it."

"Let go of the fear. I can see it building in your eyes, just like the first time I kissed you. Go in there and forget about being afraid. Just ride the hell out of that damned course and you'll win. I believe in you, baby."

Instantly, her stomach calmed and she smiled at him. The confidence he instilled in her was something she had never counted on when they had started out. How would she get along without it … or him?

"Thank you, Grant. For everything."

"You're up," he told her, gesturing to the gate.

They called her number over the loudspeaker and Heather urged Murphy onward. Nodding to the steward on her way into the ring, Heather pushed the queasy feeling in her stomach aside. She could hear the other horses, the people murmuring outside of the ring, but all of her focus was on the fences.

While making her curtesy circle, she remembered what Grant had told her in the warm-up area. Manipulating the reins, she made Murphy tuck his head, and then guided him toward the first fence—a nasty looking water jump. After clearing that jump, her eyes were on the second—a wide gate with the hosting stable's logo on it. Murphy strained against her grip on the reins, but she made him listen, counted his stride to the fence, and then at the perfect moment, let him go. Each fence in the ring she attacked with the same strategy: relax, sit back in the saddle, control Murphy, and then set up for the next one.

They had jumped a clean round when they turned for the tortuous touch and go. With all Grant's advice rolling around in her head, Heather contemplated how the combination of two simple fences had represented so much pain and so much pleasure for her. The touch and go had been her downfall when she rode under her father's watchful gaze. So many years later, the obstacle still tested her, but she had found confidence since those early days. She was no longer a scared little girl out to please a cruel father.

"Screw it," she whispered, letting Murphy have his head.

They rode to the first fence with lightning speed, and when her horse planted his feet in just the right spot, she knew she had it. He cleared the first jump, but digging in her heels, she pushed him on to the second fence, forcing him to extend his long body over the last hurdle.

When they hit the ground, a thunderous applause broke out from the audience. They had jumped the first clean round in the competition.

As soon as she was out the gate, Grant was there, clapping louder than anyone else. She felt a swell of pride when she saw him, knowing that it had not only been her success, but his as well.

"That was superb." He took Murphy's reins from her and held the horse as she dismounted.

She didn't know where the impulse came from, but instead of being concerned about who was watching them, she went to Grant, tossed her arms around his neck, and kissed him.

When she pulled back, he appeared genuinely pleased. "Well, well, that is something new. You've never kissed me like that before."

Happy—no thrilled—at completing the best ride of her life and coming out to find Grant waiting for her, Heather beamed into his twinkling eyes. "Now we really have something to celebrate tonight."

He patted her behind. "You haven't won the class yet, Heather."

"No, Grant, I've already won the prize."

A knowing smile crossed his lips and he held her to him. "That you have, baby."

"That was wonderful," Trent asserted, breaking the spell between them. "That is the best round I've ever seen you jump in a competition, Heather."

She stepped back from Grant's embrace. "Thanks, Trent."

"Whatever you said to her in the warm-up area worked, Crowley," Trent admitted. "She's never jumped better."

Grant gave Heather a smug side-glance. "I think I just helped her keep her eye on the prize."

Trent's gray eyes volleyed back and forth from Grant to Heather, and then he shook his head. "You two really aren't good at playing it low key."

Heather's eyes explored the paddock area. "Where's Rayne?"

Trent gestured to the side of the high white railing along the show ring. "I've got her set up in a chair by the ring. She's having a hard time getting comfortable."

"Any day now right?" Heather took Murphy's reins from Grant.

Trent wiped his hand over his brow, letting his gaze linger on his wife. "Any second now, actually."

Heather motioned to Rayne. "Go and sit with her, Trent."

"No, I've got to get back to the stables and check on the other riders. Rayne is fine where she is. Just keep an eye on her for me while I'm gone."

"Will do," Heather told him.

While Trent strutted away, the elation Heather had experienced exiting the show ring quickly dissolved and her nervousness rekindled. Her fingers were skimming back and forth over her reins as the wintry air finally hit her. She was amazed that she had not felt the chill before now, but like an insidious dream that permeates the depths of your waking consciousness, the cold started to sink deeper beneath her riding habit. When she shivered, Grant's arm immediately went around her shoulders.

"You should go back to the stables and get warm."

"I can't." She glimpsed the show ring over her shoulder and the barrel-chested roan bounding over the fences. "I've got to see the rest of the field ride."

"Then let me take Murphy back. I'll cool him down and come back in time to see you get the blue ribbon."

Handing off the reins, she once again felt that nervous flip in her belly. Things were different between them. He had become not only a lover, but a friend.

As he led Murphy toward the stables, Heather admired the curve of his ass beneath his jeans, only this time she vowed to spend hours holding those firm cheeks in her hands as he thrust into her again and….

"Hell of a round."

When Heather turned she was a little mystified to see Gigi standing beside her. In black jodhpur pants and a Black Sabbath T-shirt, her bobbed black hair was darting about in the brisk breeze. The smirk on her red lips added to Heather's growing sense of unease.

"You and my brother are quite the talk of the horse world." She circled the paddock area with her eyes. "It's all anyone is asking me about."

Heather refused to react to Gigi's prodding, and put on a serene smile. "Next week they'll have something new to gossip about. You know how horse people are."

"Oh, I know how they are, but what I don't understand is how you two got so close so fast. It was what … almost two weeks ago I caught you kissing in the tack room at my barn, and now here he is," her hands waved about the paddock area, "schooling you at shows and giving up his chance to compete with you. I must say I have never seen him quite so smitten."

Heather suspiciously eyed Gigi. "What are you talking about? Grant told me Maximillian was sick and he couldn't show."

"Max is fine, Heather. Grant wanted to give you a shot at the blue ribbon. Of course, he assured me that all bets would be off at state. He wants state." She uttered a fiendish-sounding snicker. "I'm glad to see he hasn't gone completely overboard with you."

The enthusiasm inside Heather fizzled. "Are you telling me he scratched Max for me?"

"Shocking, isn't it? The impervious Grant Crowley bowing out of a riding competition for a woman." Gigi edged closer, the smirk receding from her lips. "Just be careful with his heart, Heather. He may be a horse's ass on the outside, but on the inside he's just as vulnerable as the rest of us."

Heather shook her head, disgusted by Gigi's phony concern. "I'm not out to hurt him."

"But you're not exactly in this for love, are you?" She tilted back, her black eyes sweeping up and down Heather's curvy figure. "I've watched you for years on the circuit. You were always so cool, so distant with everyone. Probably why everyone thought you were a lesbian. I can't help but wonder if you can share your heart with any man. Some people cut themselves off from the world thinking they can avoid heartache, but heartache is the price we pay for being alive. If you don't embrace what you can share with another person, you might as well be dead."

Heather skeptically viewed the beautiful woman's stern features, seeing shades of Grant in them. "What's your point, Gigi?"

"I wanted you to know what he is willing to do for you. Are you willing to do the same for him, Heather?"

A crash from the show ring made them both turn. Heather looked on as the blue and white poles from the first fence in the touch and go crashed to the ground. Before the fence, a wide black gelding stood, having refused to take the last combination in the course.

"You're almost home," Gigi whispered to her. "Congratulations, on both of your victories."

While Gigi sauntered across the paddock area, Heather mulled over the ramifications of what she had disclosed. Grant had pulled out of the show for her. Instead of touching her heart, it made her furious. If she won the class, the victory would be hollow.

That bastard!

Waiting by the paddock gate, she watched as one rider after another went into the ring and failed to accomplish what she had; a clean round. By the time the last horse and rider were at the gate, waiting for their chance to enter the ring, Heather's body was so cold from standing in the freezing weather that she couldn't feel her toes.

When the last competitor entered the ring, she felt the cold dissipate around her. Rocking to the rhythm of the horse's pounding hooves, in her mind she rode the fences with the rider competing before her. Heather could feel the horse's placement before each of the fences and was counting the massive paint's strides as he approached every one of the high hurdles. With his wild tail of bright copper flying behind him, the horse proceeded to the touch and go at break neck speed. Then Heather saw it, the slight bobble on the animal's front end that signified his reservations about taking the first jump. His rider, a skinny redhead, tried her best to compensate for the horse's misstep, but the damage was done. By the time he landed after the first fence, the gelding's footing was off and the angle of approach to the second jump was going to be awkward. As the horse's thick body strained to get over the second fence, Heather cringed. When the loud bang echoed throughout the ring, Heather knew he had knocked down a pole. The blue ribbon was hers.

Her first reaction was absolute joy, but the sensation was short-lived when she remembered what Gigi had told her.

"I knew it." Arms tossed around her, lifted her into the air, and spun her about. "I knew you would win it."

When Grant set her feet back on the ground, she felt a little dizzy.

"You did it," he declared, touching his forehead to hers. His hands flew to her cheeks. "You're like ice."

Heather stepped back from him. "You pulled Maximillian so I could win, didn't you?"

His blond brows crinkled together. "No, of course not. He's sick. I told you—"

"Gigi told me everything, Grant." Her voice was as frigid as the rest of her body.

"Gigi is baiting you, Heather. Max is sick."

There it was. That first inkling of doubt.

Heather had experienced it before with men: a second-glance at something they had said, or a gesture that had left her confused, or even a declaration of emotion that had just sounded off. For her, it usually signaled that it was time to cut her losses and bolt.

Heather lowered her gaze to her pale, white hands. "She made it sound like you wanted to scratch for me."

He lifted her chin. "You know me better than that. I'd rather beat your ass than let you have a meaningless victory. I know how you would feel about me if I did that."

A shred of relief snaked through her, but still she wasn't sure.

"There you are," Trent said next to them, sounding out of breath.

Heather turned to him and immediately noticed the distress in his gray eyes. "What is it?"

"Rayne," he gasped, clutching his knees as he caught his breath. "Her water broke and her contractions have started. I've got to get her to the hospital."

Heather raised her hands, calming the panic she heard coming from him. "Trent, it's all right. You've got time."

"I need help getting her to my car." Trent took in a deep breath. "She refuses to walk back to the parking lot."

"I'll get my car and pull it up here," Grant offered. "You can't drive. You need to help her."

Trent clapped his hand over Grant's shoulder. "Thank you, Grant, but you don't have to do that."

"I want to, Trent, so no more arguments." Grant pulled his car keys from the front pocket of his jeans. "Heather, you're coming with us."

Trent waved to the ring. "She needs to collect her ribbon."

Grant swerved to Trent. "She needs to come with us. Neither one of us knows how to deliver a baby."

"He's right," Heather confirmed. "The ribbon isn't important, Trent. Your baby and wife are what matter."

Grant took her hand. "Come with me."

Pulling her toward the stables at a brisk jog, Heather looked back over her shoulder as Trent went to Rayne's lounge chair by the railing.

Grant tugged his cell phone from his front pocket. "I'll call Gigi, tell her to see to your ribbon and to Murphy. She can help Rebecca Harmon get him safely back to Southland tonight."

"Are you sure you want to drive them to the hospital, Grant? Do you know what a pregnant woman can do to your car?"

He grinned at her, seemingly caught up in the excitement of the moment. "No, but I guess I'm about to find out."

Alexandrea Weis

Chapter 21

George Ashby Newbury weighed a little over eight pounds and screamed continuously from the second he was born. Wrapped in a blue blanket and with a little light blue cap on his head, he looked like an alien creature as he lay in his bassinet. As Heather peered through the nursery visitors' window at the tiny bundle, she recalled Rayne's hand crushing hers during the car ride to the hospital. There were times that she had sworn the poor woman would not survive the strong contractions ripping her apart. But seeing the little boy cuddled in his blanket made her realize why women went through the tortuous ordeal of labor; such love was worth any price.

"He looks like Trent," Grant commented, handing her a paper cup filled with black coffee.

She took the cup and sipped from it. "He's got Rayne's nose, though. She told me they named him after her father."

"I shudder to think of any child of mine being named Tad." Grant nodded to the assortment of babies arranged in neat little rows of bassinets on the other side of the glass. "Ever think about having one of those someday?"

Heather almost choked on her coffee. "Hell no." She lowered the cup from her lips. "I'll probably raise another Jeffery Dahmer."

"I don't know. I think you would make a pretty great mother."

"No, I decided a long time ago kids weren't in the picture."

Grant pressed his shoulder against the window frame, curiously studying her. "This is a side of you I never thought existed."

She peered into her coffee, avoiding his eyes. "What side is that?"

"The uncertain Heather. You've always been so damned determined in everything you do. You're terrified of becoming a mother, aren't you?"

Heather directed her gaze to the nursery window. "If you had grown up like I did ... with the father that I had, you would never want kids, either."

"How was your father any different from mine?"

Her fingers traced the rim of her white coffee cup. "Mine wasn't domineering; he was cruel. I don't remember a lot of laughter or good times growing up. All I do remember is him pushing me and Stew. 'Be better. Ride harder. Win the class.'" She rolled her head around, working out the tension that was developing in her neck. "When I was twelve, I was diagnosed with an ulcer. At sixteen, I experimented with bulimia, because my father told me I was getting too fat to jump. Luckily, a school counselor saw me losing weight and called my mother." She raised her blue eyes to him. "It was one of the few times I can remember my mother standing up for me against my dad. Most of the time she let him do whatever and chalked it up as 'character building.'" Heather wanted to laugh, but somehow couldn't fight the tears welling up in her eyes. "I hated her for never helping me fight my father. Then when Dad went to prison and she OD'd, I cried for a week, because I never got to tell her how sorry I was for hating her."

Grant put his arm around her shoulders and held her close. "I hated my mother for leaving me with my father. I hated her for having another son and forgetting I existed."

She wiped her hand over her right eye. "You can still tell her how you feel, Grant."

He shook his head. "I put my demons to rest a long time ago. I think that is why I rode English and took to jumping like she did. I wanted to show her that I was her son, and that I mattered. I realized when I was about twenty-five that it wasn't my mother's leaving that shaped me, it was my father's staying in my life that made me what I am." He took the coffee cup from her hand and came around in front of her. "Just like your old man shaped you. All the shouting and screaming they torture us with when we're young shapes us. I guess psychologists would say it was harsh and consider it child abuse, but we survived."

"Today, at the show, I saw an older man shouting at a young girl on a horse, and the same burning in my stomach started up again like when my father yelled at me. How do I make myself forget all of that? How do I make that hurt go away?"

Grant nodded to the nursery window as he put the coffee cup down on the sill. "You replace it ... with love. You won't be like your parents, Heather, you'll be better."

"You don't know that. My parents disappointed me. I couldn't live with myself if I repeated their mistakes."

He placed his hands on her shoulders. "You'll go into parenthood knowing more than your parents, and vowing to do better. That's all any of us can do."

"What if I don't do better? What if I'm worse? Sometimes I think I'm exactly like my father. He was a cold, ruthless son of a bitch. All that mattered to him was winning. I can't take the chance of putting another human being through all the pain I went through."

"Heather, if all that mattered to you was winning, you wouldn't be here. You would have stayed at that horse show and collected your blue ribbon."

Feeling the weight of the day bearing down on her, she nestled against his chest. "I'm still going to beat your ass in the show ring. It won't be an official win until I do." She was leaning back from him when a long slow yawn snuck up on her.

Grant eased his arm around her waist, gently nudging her from the viewing window. "I think we've both had a very long day."

"I should check on Murphy. See if Rebecca got him back to Southland okay."

He chuckled, leading her down the white hospital corridor toward a silver pair of elevator doors. "I think you're already a mother to a twelve hundred pound horse."

"He's not a horse," she objected, tucking her head into his shoulder. "He's the best thing that ever happened to me."

"The best thing?" Grant questioned. "I'll have to see what I can do to change your mind about that."

* * *

It was almost ten when Heather pushed open her back door and dropped her black show boots on her shiny white-tiled floor. After insisting Grant drive her to Southland to check on Murphy, she had collected her Pathfinder from the stable parking lot and allowed

Grant to follow her home. Now as she stood in her back doorway, her body ached and all she wanted was a hot bath and a cold glass of wine.

"You look beat," Grant said, closing her back door. "Why don't you get out of those riding clothes and into a hot bath?"

She plodded along the short hallway. "You read my mind." She hugged her arms about her black riding coat. "I still haven't warmed up."

He helped to slide the jacket from around her shoulders. "You want me to get you some coffee?"

She let him take her jacket and stopped at her kitchen counter. "No, but I would really love a glass of wine."

He set her jacket on the breakfast bar. "You've got it." Motioning to her bedroom, he added, "Get in the tub, and I'll bring it to you."

Heather could not even find the strength to smile, and slowly walked from the kitchen. Once in her bathroom, she tugged off the snug riding pants and shrugged the white high-collar shirt from around her body. When the cold air in the bathroom hit her skin, she shivered.

"I must be coming down with something."

While her wide Jacuzzi tub filled with hot water, Heather wrapped a thick beige towel about her and had a seat on the edge of the tub. Splashing her hand in the water, she longed for the tub to hurry filling so she could immerse herself. The events of the long day flew across her mind, and she warmed a little inside as she pictured Trent and Rayne holding their newborn son. Despite witnessing many a birth, she treasured this experience more than any other. This was a child she hoped to watch grow, and in some small way, be a part of his life.

"One glass of sparkly wine," Grant announced, stepping into the bathroom.

Heather stood from the side of the tub and took the glass as he turned off the taps. She eagerly sipped the wine, anxious to feel that warm rush of alcohol.

"I feel like we should be drinking champagne," Grant commented.

She took the wineglass to the vanity countertop. "Feels funny thinking of Rayne and Trent as parents. I was just wondering what it will be like watching the little guy grow up at Southland."

Grant came up behind her. "If they stay at Southland. I might still get Trent to come to Crowley Stables."

"What about Gigi?"

He gently eased the towel from her body. "I'll find something else for her to do."

"What? Help you run the ranch?"

He dropped the towel on the vanity countertop. "Actually, I want her to run the whole ranch, while I'll handle Crowley Investments." He took her hand and led her to the tub. "I really need to concentrate all of my efforts on the investments."

He held her hand as she stepped into the water. "Have you ever told her this?"

"Several times, but she thinks I'm full of shit. You know Gigi, she doesn't trust anyone."

Heather sighed as she sank into the water. Scooting back against the edge of the tub, she glanced up at Grant. "Was she always that way?"

"When we were kids, we were a lot closer." Yanking the T-shirt over his head, he then dropped it on the floor. "After our mother left, she pulled away from me and my father." His hands went to the zipper on his blue jeans.

"What are you doing?" Heather asked, eyeing the still red scar on the left side of his carved chest.

He pointed to the bathtub. "Getting in with you."

"Maybe I don't want you to take a bath with me."

He quickly shoved his jeans and briefs down to his ankles and stepped out of them. "But I'm so much fun to have a bath with." Grant kicked away his clothes and bounded toward the tub.

Before she could protest, he was settling in next to her. "I can't relax if I have to share a bath with you."

"I'll help you to relax." He stretched for the controls to the tub and pressed a button, activating the jets beneath the water line. "I know a secret for helping to release all the tension of the day."

Heather smirked at him as the bubbles in the tub came to life. "I'll bet you do."

He waved at the stream of bubbles. "Can I turn this higher?"

"Why?"

"You'll see."

She nodded to a knob on the tub console to her right. "Turn the knob and the flow will increase."

As Grant turned the white knob, Heather felt the cascade of bubbles rise from a gentle rush to a forceful flow.

"That's too high," she argued, reaching for the controls.

He nudged her hand away. "Not for what I have in mind."

His arms went around her slender waist and he lifted her in the tub. Whipping her around, he set her in front of the turgid flow of bubbles. Moving in behind her, he gently pried her legs apart.

"I know just where those bubbles will do the most good." He scooted her butt higher until the bubbles were rushing against her clit.

"Oh, Grant."

He kissed her cheek. "It gets better, baby."

Grant gently raised and lowered her hips, making sure the torrent of bubbles tantalized every part of her.

The unrelenting waves of pleasure brought on by the pounding bubbles quickly sent Heather's exhausted body spiraling toward climax. When Grant slid his fingers into her, Heather cried out just as her orgasm came crashing upward. She rocked against his hand as he bit down on her earlobe.

Heather opened her eyes, relaxing as the swirl of satisfaction eased her muscles, but she did not get long to enjoy her respite. Grant spun around in the tub, lifting her in his arms.

"Do you know how much it turns me on to see you come?" he murmured, setting her hips on top of his thighs.

Heather reached below the water and fondled his erection. "You know what I really want to do to you right now?"

He pushed the damp hair away from her face. "Tell me."

She kissed him, entreating him with her mouth. Then, she bit his lower lip. "I want to ride you."

"Hold that thought." He pushed her off him, stood in the tub, and stepped over the edge.

She watched him pick up his jeans from the floor. "What are you doing?"

He dug through the back pocket of his jeans and pulled out his wallet. After he retrieved a shiny silver condom packet, he returned to the tub, hitting the water with an eager splash.

"You've got a ready supply of those things, don't you?"

He ripped the package open. "Bought several boxes yesterday." He twitched his blond brows at her. "I figured we would need them."

She watched as he slipped on the condom. "Those don't really work in water."

He reached for her. "Yes, they do." He bit into the soft flesh at the base of her neck.

Forgetting about the condom, Heather lost herself in the feel of his teeth as they nipped along to her right breast. She climbed in his lap, hungry for him. Keeping her eyes on him, Heather angled over his hips and guided his cock inside of her.

"I think I've finally broken you," he whispered as he filled her.

Clamping her hands over his shoulders, she arched her back. "Let's see how long you can last."

Grant sat back against the tub, letting her take control. "I've got a very well-disciplined body."

Running her fingertips along his rippled abdominal muscles, she grinned. "I can feel that."

His hands went along her thighs and around to her firm butt, holding her in place. Heather loved the feel of his long hands and forced his cock deeper into her as the water swirled around them. Holding on to his shoulders, she rose up and came down hard on him.

Heather did not know why he felt so good, but it was better than the other times they had been together. Going slow, determined to enjoy him, she rode him to some unknown rhythm in her head.

Grant was smiling as he watched her, but when she became more demanding, he closed his eyes and dipped his head back. His hands were urging her to go faster, but Heather kept on with her methodical, rocking motion.

The heat built steadily in her body, chasing away the last traces of cold from her bones. Shooting tendrils of electricity rose from her gut, and she quickened her rhythm, wanting more.

Soon Grant's head was buried in her chest as she rode him harder and faster. They were clinging to each other while sounds of rapid breathing and needful groans drifted through the bathroom. Digging her nails into his broad shoulders, she cried out as the orgasm raced through her.

Grant grunted beneath her, pumped his hips upward, and exploded into her. Sighing into her neck, he squeezed his arms around her right before he breathed her name.

Cradling her in his arms, Grant sat back against the tub with her head curled into his chest. "I know you're going to hate me for saying this." He rubbed his stubble-covered cheek against hers. "But I think I want to put one of these tubs in every room of my house."

Heather let her hand run through the bubbles coming out of the jet next to her. She couldn't remember when it had felt so right with a man. Unfortunately, the more that sense of comfort pervaded her heart, the greater her apprehension.

"I will certainly never look at Jacuzzi bubbles the same way again," she reflected.

"What do you say to a different color tub in each room? We could use a different one every night of the week."

"You might get tired of taking baths with me after a while."

"Never," he confessed, tightening his arms around her. "I want you with me every night from now on." She looked up at him. "I was serious before about letting Gigi run the ranch. Dad can't keep going, and I need to be in Dallas more. Once Gigi is comfortable overseeing the ranch, I'm going to move permanently to Dallas. I want you to come with me."

Heather's heart almost stopped. Her first reaction wasn't happiness, it was panic.

"I thought we agreed this was only for fun. You said you didn't want any more than that with any woman."

He nuzzled her neck. "Now I want more ... with you."

"But I have a life here, and a job—"

"We can have a new life in Dallas." He smiled, trying to reassure her. "You can get a job at any hospital."

"And Murphy. What about him? Dallas is a long drive from Southland Stables."

He took in a deep breath, gauging her reaction. "I'll find another stable closer for Maximillian and Murphy, whatever it takes."

She eased back from him in the water. "I don't know, Grant. Don't you think we should give this more time? We barely know each other."

His chuckle sounded more anxious than amused. "I thought that was supposed to be my line." He inched closer to her, letting the first signs of worry surface in his eyes. "We've known each other for several months; whether or not that was as lovers shouldn't matter. This is right between us."

She bit down on her lower lip while her stomach churned with reservations. "Is it?"

He took a few seconds to collect his thoughts while keeping his eyes locked on her. "Heather, I know how strong and independent you like to think you are, but I don't want you to be alone anymore. I want you to be with me. I'm not suggesting we get married, just move in together and see how it goes."

Shades of her conversation with Ben came back to haunt her, and the same sickening feeling she had felt then resurfaced with Grant. Why did she feel this way? She knew he was right, wanted to say yes, but she was terrified of making a mistake; another mistake that would prove her father right.

Wanting to put some distance between them, Heather climbed from the tub. "I've been alone for a long time, Grant. I'm better off on my own." She went to the vanity and retrieved the towel he had left there. "I can't go back to Dallas. After everything that happened there, I swore I would never go back."

He came out of the tub after her. "Heather, it's time to put the past behind you."

"It's not that easy for me, Grant. I went through hell in Dallas, and moved here to get away from the publicity. You don't understand. You've never had to run away from your family's failures."

"Hey, what's this all about?" He came up behind her. "What is going on with you?" His arms went around her shoulders. "Talk to me. You wouldn't talk to me earlier today when you were about to go into the ring. I knew you were afraid then, and I can see that same fear in your eyes now."

"I wasn't afraid." She tried to wiggle free of his embrace, but he held her close. "I was thinking."

He lowered his mouth to her ear. "Thinking about what?"

She glared at his reflection in the vanity mirror. "Did you let me win today? Did you keep Maximillian at Crowley Stables so I could win the class?"

The sigh she heard from him already told her what she had suspected. "What difference does any of that make, Heather? You won, and I was proud of you."

She spun around to him. "I didn't win, Grant. If anything, I lost today."

"No you didn't, baby. You won me."

Heather stood in front of him as the heat from his skin warmed her. He felt so strong next to her, so sure, but could she trust that? He had lied to her. In her experience, the first lie always led to others. Her father had lied to her, promising that everything would be all right and he wouldn't go to prison. Her mother had lied, swearing she would always be there for her. Could she count on Grant like she had counted on her parents? In the end, they had lied and eventually left her. Would Grant leave her, too? Heather knew what she had to do. She had to protect her heart.

"I can't move in with you, Grant. Me and relationships ... they always end in disaster."

He caressed her cheek, attempting to soothe her. "Maybe I'll be different. We should try."

"Maybe we should just stick to what we have," she firmly countered.

"I'm not willing to do that, Heather. I know what you need. I can read your every thought, every mood. You need to talk to me, right now. Tell me what you're really feeling."

Heather knew what she was feeling, but everything she had been taught as a child—all the rules and dictates her father had pounded into her—refused to let those emotions show. Telling someone how she felt was a sign of weakness.

"Wearing your heart on your sleeve," her father had always insisted, "tells the world that you are worthless and weak. And we are not weak, Heather. You can never be weak."

Her father's voice, like a jackhammer in cement, pounded in her head. All her life it had been the same message—never be weak, never let them see your true heart.

Heather proudly raised her head, remembering the woman her father wanted her to be. "You know I'm right, Grant. You have a history with women that you will eventually go back to when you get bored with me, and I ... I'm not going to inconvenience myself on a whim."

Shock registered in his eyes. Grant recoiled from her. "A whim? This isn't a whim."

Heather clenched her fists, steadying her resolve. "Come on, Grant. We both know better."

He ran his hand through his damp hair, seemingly stunned by her admission. "Is that all I am to you? A whim?"

The pain in his voice seared through her. She didn't want to hurt him, but reason told her the time had come to finish this.

It's for the best.

"We had a good time, but perhaps we should go our separate ways." She swallowed back the bitter taste rising in her throat. "I'm not ready to get serious with anyone … especially someone like you."

"Someone like me? Jesus." He started picking up his clothes from the floor. "When you want to rip a guy apart, you certainly don't waste any time. I thought we meant something to each other, Heather."

"I care for you, Grant. I really do, but what you're asking…." She had to choke back the emotion in her voice. This was killing her.

"I get it." He shoved his legs through his pants, yanking them up his hips. "Fucking me was just a good time." He zipped up his jeans. "It was just about the sex for you, after all."

She wanted to beg him to forgive her callous words. Yes, she would live with him, and yes she wanted him, but instead of speaking out, she stood by the vanity, clutching her white towel to her shivering body and watching him dress.

"You really had me going," he snarled, shrugging on his shirt. "Stupid me. To think you could actually care for anyone other than your horse." He stared at her; his amber eyes ripping her apart. "See you around the show ring, Ms. Phillips."

He bolted from her bathroom. After the slam of her front door carried all the way to her bedroom, Heather flopped down on her bed. The black emptiness creeping up from the pit of her stomach closed in around the borders of her heart. As she lay on her bed, staring up at her two-tiered white ceiling, she let those murky fingers of indifference enshroud her.

It was over. She had shoved yet another man from her life and spared herself the indignity of an ugly break up. Heather was safe; she was protected by a future she could predict. But above all, she had stuck to her father's one abiding rule; never let them see you cry. Pulling the white comforter around her wet body, she curled into a ball. Tightly shutting her eyes, Heather prayed like hell for the pain in her heart to hurry away before she changed her mind.

Chapter 22

A chilly November breeze was whipping around the back jumping ring at Southland Stables. As Heather pulled Murphy up after taking a large green and white fence, she spotted Trent coming into the ring. Strutting with his typical arrogant gate, he was still dressed in a black suit and yellow tie, but his usually sharp gray eyes were a little dull, and his taut and tanned face appeared haggard. Heather wasn't sure if his apparent fatigue could be blamed on a long day at the office or being up all night with his new son.

Bringing Murphy to the center of the ring, she waited as Trent came up to her.

"Thought I'd find you out here," he said, patting Murphy's neck. "You okay? You look tired."

Heather let the reins slacken in her hands. "I was about to say the same thing to you."

He came around the horse's head and gazed up at her. "I've got a newborn at home. What's your excuse?"

"Just a bug I picked up and can't shake."

"You've been out here every day until well after sundown for damn near two weeks. Perhaps you should take a break."

"Can't," she insisted. "State is this weekend."

"Take an evening off and spend it with Grant. You two can't have had a lot of time together with you being here every evening."

Tightening the grip on her reins at the mention of Grant's name, Heather concentrated on keeping any hint of emotion from her face. "You know me. The show is the most important thing."

Trent cocked his head to the side, examining her blue eyes. "Yeah, I know you. I also know when you're upset, or have something on your mind, you spend more time in the ring. So what is it?" She shortened her reins and was about to guide Murphy to the rail when he held the horse. "That day at the hospital when George was born, I may have been a tad distracted, but I saw how you two were with each other. You want to tell me what happened?"

"Why not ask Grant? He said you two were friends."

"Business acquaintances, not friends." He let go of the reins and wiped his hands. "Not close ones anyway. I thought I would ask you, since you're my friend."

Heather wanted to dash from the ring, but knew that would never sit well with Trent. At times, he could be just as relentless as Grant. But he wasn't Grant, and what Heather really needed was a friend. Despite the ever-present voice of Carl Phillips in her head, Heather craved someone to share her feelings with.

"He wanted to move in together—actually, move to Dallas together—and I ... I called it off."

Trent crossed his arms and focused his disconcerting eyes on her. "Why did you do that?"

"It wouldn't have worked." She dropped her eyes to Murphy's black mane, growing uncomfortable with his penetrating stare.

"You got afraid again, didn't you?"

Her mouth dropped open and she scanned the ring, appearing incredulous at the suggestion. "What is it with men thinking I'm afraid all the time? You, Ben, and even Grant said—"

"Because you are afraid, Heather. You're terrified of letting someone in. I've watched you for years, running away from any man who showed the slightest interest in you. I was one of them, remember? I tried getting through to you, tried to get you to trust me, but you were always so closed off, so hard to reach." He shrugged. "I gave up, but Grant didn't. You need to ask yourself ... do you want to push away someone willing to work that hard to get you?"

"Come on, Trent," she shouted, making Murphy raise his head. "He didn't work hard for me. It was just sex, like all men want. Sex without strings."

"If that were the case, Heather, then why do you think he asked you to move in with him? That wasn't about sex, it was about a relationship. When a man finds a woman he wants, he makes her his. Keeps her safe and does everything he can to make sure she never doubts him."

Heather had no reply and instead sniffed loudly. "How many women did you live with, Trent? I didn't see any of those relationships lasting."

"I'm not Grant, Heather. As far as I know, that man has never lived with any woman. Seems to me he thought you were pretty damned special to want to make such a public statement about his feelings."

"I thought you didn't want me seeing him."

Trent took a look around the ring, nodding his head. "I didn't, in the beginning. I thought he would be a distraction for you, but he wasn't. You rode your best with him. I decided if he could do that for you, then he wasn't bad for you."

She shook her head, as if trying to shut out his words. "When it all falls apart, it will be bad for me. It will be another ugly story about me that everyone will know. Something else they can whisper as I go by." She tossed a hand in the air above Murphy's neck. "See, there goes the woman Grant Crowley dumped, the daughter of that doctor who murdered his patients."

He pointed at her, scowling. "No one has ever said that about you, Heather, ever. When are you going to let that shit go?"

"How can I let it go, Trent?" Tears flooded her eyes. "It is part of me ... haunting me day and night."

"You just choose to not let it rule your life. You have to let it go. You won't move on until you do. Do it now, Heather, before you wake up an old woman and realize you wasted your life because of your father's mistakes. Make some happiness for yourself, because no one else will. You have to fight for happiness just like you have to fight for that blue ribbon."

"I appreciate the pep talk, Trent, but Grant and I are over."

"Damn, you're stubborn." He patted Murphy's neck. "You remind me of Rayne. Took me a while to convince her I was sincere."

"What changed her mind?"

He chuckled. "A miracle. Maybe that's what you need."

She smirked at him. "I'm thinking more of an extinction level event. You know, the 'if he were the last man on earth' scenario … then I might consider it." She turned Murphy to the rail.

"How is Murphy coming along?" Trent called behind her. "Is he ready for State?"

"He's ready."

"Are you ready to face Crowley again?"

Heather clucked to Murphy, asking him to canter. "Hell no," she whispered and then yelled, "I'll be fine, Trent."

Turning Murphy toward a stack of metal barrels lined up side by side, she guided the horse to the jump. Keenly aware that Trent was watching her every move, she concentrated on riding through the fence. After sailing over the hurdle without incident, she patted Murphy's neck.

"Good." Trent clapped from the inside of the ring. "Do that ten times in a row at State and you'll win."

"I'll win," she declared, coming back to the center of the ring. "I'm going to get that blue ribbon and nothing will stop me."

Trent sported a dubious grin. "Nothing? We'll see about that."

* * *

It was well after dark when Heather finally trudged through her back door. The eerie quiet of her house had become overbearing after Grant had walked out of her life. The nights she had shared with him had made her home feel more appealing, more comforting. Now it seemed lifeless and dead without him.

"Yeah, I'm definitely going to get that dog," she mumbled as she went to her refrigerator and reached for the bottle of sparkling wine.

She had just worked the cork from the bottle and was stretching for a glass from an overhead cabinet when the incessant chirp of her doorbell rattled her nerves.

Her first thought was of Grant. It would be just like him to come back. For an instant, she was afraid of opening the door. What if she could not tell him no this time?

"Screw it," she huffed, and took off for the front door.

Raising her head and preparing for another round of heated discussion, she yanked the heavy front door open. But it wasn't Grant on her short porch.

Wearing his usual pleated jeans, crisp white dress shirt, and black cowboy boots, Tad Crowley was leaning into her threshold and holding a black cowboy hat in his hands.

"We need to have a little chat."

Defiantly, Heather rested her hand on her hip. "What, are you here to give me another check, Mr. Crowley? I've already called it off with your son. I thought you would be pleased."

"Pleased? You really don't know me, Ms. Phillips." He pointed inside her home. "May I?"

Heather waved him in. "I'm not sure why you're here."

Halting in her entryway, his beady amber eyes took in her decorative plaster inlay. Before he faced her, he slapped his hat against his jeans. "I wanted to talk to you about Grant."

Heather shut her front door. "Why? I think you made everything perfectly clear the last time we spoke."

"I know I came across as a real bastard, but I had my son's best interests at heart. I thought you were only out to get his money ... seems I was wrong about you."

Heather's bare feet fidgeted on her stone floor. Unsure of what to say or do, she caught sight of her tightly clasped hands.

This is all I need!

"The reason I came here tonight was to ask you a question," he went on. "Why did you end things with my son?"

She bit back the tirade she wanted to let loose on the man. Instead, she raised her head, looked him in the eye. "I think that is something you need to take up with Grant, not me."

"He won't talk to me. I came here because I was hoping you would." He gave her a half-grin, the kind usually used by wily, wrinkled cowboys in old black and white movies. "I know you're stubborn and driven, a lot like my son, but when things get to Grant, he shuts down and turns away from me. I was hoping you could give me some answers." He took a step closer to her. "So why did you call it off?"

243

"How do you know I was the one who ended it?"

His chuckle resonated in the short entrance hall. "Grant and I had an argument when Gigi told me about the two of you. I insisted he give you up, but he staunchly refused. After, he left the ranch and stayed in Dallas. I thought he would come home eventually. My boy isn't prone to long term relationships, so I figured I would let him get you out of his system. And then one day he did come home, but I'll be damned if he wasn't the same man I knew. He's changed." He pointed his cowboy hat at her. "You changed him. My question is, why didn't you want him?"

"That's really none of your business, Mr. Crowley."

"Excuse me, Ms. Phillips, but it is my business. He's my son, and despite what you may think of me, his happiness is my primary concern."

She let her eyes drift up and down his tall figure. He reminded her of Grant, making her ache for the man even more. "What about Vanessa? I thought I was getting in the way of your plans for your ranch."

He shrugged his wide shoulders. "Plans change, especially when you start seeing those plans from a different vantage point."

Heather shook her head, not quite sure where this was going. "I don't understand. What has any of this got to do with me?"

"It's pretty simple." He tilted his head slightly to the left. "My son became his own man with you. He stood up to me, he told me to go to hell, and he stopped trying to appease me. You gave me back the Grant I knew. The stubborn, ornery, son of a bitch I spent more time fighting with than agreeing with. But that's my son, and I liked him that way. Ever since I got sick a few years back, he's been avoiding those arguments with me, doing everything I asked, and not being the man I wanted him to be. You brought back his fire. Any woman who could do that certainly meant something to him. I guess I wanted to thank you for returning my son to me."

She nervously fiddled with the pocket on her riding pants. "Grant told me what happened that day you two argued and you ended up in the hospital. Not fighting with you was his way of keeping you safe, Mr. Crowley. He's scared if he fights with you, you'll have a heart attack."

Tad Crowley nodded. "I know that. It's just that I never wanted my son to stop being himself because I was sick. It only made me feel more like an invalid. I like it when we fight … makes me know that he has an opinion, that he's a winner. Hell, he's always been a winner to me."

"Maybe you should tell him that."

"I just might." He ran his finger over the brim of his cowboy hat. "Parents never set out to alienate their children, Ms. Phillips. We're simply trying to prepare them for the real world. Your old man did the same thing with you and your brother, but he was always damned proud of the two of you … real damned proud."

Heather was waylaid by his comment. "How would you know that?"

He made a move toward the door. "First time I met your father, I was at a fundraiser for Baylor Hospital. After shaking my hand, he reached into his wallet and pulled out a picture of you. You were seven or eight, sitting atop your horse and holding a blue ribbon in your hand. I remember he told me that nothing he could ever do in the operating room was going to be better than what he had in you." He stretched for the doorknob. "If you ask me, that sounds like a man who knew a thing or two about what really matters in life."

Heather cracked a small grin. "So you came all the way out here to tell me that."

He opened the door. "I came to tell you that I was wrong … about you and my son. Sometimes you've got to admit you're wrong in person. Only way it sounds genuine. My wife taught me that."

She followed him out the door. "Thank you, Mr. Crowley. I appreciate your vote of confidence, but your son and I are over. I think it's for the best. We were never going to work."

He put his hat on his head. "Well, that's it then." He went to the edge of her short porch and looked out at her quiet street. "I may be an old cattle rancher, Ms. Phillips, but you know I can still smell bullshit from a mile away." He turned to her and winked. "You have a good evenin'."

The lean cowboy sauntered to his waiting gray Hummer H3 and climbed in the driver's seat. With her arms wrapped around her, Heather watched Tad Crowley's car pull away from the curb. Shaking her head, she ducked back inside her front door.

It would seem she had been wrong about Tad Crowley. Perhaps she had been wrong about his son, too.

Forget it, Heather. It's over.

Her little voice was right; they were beyond all hope. It would take a miracle to get her and Grant back together. She thought of Trent's words earlier that day. Unlike her riding master, Heather had stopped believing in such divine intervention a long time ago. She reasoned God wasn't interested in her problems. He had bigger battles to fight.

Chapter 23

It was two days before the state horse show and Heather was scurrying about the halls of the Lewisville Medical Center ER, trying to keep a crying four-year-old with a broken arm happy in exam room two, cleaning up the car accident victim that had just been admitted in exam room six, getting ice for the patient with chest pain in exam room five, and setting up a suture tray for Dr. Eisenberg for the dog bite in exam room eight.

Her blue scrub suit was damp, her stomach was queasy, and she swore her legs were going to give out on her. When Heather finally got the supplies to the exam room where the young man who had been bitten by his Dalmatian was waiting, she ached to have a seat and place a damp towel over her pounding head.

"Where were you?" Ben snapped. "I needed that suture set five minutes ago."

"Sorry. I got held up in two with the broken arm."

Heather went to the bedside and situated a flat silver tray close to his side. She carefully ripped the plastic bag in her hand open and reached in for the square box covered in white paper. After setting the box down on the silver tray, she pulled the edges of the paper away with her fingertips, careful not to cross the sterile field of the suture set, and then stepped back.

Ben lifted the packet of gloves on top of the set. "What is wrong with you today, Heather?"

Heather eyed the young man on the bed as Ben carefully slipped on the sterile gloves. "I'm still fighting this bug."

Ben closely examined the young man's right leg where the dog had taken a chunk out of his calf. "That's been going on over two weeks with you and this bug." He lifted the needle holder from the set and then reached for the green foil packet filled with the black nylon suture. "You think maybe you should see someone about it?" He pointed to the bright lamp set up next to the bed. "Shine that more on the wound."

Heather jumped around Ben's stool and adjusted the lamp. "I'm just run down," she explained. "I've been working with Murphy every evening to get ready for the show Saturday."

Ben loaded the suture needle onto the needle holder. "Ah, yes, your big state competition." Ben looked up at the young freckle-faced man on the exam bed. "Our Nurse Phillips here is a champion show jumper."

The young man nodded. "That's cool."

Ben inspected the ugly bite that was still oozing blood. "Hold still. I deadened the area so you won't feel a thing."

"Sure, Doc."

Ben lifted the needle holder with one hand as he held the edges of the wound together with the other. "Is your boyfriend going to be at the show?"

The question took Heather by surprise and she immediately raised her eyes to their patient. "No." She cleared her throat. "I don't have a boyfriend, Dr. Eisenberg."

Ben kept his concentration on the wound as he carefully pinched the two jagged sides together and ran the needle through the skin. "Really? I thought you were seeing someone." He pulled the needle up as he brought the skin together with the suture. "A certain cattle rancher?"

Heather angrily pressed her lips together as he sewed the wound closed. She hated it when he got like this. Ben was known all over the unit for putting staff in their place—staff he didn't like. After their first break up, his snide comments had her changing her schedule to avoid being around him.

"There is no cattle rancher, not anymore," she finally disclosed.

Ben stopped sewing and gazed up at her. "When did this happen?"

She motioned to the waiting laceration before him. "You should finish so Mr. Backer can be on his way back home to his dog."

Ben sat back on his stool, giving her a thorough going over with his blue eyes. "When?"

She nervously looked to her patient. "Two weeks ago."

"Why didn't you say anything to me?"

"Perhaps we should discuss this later," Heather proposed.

The very slender Mr. Backer shrugged. "Don't mind me. I just broke up with my girl, too."

Ben glared at him. "Yes, but you still have your adoring Cujo waiting at home to eat your other leg."

"Dr. Eisenberg," Heather scolded. "Please."

Ben stood from the stool and dropped the needle holder on the tray. "Mr. Backer, will you excuse us?"

"What are you doing?" Heather whispered to him, alarmed he had broken the sterile field on the tray.

Ben yanked off his gloves and grabbed her elbow. "Come with me."

They were not even two steps out of the room when he maneuvered her into the wall. He stood before her, his wide shoulders blocking her view of the hallway and nurses' station.

"What is with you?" She thumbed the door. "You don't walk out halfway through finishing a wound. You know that, Ben. It's unprofessional."

"When were you going to tell me you had broken up with Grant Crowley?" His eyes were two blue flames, burning into her. His wide mouth was pulled back in an angry frown as he angled over her, intimidating her with his size.

"It's none of your goddamned business, Ben." She defensively folded her arms over her chest.

Ben's eyes scrutinized her face, and then his hand went to her forehead.

She slapped his hand away. "Don't touch me."

He ignored her and palpated the nodes along the side of her neck. "How long have you been like this, Heather? You're so pale."

She shoved him away. "I mean it, cut it out, Ben. When I need a doctor, I'll make an appointment and go—"

"Go to room three," he interrupted. "Wait for me there. You're sick, Heather. You're no good to me, or the patients, if you can't do your job."

"Forget it, Ben."

She was attempting to move his heavy body aside when her vision suddenly became fuzzy. Freezing in mid-step, Heather lowered her head as everything around her turned into slow motion.

"Heather?" she heard him call to her, but she could not move. The fuzziness was growing darker and her head was feeling lighter.

"Ben!" She grabbed for his arm.

Her legs were giving out beneath her and the floor was coming toward her face, but there was nothing she could do to stop her fall. Heather was powerless, as if her body was not hers anymore and her will had been instantly usurped.

Then, arms grabbed her and lifted her into the air. That was the last thing she felt before the bright fluorescent lights in the ceiling above were instantly snuffed out.

* * *

Heather was sitting on an exam bed, picking at the tape on her inner arm where the lab technician had drawn her blood and feeling utterly foolish. She was a nurse and should be taking care of her patients, not occupying a needed emergency room bed.

After coming out of her spell—that's what she was calling it, because fainting sounded too hokey for a modern woman like her—Ben had insisted she be taken to an exam room and worked up. That he was doing her assessment made her even more uncomfortable. When he started asking intimate questions about her and Grant, she almost walked out on him.

"Well, your labs are back," Ben announced, rushing through her open exam room door.

Heather perked up on her gurney. "Let me take a look." She reached out for the paperwork in his hands, but Ben held it away from her eager grip.

He pushed a stool beside her bed and had a seat. The grim look on his face frightened Heather … it frightened her to death.

"What is it, Ben?"

He shook his head. "You're going to have to change your plans for that horse show tomorrow. You're not going to be able to ride for a while."

She sank into the bed. "What do you mean? I have to show tomorrow. I've been busting my ass for weeks to get ready. I can't just—"

"Heather, you need to listen very carefully to what I'm about to say."

Slowly, she nodded her head and waited for the bad news.

Alexandrea Weis

Chapter 24

The crisp fall air about the Tandy Park show grounds was making the white check-in tent set up outside of the jumping ring loudly billow, much to the regret of the few riders whose horses kept spooking at the phenomenon. The sun was shining down on the array of fences set up in the ring. Large red British telephone boxes flanked one wide oxer, while a group of exuberant jazz musicians were painted on a solid wall that led to a futuristic touch and go. All the jumps were meant to confound and give a horse pause, but few of the animals at this level of competition were easily put off by such fences. Or at least, every rider hoped that was the case.

A light bay with the black legs and bright white blaze on his face was having second thoughts about a fence with the front and back ends of a Venetian gondola set on either side of the triple-tiered array of red and white poles. The horse had refused twice already, and Heather waited to see if the creature would actually take the jump or be eliminated for performing the dreaded three refusals. As the rider approached the fence for a third time, kicking her heels furiously into the sides of the clunky beast, Heather knew the animal would stop right before the hurdle. A few seconds later when the big bay did exactly that, she tossed her hand into the air, feeling the rider's pain. No one wanted to be eliminated for refusals at a horse show. It was the ultimate humiliation.

"She should have taken him in at an angle," Heather muttered as a round of applause for the rider sounded outside of the ring. "Might have given him less time to think about it."

"She's a young rider," Trent said next to her. "A more experienced rider would have known that." His eyes scanned her profile as she stared into the ring. "Sorry you're not riding in the class?"

Heather turned to him, pushing back the long brown hair the wind had loosened from her ponytail. "I'm sorry I'm here."

"I told you, it's your job to be here and support the other riders from Southland Stables. If you hadn't shown up, I would have fired your ass."

She nervously scanned the show grounds. "Coming here was a bad idea."

Trent leaned against the white railing next to him. "For you or for him?"

"Don't start that again," she fumed. "It's bad enough I have to stand here and watch the other riders compete in my class."

"There's still a good chance you'll win reserve champion in your division even after not showing today. You and Grant have been one and two all season in the Junior Division. No one else comes close to your points."

Heather lightly pounded her fist against the white railing in front of her. "Yeah, well, second place isn't first."

"Any idea what he will say when Grant finds out you're not riding?"

Heather gazed at the crowd gathered around the ring. Parents, spouses, children, and friends of the competitors were reclining in lounge chairs, standing by the gate, seated on blankets, or had a place in the small set of bleachers next to the ring. Amid the myriad of faces, she saw no one she knew, but worst of all since arriving at the show grounds, Heather had seen no sign of Grant.

"Maybe you should tell him before he finds out you're not in the class," Trent suggested.

She examined his pristine white riding shirt and snug black jodhpur pants. "Shouldn't you be getting ready for your class?"

He toed the dusty ground with his shiny black boot. "Ignoring him isn't going to make it any easier, Heather. He's going to ask why you're not riding. He needs to know."

"I knew I should never have said anything to you." Her blue eyes turned cold and she leaned against the white railing in front of her. "It's my problem, Trent. Telling Grant about my condition ... he doesn't need to know. He can't help me."

"You should let him decide that."

Setting her hands on top of the railing, she sighed. "I don't need anybody, Trent. If I run into Grant, I'll tell him that, too."

Trent stood from the fence. "Well, here's your chance."

Her heart plummeted to her shoes. Her eyes searched his, dreading the possibility of what was to come.

Trent motioned to the ring entrance a few yards down. "He just rode up to the gate and spotted you."

Heather could not turn around, she could not even breathe. She knew coming to the show would eventually lead to her crossing paths with Grant, and she had been preparing herself for that moment since their break up. Unfortunately, the confrontation she had imagined was supposed to take place in the show ring, and not outside of it.

Trent patted her shoulder. "Just tell him he's an asshole, like you always do."

She gripped his hand, terrified at the prospect of being alone with Grant. "Don't leave me."

He pried her hand from his. "I have to get to the stables and saddle up Bob for our class. Besides, I thought you said you didn't need anyone."

With a knowing smirk, Trent went around her and walked away. She heard him say Grant's name over her right shoulder. Her stomach shrank to the size of a pea as she watched the shadow of a horse and rider growing bigger on the ground in front of her. Mustering all of her fortitude, she raised her head and slowly twisted around to meet those devilish eyes head on.

He was wearing his usual black jacket, white high collar shirt, and black jodhpur pants, but the black velvet riding helmet was in his hand. Maximillian snorted loudly as Grant threw the hat to her feet and promptly dismounted his horse.

"What's wrong?" He came up to her, his eyes eviscerating her strength. "Why aren't you dressed out? Where's Murphy?"

Heather stood fast, keeping a ramrod posture before him. "He's at Southland. I'm not showing today."

Maximillian tugged against the reins as Grant moved warily closer to her. "Why aren't you showing, Heather?" The concern was evident in his strained voice. "Is something wrong with Murphy?"

She couldn't take his eyes anymore, and wringing her shaking hands together, she lowered her gaze. "It's not Murphy. It's me. The doctor told me I couldn't ride today."

He dropped Maximillian's reins and gripped her arms. "What is it? What's wrong?"

Heather careened her head around him to see Maximillian taking full advantage of his freedom by attacking the green grass. "You should get your horse."

"Forget the horse," he all but shouted. "What's wrong with you? And what doctors? You went to a doctor? When?"

The change in him, from the stoic, cold competitor she had known to the caring lover before her, made her smile. Then, remembering everything that had happened between them, she forced the smile from her lips.

"I've been sick for over two weeks now, and the other day at work," she eased out of his clutches, "I kind of ... passed out."

"Passed out!" He combed his hand through his hair. "Why didn't you call me? Text me? Something!"

Several of the onlookers gathered around their spot at the rail gave Grant a scornful gaze; one even held her finger to her lips and pointed to the horse jumping in the show ring.

Grant took her hand and was about to lead her away from the side of the ring when he remembered Maximillian still grazing away. He let her go, walked over to his horse, and picked up his reins. Marching back to Heather with Maximillian in tow, he came up to her, his amber eyes blazing.

"Now what in the hell is going on with you?"

Bolstered by his reaction, and moved by his show of concern, Heather's nerves settled as he took her elbow, ushering her away from the ring.

"Heather? Tell me." His voice tugged at her heart. "Whatever it is, I'm here for you. I want to help. I'll do whatever it takes."

She let out a breath and motioned to the tent by the entrance gate to the show ring. "Don't you have to check in for your class?"

He waved his hand at the ring, nonplussed. "Forget the class."

"Grant, you can't forget the class. You're the best rider in it. You have to win the blue ribbon to get your state championship."

He came closer to her. "Heather, I don't give a damn about blue ribbons or state championships. I care about you."

Her insides trembled at the nearness of him. "Grant, please don't do that. Don't make this out to be more than it is. You don't want me."

"Jesus, there you go again." He threw his free hand up in the air. "When will you realize that it's not you against the world? You walk around thinking you're not worthy because of your past and your father, but you are deserving of love, Heather. Everyone is. Love is an inalienable right, and not a platitude used to sell greeting cards."

Her anger rekindled. "What love, Grant? We had sex ... that was it." She felt that itch to run away again. "We had a good time and neither one of us should have expected more."

"Dammit, Heather! When are you going to give me some credit for having feelings for you?" His lips slammed together. "Now, would you just tell me what is wrong with you? I know you and you wouldn't miss this show unless it was something pretty damned serious. So out with it. What are we dealing with?"

"'We'? We're not a 'we,' Grant."

His hand sliced through the air. "Heather, stop ... enough. I'm sorry I left that night. I popped that living together shit on you and should have known you would react the way you did. But this is different. I love you too damn much to let you—"

"You love me?" she blurted out.

He appeared shocked. "Of course I love you. Would I have asked you to live with me if I didn't love you?"

Suddenly, everything felt different to Heather. Her world had been upended by his confession. This wasn't supposed to happen.

"Why didn't you say that before?" she warily pressed.

He shook his head. "You never gave me the chance. First, I ask you to live with me, and then you're calling what we had a whim.

So, I got pissed. There I was spilling my heart out to you and all you could do was ignore me."

"I wasn't ignoring you. I was sparing you a tedious break up and eventual—"

He pointed the reins in his other hand at her. "There you go again. I'm telling you that I love you, and all you can do is ignore me."

Love. The word sunk like a stone to the depths of her being. Other men had used the same word, but none had impacted her quite like this. The fuzzy warm feeling that spread to her toes dissolved her determination to shut him out. Perhaps she had been wrong about him. For just once in her life, she wanted to take a chance with a man and know the kind of joy that she saw so many others experiencing.

Smiling coyly, she tilted her head to the side. "So you still love me, even after everything that happened between us?"

Grant let his gaze wander over the show grounds. "Maybe I found out how much I love you because of what happened. I learned that loving someone means never giving up, even when the one you love already has." His striking eyes found their way back to her. "Besides, without you, I was pretty damn miserable."

She tucked her hands in the front pockets of her jeans. "Yeah, I know what you mean. I wasn't right without you, either."

He let Maximillian's reins fall from his hand, and the horse trotted off to a lush piece of green grass not far away. "Does that mean you do feel something for me, Ms. Phillips?"

She slowly nodded. "Yes, Mr. Crowley, it does."

He inched closer, his stern features softening. "So what's wrong with you? What kind of doctors do I need to hire to care for you? You'll have the best specialist. I'll do whatever it takes to get you well."

Moved beyond measure, Heather cupped his angular jaw. All her life she had yearned for such an admission, but had never met a man she felt could make her happy. Now, for the first time, here was someone she wanted to take a chance on. With one word, the doubts of her past had been replaced by the hope for a happy future. Such was the power of love.

She lowered her hand from his face. "I'll get well, Grant, eventually."

"Eventually?" He flung his arms around her. "That's it. From now on, I'm sticking to you like glue, you hear me? And if that means I have to move in with you, drive you to the doctors, or take care of Murphy, you are going to let me, all right?"

She giggled against him, happy to be in his arms once again. "Whatever you say, Grant. But you really don't have to worry. I'm assured I'll make a full recovery. It will just take some time."

"How much time, Heather?"

Raising her head, she smiled into his stunning eyes. "About nine months."

Alexandrea Weis

Epilogue

Winter storm clouds were gathering on the horizon as Heather eyed the combination of brightly colored fences Trent had set up in the center of the jumping ring. The long-sleeved T-shirt and vest she had donned to stave off the cold weren't helping as she guided Murphy to the white railing. A pretty chestnut filly in the paddock adjacent to her side of the ring gave a short whinny to Murphy, making her horse prance at the rail.

"Flirt," she murmured to the horse.

Passing below the shade of a grand oak tree next to the ring in the paddock, Heather heard the call of several of the horses in the open field situated in the rear of the blue and white stables beside her.

"This time take it at a steady canter, Heather. And keep his head in place; he's still got too much of it for his own good."

Heather felt the muscles in her arms straining against the pull of Murphy's bit as she directed him to the combination of fences. Holding back until she felt he was in just the right spot, Heather then eased up on the reins and allowed the horse to take off. Clearing the first fence with room to spare, she proceeded to the touch and go at the end of the combination. Recalling all that she had learned over the past year, all the things Grant and Trent had taught her, Heather became empowered when she approached the fences; what had once been intimidating was now just another set of jumps to her. The tricky combination had lost its sinister luster.

Applause broke out from the side of the ring. Heather veered Murphy around to see Grant standing by the fence with an infant covered in thick pink pajamas propped up in his arms.

"Yay, clap for Mommy," he told his daughter.

"Quite a cheering section," Trent professed, coming alongside Murphy.

Heather beamed. "The best cheering section a woman could ask for."

"How's it feel to be back in the saddle after a year?" he questioned, patting Murphy's thick neck.

"Good." She nodded and then took in the majestic setting of Crowley stables. "Never thought I would be here, though."

Trent's musical laughter filled the air. "That makes two of us, but your man can be pretty persuasive."

"When is Rayne bringing up George?"

Trent waved to Grant. "She'll be here shortly. She went to pick up her mother. Estelle wants to see where I'm riding master now." Trent glanced up at her. "You making any headway with him in that department?"

She nodded as Grant swooped between the white fence railings, carrying the pink bundle securely in his arms. "He called Maureen after Mandy was born. I figure with time he'll introduce his daughter to her grandmother. Old scars take a while to heal, but eventually they do fade from view."

"I guess you found the cure for your scars, eh, Heather? Funny how those little miracles pop up right when you need them most."

She watched Grant making his way across the ring, his long legs kicking out in front of him, and Heather felt a surge of happiness. "I guess you were right, Trent. Nothing like a bright future to close the door on a painful past," she mused, admiring Grant's toned body and curly blond hair.

"She's looking good," Grant asserted as he stood next to Trent.

"She still needs lots of work," Trent grudgingly advised. "But we should be able to put her and Murphy in a few shows in the spring."

Grant bounced the baby in his arms, making a happy face for the gurgling child. "And Olive Girl will get to go to her first show with Mommy."

Trent furrowed his brow as he eyed Grant and the baby. "Why do you call her Olive Girl? I thought her name was Amanda."

"You don't want to know." Heather snickered as she climbed down from Murphy's back.

She walked up to Grant and removed the pink hoodie cap from the baby's head. A jumble of blonde curls bounced to life. Rubbing her hand lovingly over the curls, Heather smiled.

Trent took Murphy's reins from her. "I'll take him back to the stable for you."

Grant grinned at him. "Thank you, riding master."

Trent scowled. "It's only because you're paying me an exorbitant amount of money that I won't punch you in the nose for that, Crowley."

"I needed someone to replace Gigi, Trent, and you're the best I know."

Trent nodded. "How does she like handling the ranch instead of running the stables?"

Grant handed the baby to Heather. "I think she has found her calling. Bossing men and cows around all day suits her. Even my father is impressed with her."

Trent chuckled and clucked to Murphy. When he was out of earshot, Heather arched a scolding eyebrow at Grant.

"You need to stop calling her Olive Girl."

He gave her a cocky grin. "Would you prefer Jacuzzi girl?"

Heather pressed her cheek to her baby's fine curls. "Your daddy's an asshole, Mandy."

"Glad to see your hormones are back to normal." He hooked his finger through the belt loop of his jeans as his face sobered. "Did you get my offer this morning?"

She avoided his eyes. "The one you left on the kitchen table? I saw it."

"I figured I'd better type it out formally so you wouldn't freak out like before."

"I didn't freak out, Grant. I was just ... surprised, that's all."

"You dumped me," he argued.

She bounced her baby in her arms. "You're the one who ran out my front door, as I recall."

"Let's not rehash that again." He rubbed his hand over his face. "So, what's your answer?"

"I need more time to weigh my options."

"What options? It's a straightforward offer. Yes or no, Heather."

She smirked at him. "You want me to freak out again?"

He held up his hands, assuaging her. "Hell no. Last time I was suggesting just living together. I can't imagine what you'll do now that I want to marry you." His cheeky grin reappeared. "Would you even consider marrying your former rival, Ms. Phillips?"

"You're still my rival, Mr. Crowley."

"After all we've been through? You've got to be kidding me, Heather?"

Heather delighted in his exasperation. "Don't worry, Grant. I'll marry you … one day."

"When, for Christ's sake?"

"When I beat you in the show ring. Then we'll get married."

Grant flourished a playful frown. "I think I would prefer to buy more Olive Girl olive oil. If I get you pregnant again, then you'll have to marry me."

"That would be cheating. Don't you want to win me fair and square?"

He came up to her and kissed his daughter's head. Then, snuggling his arms around his family, he uttered a soulful sigh. "I've already won you, Heather. Can't you see that?"

Relishing the feel of her baby in her arms and the warmth of Grant's hug, Heather reasoned it didn't get much better than this.

"So what do you say? Or should I take you over my knee to convince you that I am the perfect man for you?"

"I don't need any more convincing." She put her lips close to his ear, and whispered, "I love you, Grant Crowley. I'll marry you any time you want."

"Thank God. You had me worried, baby. Thought it might be touch and go there for a minute."

"Touch and go?" Heather caught a glimpse of the jumps in the ring, and reflected on all the obstacles she had overcome. "That's all behind me. From now on, I'm going to grab every opportunity and embrace every happiness."

"No more running away?" Grant's arm slipped around her waist. "I like the sound of that."

"I'm done running." Heather glanced up at Grant and reveled in his loving gaze. "I'm right where I always wanted to be."

THE END

Book 7 in the Cover to Covers Series
The Bond
Coming 1/27/15

Clenching her fist, she knocked gently above the letter B painted in gold on his door. At first, she heard nothing. Then there seemed to be some commotion, as if things were being tossed around. She swore a curse word or two were uttered, and then the door flew open.

Sam's first reaction was, "Holy shit," and she almost said it our loud when she saw the man in the doorway, towering over her.

Wearing only a dirty pair of faded jeans, his abs were the first thing she saw. Rippled, chiseled and utterly defined, he was beyond in good shape, he was fucking perfect. His arms were muscular, his skin was tan, his chest was wide and she ached to run her hands over his well-proportioned pecs. However, when her eyes rose to his face, her enthusiasm fizzled.

With almost arctic blue eyes and an impatient sneer on his cruel lips, he appeared far from friendly. His wavy hair was thick, and a rich shade of dark brown. He had an edgy face. Not handsome, not cute, but mesmerizing. His eyes drew her in first, then his lips, and by the time Sam's gaze was gliding along his perfectly carved jaw, she was captivated.

"Can I help you?"

Sam was immediately bewitched by his voice. It was deep, hypnotic, and something like a fog horn on the river in the middle of a misty night.

Shit. Focus.

"Ah, I live next door, and your banging woke me up." She pointed to her open door.

"You're my neighbor? From apartment A?"

That velvety deep voice was lulling her into you into a false sense of lust. "Ah, yes, and your banging on the wall woke me."

His eyes went up and down her figure. She wondered why she suddenly felt cold and then realized her robe had fallen open, showing off her short nightshirt. Grabbing at the robe, she quickly covered herself.

"Look, I'd appreciate it if you could save the decorating for the day," she got out, trying not to turn red. "I'm a nurse, and I've got day shift all this week. I really need my sleep."

He folded his arms over his chest and Sam thought her heart was going to explode. "Sorry. I was just getting something set up." He held out his hand. "I'm Doug, by the way. Doug Morgan."

She took his hand. It was warm, thick, and she instantly got a sense of his strength. "I'm Sam, Sam Woods."

His eyes were studying her face, making her toes curl. "What's the Sam stand for?"

"Samantha, but I hate the name."

He grinned. It was one of those mischievous kind of grins that hinted to the bad thoughts motivating it. "Well, I know what to call you from now on, Samantha."

She gaped at him. *Seriously?* The only neighbor on her floor and he was going to be an asshole. She shook her head. "Look, just please keep the banging to daytime hours when I'm not home. You can renovate to your heart's delight then."

Feeling the need to make a hasty exit, she turned for her door.

"I'll keep it down just for you, Samantha."

She stopped at her door and turned to him. He was standing out in the hallway, watching her. Sam got an uncanny feeling, like they had met before, but she was sure she had never met anyone before with those abs ... ah, eyes.

"It's just Sam, Mr. Morgan." Hurrying inside, she slammed her door. Sam set the deadbolt and then thumped her head against the thick door.

"Oh my God. I'm so screwed."

This was not what she needed right now. It was bad enough he was a fantasy in the flesh, but his attitude was going to bother

her immensely. Why can't he be great looking with a wonderful personality to match?

"Then he'd be married," she mused. "The good ones always are."

Alexandrea Weis is an advanced practice registered nurse who was born and raised in New Orleans. Having been brought up in the motion picture industry, she learned to tell stories from a different perspective and began writing at the age of eight. Infusing the rich tapestry of her hometown into her award-winning novels, she believes that creating vivid characters makes a story moving and memorable. A permitted/certified wildlife rehabber with the Louisiana Wildlife and Fisheries, Weis rescues orphaned and injured wildlife. She lives with her husband and pets in New Orleans.

To read more about Alexandrea Weis or her books, you can go to the following sites:
Website: http://www.alexandreaweis.com/
Facebook: http://www.facebook.com/authoralexandreaweis
Twitter: https://twitter.com/alexandreaweis
Goodreads: http://www.goodreads.com/author/show/1211671.Alexandrea_Weis